THE PACHYDERMS' LAMENT

THE PACHYDERMS' LAMENT

THE HYPATOMANCER'S TALE
BOOK TWO

BEING THE ELEVENTH ROMANCE OF NOVA EUROPA

ROBERT REGINALD

THE BORGO PRESS
MMXI

THE PACHYDERMS' LAMENT

FIRST EDITION

Published by Wildside Press LLC

www.wildsidebooks.com

DEDICATION

To the memory of
Edmond Hamilton and **Leigh Brackett**,
And the kindness they extended to a young fan
attending his first SF con 43 years ago;

And for
Francis Jarman,
Friend, Roman, countryman in the exotic lands
of ancient numismatics and modern literature.

CONTENTS

PROLOGUE
"ALL WILL BE REVEALED"

ANNO DOMINI 1622-1625
ANNO JULIANA 1262-1265

Transiting through ætherspace was something that I learned during my pubertal years as a student of *grande-magie* at the Monastery of Saint-Arthémie in Antioche. Brother Lave would stand by a large *argentaurum* mirror in one room, and Brother Crèche next to a second device in the adjoining room, and we were expected to jump back and forth, forth and back, over and over again, until the action became second-nature to us, and required little conscious thought on our part.

There was never any sense of a passage of time while we moved through the ætherial realm; first we were "here," and then we were "there," instantaneously—or so it seemed.

Later, the good brethren sent us on much longer journeys to affiliated abbeys in other lands; but once again, I never felt that my trip through the void took any "time" away from my life. The transit just happened when I found and twisted the leys properly—and I soon became very proficient at doing just that. The voyage seemed to happen without any lapse in consciousness; and so we assumed—all of us—that every such transit would always take place in exactly the same fashion.

But so few of my colleagues had ever make the leap from Nova Europa to the Otherworlds—and returned—that none of us had any experience at making such long-jumps through the æthersphere—or to talk with someone who had. Only Doctor Scarabbaios had ventured so far as the Fifth Circle—an unimaginable distance—and returned decades later to tell the tale—but almost no one believed him—no one except me!

And now that same not-so-gentleman had dispatched me and mine headlong into the æther—sent us on a trip from somewhere here to…nowhere there.

But perhaps I jump ahead of myself, if you'll pardon the expression. Perhaps I should first tell you about how I reached this point in my existence.

* * * * * * *

My name is Morpheús—Morpheús the Mage. My story begins in Barstölný, in the Kingdom of Kórynthia in Nova Europa—which is what we call our world—and also the continent on which I dwell. I know now that there exists an infinity of such planets scattered throughout the cosmos, like jewels on a sequined skirt, arrayed in a series of probabilities that we call "spheres" or "circles."

Those places that most resemble Nova Europa we categorize in the First Circle; the most divergent ones we place in the Fifth Circle; and outside the latter sphere, in the Sixth Circle and beyond, lies a Chaos of uncertainty, filled with places that may be unfathomable, unreachable, or simply not understandable by the likes of humankind.

So, why try to travel there?

This is what happened.

* * * * * * *

Scooter (my wherret familiar) and I were skrying the æther one day in the Year of Our Lord 1622. I encountered a female presence—a Lady who called herself Niobë—who begged for my help to free her from an intolerable prison on a Fifth-Circle world, Naprimér. Somehow, she touched a place deep within my soul—a place that hadn't felt any emotion in quite some time.

After my years of education, I'd worked very hard to develop my peculiar and rare talent—hypatomancy, the ability to forecast the future—and to make it the engine of my progress in society. I'd succeeded beyond any childhood dream, and was eventually named Scanner Prime of the Kingdom of Kórynthia by Queen Evetéria. I now had status, I had money, I had property. I'd risen very rapidly through the ranks of my peers, and stood just a step away from the premier position in the state for mages, the post of Minister of Magical Affairs—and given time, I would probably have attained that role when the current Magister retired or expired.

But the years of toiling had taken their toll. I'd grown weary of telling my clients their much-sweetened lies. For the truth is, no one wants to hear the *real* truth about their futures, not ever. And as for my own future?—the laws of *l'art magique* prevented me from discerning that end, or anything connected with it. I grew increasingly frustrated as time went on.

The "Lady" gave me a reason to leave—a quest or a purpose, if you will, that might re-energize my life and my spirit, both of which had grown stale with disuse. And so, even though I couldn't physically *touch* her, stranded as she was in a place so far distant from my own, she managed to touch *me* in ways that moved me very deeply. In the end, I *had* to do this thing, and I had to do it now.

I resigned my position as Scanner Prime, and sought out Doctor Scarabbaios, the only person who knew anything about off-world transit. But the old mage was unwilling to assist me without something in return: a copy of an exceedingly rare tome called *The Necropompeion*, an almost mythical artifact said to have been generated in the depths of Hades itself.

To secure the only accessible copy of this work, I assembled a team of retired soldiers, headed by Sergeant Strook (who called himself "Hawk"), and took them to Indushia, halfway around the world. After many adventures there, we succeeded in acquiring the precious volume, and Scooter and I brought it to Doctor S.'s lair high in the Alps of central Nova Europa.

As he'd promised, Scarabbaios then told us in detail about his travels through the Five Circles of the Otherworlds—and about the Overworld that wanted to control them all. Then he showed us his marvelous laboratory, filled with transit-devices of all kinds, including an *atraurum*, a round black mirror that couldn't possibly exist—but obviously did!

Something went wrong then. Something went seriously wrong very fast.

"All will be revealed," the Doctor abruptly said to us, "when you reach the other side."

Suddenly, the black-gold mirror activated without warning, and before I could react, generated a psychic whirlpool that began drawing me and Scooter into its bowels. I tried shouting a few spells to break the link, but not knowing how the device worked, I couldn't find the right combination. I was beginning to reach for my magical pouch when I and my familiar were abruptly yanked by the suction of the æther right into its depths.

It was like falling down a long shaft without ever hitting bottom. I know I screamed my lungs out as I tumbled, head over heel, the wherret desperately clinging to my shirt. We were transited—I knew not where.

And then we were there!

CHAPTER ONE
"WHAT *IS* THE FOURTH ELEPHANT'S EGG?"

I recognized the place immediately from Doctor Scarabbaios's description. We were on the Overworld, a fact that I confirmed by tasting the æther.

"He betrayed us!" the wherret said. It sounded almost hurt.

"Perhaps," I said. "But this was a place that we ultimately needed to reach, so perhaps he's really done us a favor in the end."

The room reminded me of the stone receptacle where we'd originally landed on the old mage's mountain hideaway—except that the walls were decorated with fancy lettering and ornate designs. A mirror was inset into the décor behind us—but like Scarabbaios's receiver, it had gone inert, and I could not reactivate it. There was a hole in one edge of the metal—it almost appeared to me that something had once been plugged in there.

I went to the only door, and found, much to my surprise, that it readily opened to me. The suite of rooms was lushly furnished and carpeted. I hadn't seen such rampant luxury so carelessly displayed since visiting the Kaisareion Palace in Julianople.

In the dining area, we found a small table laid out for three, plus an apparatus obviously intended for Scooter's use. When I sat down, the candelabra suddenly lighted, and I heard a door open and close somewhere in the distance. Two sets of footsteps came down a corridor towards us.

A man and a woman sat down opposite me. They were both

petite in size, slim and almost pinched in the cheeks, with narrow bands of hair down the middle and sides of their heads. The areas in between appear to have been shaved or trimmed in some fashion, and the skin dyed with the same kinds of designs that I'd seen on the walls of the room to which we'd transited.

"You must be Morpheús," the woman said to me in passable Greek; her accent had an antique flavor, as if she'd learned the language during Classical times. "And Scooter the wherret, of course," she added, nodding at my friend. "You can call me Mistress Zalmanna. My companion is High Master Phenneïlonn. He does not speak your tongue, so please direct all questions to me."

"Why have you brought us here?" I asked in an abrupt tone.

She smiled at me. "This is where you wanted to be, is it not? But let us enjoy our meal before we get down to business, shall we?"

She made no signal, but immediately servants appeared along either wall, bringing us small bowls of warm, scented water in which to wash our hands and faces, and towels of some soft substance with which to wipe them.

Then the courses were placed in front of us, one at a time. I have no idea what they actually served us. Each plate contained an ort of something spicy or sweet or tangy, just enough to whet the appetite. There might have been a hundred of these dishes all told, and some of the flavors featured therein were extraordinary beyond description. I'm no gourmand, but even I could sense the subtle tastes buried within. As for Scooter, they gave the creature its own set of platters, and even though I saw nothing live on any of them, it too seemed to be completely satisfied at the end.

The final offering was a small chilled glass of something that reminded me of an old, sweet liquor that I'd once tasted at the Four Corners of the World Inn at Arbyll in Asshyria. Extraordinary!

When everything was cleared away, Zalmanna touched a cloth to her small pink lips, and smiled a second time.

"I hope that met your expectations," she said. "We enjoy variety, you see, and have access to the culinary masterpieces of thousands of worlds. Even I have never experienced some of the sensations that we featured tonight—and some will never be served here again.

"But—our old mutual friend informs us that you have an itch that you are unable to scratch, so to speak. We can supply your needs in every respect. But, as usual with such transactions, they seem to work best when both parties give something and gain something, each unto each. And so it is with us. We are happy to facilitate the attainment of your desires, but we also have things that we want and cannot retrieve ourselves, for a variety of reasons.

"I am authorized by Master Phenneïlonn"—he bowed his head when his name was spoken—"to offer you and yours free transport to any place that you may desire to go in the Fifth Circle, provided that you first bring us The Fourth Elephant's Egg.

"What if I don't know the address of the world that I seek?" I asked.

"We can find it for you with some basic information. Our database is astonishingly vast. And if by chance we do not currently reference the particular place that you wish to go, we will continue searching for it for however long it takes."

"How do I know that you'll fulfill your end of the bargain?"

"Our word is good. Ask anyone. Ask Doctor Scarabbaios. We never break a contract. Our laws forbid it, our society prevents it, our very nature abhors it. No, we will complete the transaction, of that you may be assured."

"What about our return from the Fifth Circle back to our own world?"

"Ah, that we cannot facilitate without some additional payment being made. And the chances of you surviving two such challenges are unlikely at best."

"So, what *is* The Fourth Elephant's Egg?" Scooter asked. That was the question that I really didn't want to pose, but it had to be said just the same.

For the first time, "Mistress" paused before speaking.

"We do not really know for sure," she finally said. "You must understand that the cosmos contains an almost infinite number of worlds—indeed, it is infinity minus one. Some of these lie in the Sixth Circle and above."

"The Sixth Circle?—but there are only five, I understand."

"There are five that we can readily visit. Our ætheromath-ematicians postulate, however, that many more circles actually exist, perhaps an unlimited number—no one knows. But most of these cannot be sampled by such as we, at least not without some special apparatus, and many not at all. To do so would be instant death for humans. The environment there is not condu-cive to our style of life.

"But the circles are never that rigidly defined. The line between the Fourth and Fifth Circle blurs as you approach it, and so does the demarcation point between the Fifth and Sixth. Hence, there are Sixth Circle worlds that we *could* visit, if we knew about them, had their signatures recorded, and had the energy to reach them. All of these are major difficulties, as you might imagine. There are worlds for which we have descrip-tions that we cannot presently reach, because we have insuf-ficient power available to boost a transit signal that far. But they are much more readily accessible from certain points in the Fifth Circle.

"On one such world just beyond or at the line separating the Fifth and Sixth Spheres, there exists a source of power or energy or radiance known as The Fourth Elephant's Egg. We have no more information about it than that. But it sounds very interesting to us. We are the ultimate collectors of the universe. We exist to trade new information and new experiences. We want this thing, whatever it is, and we want you to get it for us."

"But if that particular world is inaccessible to you, then how can we transit there?" I asked. This seemed to me such an obvious obstacle that I wondered how and why they hadn't considered it before.

"We can get you to a nearby Fifth Circle world known as Yelloweyen. We can even give you a transit-device that will work in that part of the æther (most do not), with enough power to get you to and from the place where this Egg is supposedly located, and with a return link to one of our great mirrors here. Our scientists have determined that all of this is possible. But how you find the object itself and get it disassembled to a stage where it can be moved—well, all of that is up to you."

I sighed. "Very well," I said. "I might need to take some trained men and special materiel with me, and have the ability to bring them back again—before you send me to Naprimér, the place that I ultimately wish to go. These men—whichever of them survives—must be returned to their homes in Nova Europa. That's a minimum requirement, since I must make the same pledge to them."

Zalmanna turned to her companion and rattled off an exchange with him in their own tongue. He appeared to disapprove, but then seemed to change his mind after a further conversation. Finally she turned to me and said, "This is agreed. We will return your comrades to their homes without reservation."

"Including the wherret?"

"But...that was not what you stated."

"*All* my companions!" I said.

She spoke something to Phenneïlonn, who responded with an angry retort, shaking his head.

"Master," Scooter whispered in my ear, "You do not need to do this. I am bound to you of my own free will for seven times seven years, and I will honor that agreement."

"Nonetheless, I won't hold you to it if you get a chance to return to your homeworld. At least you'll have the choice."

"Thank you," it said, and licked the lower lobe of my ear.

Finally Phenneïlonn looked right at me and said something like: "*Shoskí eskhályon notsálmy.*"

"So mote it be," Zalmanna stated. "The Master agrees—and I must tell you, Morpheús, that this is the first time in my experience that he has ever altered a contract in this fashion. You need to be cognizant that this is not a usual event here."

"You'll have to arrange for one or more transit-trips between here and Nova Europa so that I can prepare properly for this expedition," I said. "But I assume you knew that already."

I looked around the room at the richness everywhere displayed. Too much, I thought: it was almost cloying in its intensity.

She sat back in her chair.

"Do you approve of our *décor*?" she asked.

"It is...overwhelming, Mistress," I said. "Where are the green spaces on this world? I was told you had none."

"We needed those places for our technology," Zalmanna said. "We do maintain a few small parks in each district, but we devote ourselves to other pursuits most of the time. You would not understand, I think."

"I wonder," I said. I was going to say more on this topic, but Scooter nipped me on the earlobe, a sign that I needed to shut my trap—and right now!

"I think you are really a bit of a fool, Morpheús," Zalmanna continued, "but then so many of you shadow-men are. You don't understand the reality of the universe, or our place (or your place) within it.

"This conversation is now over. You will find that the mirror in the room where you arrived is functional again. Use it to return to Nova Europa. Gather whatever men and materiel you need, and return to us here whenever you are ready."

She slid a small, eight-sided medallion of black-gold across the table to me. "This has the potency to achieve part of your desires. Use it wisely and use it well. Place it on your chest—here!" Zalmanna parted the silk of her green gown until I could spy the tops of her small white breasts, lying there like two large, limp slugs on a log. She thumped the bone between them with her right index finger, creating an almost hollow sound. I shuddered in disgust.

Then she and Phenneïlonn rose from their seats, bowed, and marched away down that long, long corridor again. At the end of their rattling step-step-steps I heard a door click open—and then close again with a loud clunk.

It was time for us to get down to work.

CHAPTER TWO
"YOU DIRTY SON OF A WITCH!"

I used the medallion that Zalmanna the Overseer had given me to take us back to Doctor Scarabbaios's Hall of Mirrors. As instructed, I'd placed it over my breastbone, where it had quickly and firmly attached itself, and now seemed almost a part of my skin. I wondered how I would ever get it loose again.

We emerged from the same black-gold transit-device that the old mage had employed to send us to the Overworld. The room was as dark as my spirit, after our experiences with the Overseers, but I activated a nearby glowlight, which, when it finally sputtered to life, cast a pale emerald hue over the machinery scattered around us. But I wasn't interested in the "good" Doctor's collection of fancy wall mirrors, or even the *outré* implements littering the experimental tables.

We rousted the magus out of his bed in a far corner of the manse.

"You dirty son of a witch!" I yelled in his wrinkled face, grabbing him by his nightshirt and pulling him up to within an inch of my eyes, "you sold us out!"

"I…I…," he sputtered.

"You violated the Code of Magely Conduct. I should bring you up on charges before the Brotherhood of Tighris. You know what they'd do to you, in spite of your reputation."

"You can't do that," he said, "you can't! I'm an old man. I'm…I'm retired. This place is all I have left."

"Then you'd better tell me what I need to know—tell it to me straight—and lend Scooter access to your consciousness, freely and openly, so it can test your responses.

"What say you, Doctor Scarabbaios?"

"I agree! I agree! Just don't report me!" he said.

I released my grip and let his body drop the remaining two feet to the bed. Then I bore down on him with my will, using the fear that I'd generated to penetrate his defenses.

"Scooter!" I said—and the wherret jumped from my shoulder onto his chest, further intimidating him, and scratching a line of blood down the stubble of his right cheek. The wherret then touched the magus's face with its long, serrated tongue, establishing psychic contact.

"Ahhh!" the old man exclaimed, as he tried to burrow back into his pillow. "Stop that! No!"

But he couldn't resist the double onslaught of a Psairothi master plus a wherret.

"Did Master Melanchthon have a wherretian servant named Grit?"

"Yes, yes." Scarabbaios was almost babbling by this time.

"How did he acquire it?" I asked.

"He drew it from the Fifth Circle of the Otherworlds."

"Tell me of the circumstances."

"Melanchthon was not of this world," Scarabbaios said. "He never told me where he was born or how he came to be here, but I know that he brought Grit with him at the time—and that the wherret derived from a place deep within the Fifth Circle. He said that if I knew any of the details, my life would be in danger. But he understood things about the Otherworlds that no one from Nova Europa could possibly know.

"In his laboratory high on the ridge above the Bosporus Strait, he'd assembled a collection of very curious instruments—plus a set of transit-mirrors unlike any others I'd ever seen. Some of them I managed to save after his death, although others were carried off by the Turks when they pillaged the place early in 1453. I never knew what happened to the great Ouroboros Mirror, the ancient device that he claimed could take him anywhere in the universe."

"But if that's so," I said, "Where did he find the power?"

"Ah. Well, as to that, he once told me that the answer lay within the pages of a book—*The Necropompeion*, to be precise—but he never indicated exactly how the volume needed to be manipulated in order to generate the vast amounts of energy necessary to travel from here to the other circles. But he seemed confident that he could do so at will."

"So, what prevented him?" Scooter asked.

"He said once that the Overseers constantly monitor the æthernet for surges that might indicate trans-circle travel. He didn't want to be found by them. I had the impression that he'd done something of which they'd disapproved, and that he'd be punished by them if they ever managed to locate him. I think that's what must have happened in the end."

"What do you mean?" I asked.

"Just before the Turks closed their claws around the walls of Julianople, Melanchthon moved the Ouroboros Mirror to his residence in the city. We were fighting daily to resist the magical attacks of the Turkish Imams, led by the Kalifah, their greatest mage. Near the end of May, it became obvious to my Master that we could not hold off the infidels much longer, and he said as much to the Autokratôr Kônstantinos.

"'What else can we do?' the Basileus asked.

"'There may be a way, Majesty, but it is a very, very risky procedure, possibly even imperiling your immortal soul. I could call up a creature from the Otherworlds, a behemoth that would ravage the enemy, but might also prove uncontrollable afterwards. Do you wish me take that risk?'

"The Emperor aged ten years in ten minutes while considering the problem—as you know, he did not long survive the victory—but he finally said, 'Do what you have to do to save the city, but keep the solution a secret from everyone.'

"So Melanchthon asked me to join him in his workshop at his home near the Kaisareion Palace, together with Grit and another mage, Igniferus of Pontus, and then he did something that chilled me to my bones. He made the image of the ouro-boros that encircled the great mirror somehow come alive. It began to twist 'round and 'round the rim of the structure, its forked tongue shooting out in front, like some great double stinger. I heard a whine from deep within the transit-mirror as it began to activate and build its charge.

"He opened *The Necropompeion* and began reading from it—but nothing he said made any sense, and the words were jumbled in such a way that I cannot now recall any of it. ['This is true, Master,' Scooter interjected]. Then something from the book transferred itself into the mirror, and the transit-device came alive and open to somewhere out in the void—I don't know where. Melanchthon literally stepped forward, reached his right hand through the metal surface, and pulled the crea-ture that I later called Blosk into Nova Europa. Somehow he communicated with the thing and made the bargain of which I told you—and the creature knew our language almost immedi-ately, although I don't know how it acquired such a facility.

"Then the mage turned to us and said: 'You stand as my witness, Scarabbaios and Igniferus, that if something should happen to me to prevent the fulfillment of the contract, you'—he pointed at me—'and you'—he pointed at my companion—'will bear the burden of completing these terms, lest Blosk return to destroy the city of Julianople.'

"We both swore mighty oaths that we would fulfill his promise, but before we'd even finished reciting our pledges, the Ouroboros Mirror activated again, this time by itself, and a small man transited through.

"'So, Melanchthon, we meet again,' he said, and nodded at Grit. 'You will come with me now, or I will send this creature back to where it originated.'

"'Remember what I told you,' the Master Mage said to us—and then he and the wherret left, just like that. We turned Blosk against the Turks, and they were destroyed and the Kalifah defeated, as had been promised. No one could stand against it. But afterwards, Igniferus perished a few days later in a magical skirmish with the remnants of the heathen forces, so I was left alone with the burden of making certain that Blosk found its way back to its homeworld."

"So Melanchthon didn't die in the siege," I said.

"No, but the Emperor counted him among the national martyrs who gave their lives for the city, even though his body was never found. Many were lost in this way, so no one ever questioned what had happened to the Great Mage. He is still accounted the savior of the nation."

"And the man who came for Melanchthon…?"

"…was an Overseer, I think. But I'm not sure. I had the sense—and it was only a feeling—that he could not have compelled the Master against his will. And *that* is all I know, Master Morpheús. I've been trying to fathom the secrets of *The Necropompeion* ever since you left, and I…cannot. Perhaps it needs the Ouroboros Mirror as a counterpart in the equation. I just don't know."

"Then give me the book and let me try," I said.

His face fell even further into despondency, but he finally nodded his head. "It's on the shelf over there," he said, indicating an alcove across the room. "Take it—you've taken everything else."

"No, Scarabbaios, whatever's happened to you is something that you did to yourself. You made your choices, and now you must live with the consequences, good or ill. That's all life is. You may be old, but no one's keeping you confined in this self-prison. Wake up, old man, and learn to live again. Get out into the world and enjoy a summer's day."

"I don't know if I can."

"Well, try."

In the end, I have very little patience for whiners.

CHAPTER THREE
"OH POOPY, POOPY DOO"

Scooter and I transited home to Barstölný a few moments later, and found my household in an uproar.

"I...I will not tolerate that...woman!" Martana yelled at me, right after I stepped through the transit-mirror.

"What woman?" I asked, caught completely without warning by her onslaught.

"That...Shah'rah," she said. "She is a bad person, Sir. She wants this and she wants that, she wants everything to be 'just so.' She is never happy with what Martana does for her. She must go!—or I must go!"

"Shah'rah!" I shouted. When she appeared, I asked her what was going on.

"She washed, uh, shawl Grandmama had knit"—her diction had greatly improved in my absence—"It...only thing left of her. She ruined—tassels now all gone!"

"Martana?" I asked.

"That knitty thing, 'twas filthy-nasty, Master," she said. "It needed a good wash. That...that woman needs a good wash, too. I give her a good wash, you see!"

"And I thought you two were getting along so well," I said. "You'll stop this bickering at once, is that understood?"

"Yes, Master," they both said.

"Martana, Shah'rah is an indentured servant. She lives in this household. You do not. You will treat each other with respect. Shah'rah, you'll be responsible for cleaning your own room and your own things in the future. Martana, you'll stay out of Shah'rah's room and Shah'rah's belongings. Agreed?"

"Yes, Master," they said.

"Very well. Shah'rah, please fix me something to eat while I check for messages. Scooter, you're free until I call you again. Martana, please get back to work."

"Yes, Master," they all said. Gadzooks: sometimes it was like managing a household full of unruly children!

In the privacy of my laboratory (for the first time in memory, I actually locked the door!), I surveyed the recorder sky-orb: two calls from Hawk, one from Doctor Árbogast, one half-word that may have come from the Lady, and twenty-two messages from various purveyors of magical implements and supplies; Doctor Flox, for example had left me this witty little ditty:

> "Crap-a-Lot!
> Crap-a-Lot!
> It's just so good for what ails you.
> With Crap-a-Lot!
> Oh, Crap-a-Lot!
> You're never in a stew.
> Oh poopy, poopy doo!"

and so on. He must have overbought this particular drug, and now had to flush some of the product out of his system, so to speak. Maybe he could give some to Kolkus. I chuckled at the thought.

"What's so funny, Master?" Scooter said. I just about jumped out of my skin.

"How did you unlock the door?" I asked.

"I didn't. Remember?"

Of course—wherrets are animorphs. When stretched, they could fit through almost any crack.

"In any case, what are you doing here?"

"I had a message of my own that I thought you'd want to hear," Scooter said.

"A message? But you don't have a sky-orb," I said.

"No, I don't, Master, and this particular communication didn't arrive through the æther. That's one of the things that makes it so puzzling. It was waiting for me in my alcove."

The wherret pulled a small square envelope out of its traveling harness; there was some kind of writing on it, but I couldn't make it out.

"What's remarkable is that it's written in my native tongue, which no one here should know or understand. What's even more astonishing is the message itself: 'We need to talk. Grit.'"

"But I thought that Grit had been taken with its master to the Overworld."

"That was 169 years ago, Sir."

"How long do wherrets live?" I asked.

"As long as we want," my friend said. "Obviously, Grit's still alive, and it's somewhere on Nova Europa. Perhaps it can tell us what happened to Melanchthon."

"But how do we contact it?"

"We don't—not directly. But we can let it know that it's welcome here. If you give me permission, I'll ink a character from our language on the garden wall out back. The word will be passed."

"Very well," I said. "Do it."

At that moment, there was a rat-tat-rapping on my chamber door. I unlocked it, and found Shah'rah standing there.

"Dinner, I serve," she said.

And it was, too, but the meat was stringy and overcooked, the vegetables were overripe and undercooked, the bread was hard and moldy, and the wine was a tad sour. I tried not to grimace.

"So sorry, Sir," she said, smiling sweetly, "But did not know you come home today, so do not shop for the foods. If you tell me when...."

I pushed my plate back with most of my portion untouched.

"I'm not really hungry," I said.

"And I have things to do," the wherret added, jumping from its perch and scooting out the door.

Shah'rah began clearing the table. Out in the kitchen, I could hear Martana clanging and banging around while scrubbing up the mess.

"What *is* this!" I heard her yell to my new cook.

Oh, Lord! I could see that this was going to be a truly joyous homecoming!

CHAPTER FOUR
"WE WANT THAT
ELEPHANT'S EGG!"

That evening, I locked myself in the laboratory and again tried contacting Niobë of Naprimér, whom I'd labeled in my own mind "The Lady." As best as I could figure, it should have been early afternoon there, but I got no response to my hail. Sometimes the captive woman was surprisingly easy to reach, but often all I received for my effort was ætherial static.

I took a break, and decided to do some research in my library on the background of the infamous Melanchthon of Byzantion. Adrianos's *Mages of Antiquity* (*Magi Antiquitatis*) was always the first place to look for information, and sure enough, the old reliable researcher had all the basic information:

> MELANCHTHON or MELANCHTHONIUS, called Malitiosus ("The Crafty") and The Great Mage, fl. A.J. 1017-1093 (A.D. 1377-1453). He is first recorded by Juniperos as paying the magerly tax in Alexandria Ægyptia in 1017, and again in 1020, although his precise station there is unknown. Prolix associates him (under the name Melanchthonius) with Mar-Tib-Lumu in Kalleh Assyriana ca. 1025, where he worked with that mage on long-range transit experiments, evidently without success. Marcus Eugenius is the first to mention his familiar, the ferret Grit, in 1037, and the first to call him "Malitiosus." However, Scotus states that Grit

was not a ferret, but a creature similar in features that derived from the Otherworlds; and also implies that Master Melanchthon himself transited to Nova Europa from some other place in the æther ca. 1015. The Great Mage's residence during the 1030s is unknown.

Melanchthon is first noted as being received at the Golden Throne of Julianople in the year 1041, under the reign of Autokratôr Kônstantinos x, and after his death, by his son, Nikomedês ɪɪ, and his grandsons, Dêmêtrios ɪv and Kônstantinos xɪ. He quickly attached himself to the official magical apparatus of the state, and by 1052 is being called "First Mage" in court documents. He held that position for the next four decades.

During the Turkish Crisis of 1081-1093, Melanchthon is said to have been instrumental in saving Julianople from destruction through the two attacks on the city, although the exact nature of his magical intervention remains unknown. Fraich believes that the Great Mage defeated the Chief Magus or Kalifah of the Musselmans, Abduläziz, in personal combat, but the fact that Abduläziz is known to have survived for another half dozen years after the siege of Julianople would seem to mitigate against this notion.

In any event, Melanchthon disappeared during the final conflict in 1093, and was succeeded by his assistant, Second Mage Karôlinos Scarabbaios. His body was never found, although he was added to the list of martyrs of the state by Autokratôr Julian vɪɪɪ. Some historians believe that Melanchthon returned to the Otherworlds, where he abideth even to this day.

I read the entry to Scooter, who said: "I wonder where he could have gone, Master. Maybe to the Overworld."

"Indeed. I wonder if I can persuade Mistress Zalmanna to search their records," I said.

"If, that is, she speaks truly, Sir. While I believe that she has spoken no direct untruth as yet, I do sense that she only relates that which *must* be conveyed, and often not the entire tale."

"I felt the same," I said, "but I don't know the right questions to ask. Perhaps Niobë might have some ideas."

So I went back to my *officina* and tried again to contact the Lady of Naprimér. This time I had no problem establishing the link.

I felt a tingle as the twin sky-orbs suddenly came alive. "Morpheús!" I heard, but very, very faintly. Still, I recognized that voice!

"Milady," I said, sitting straight up in my chair, and twisting the leys to focus on that distant signal; but although I could hear her speaking, I could not retrieve an image, try as I might.

"Whatever happened to you? It's been three months! I'd almost given up hearing from you again."

Three months? How was that possible? Time elapsed or flowed on Naprimér at a different rate than on Nova Europa—and we thought we'd calculated a rough correspondence during our previous contacts. Now all of our sensibilities seemed turned topsy-turvy.

"I tried reaching you earlier today," I said. "But I couldn't make contact, I don't know why. And the time that's elapsed here has not been nearly as long—perhaps a week. Something strange has been going on in the æthersphere."

"What?" she said. "I can't hear you very well, Morpheús. And who's that other person in the link?"

"*What* other person?" I asked, for I could hear no one, although the connection was truly terrible, full of gaps and a hissing noise that permeated everything.

"Why are you saying such things?" she said. "Who *are* you? Morphy, they're telling me that unless you do this 'thing' for them, I'll never be able to talk to you again."

"*Who* is?"

Then I heard a third person enunciate quite, quite clearly: "Master Morpheús, we want that Elephant's Egg! It is time that you focus on the problem at hand, and begin your work for us."

I recognized the dulcet diction of Mistress Zalmanna, the junior Overseer.

"How I prepare for my task and what I do about it is *my* choice, not yours," I said. "I will simply not rush into something this delicate and this dangerous. Leave me alone until I contact you. That's my final word on the subject.

"Oh, and remove the Lady Niobë from the equation. She has nothing to do with you."

"She has everything to do with us," Zalmanna said. "She motivates you, and that motivates me to seek discourse with her directly. And you cannot stop me, mage, nor any of my ilk. We will expect you here within the week. And do not think—ever—that you can escape our scrutiny."

I spoke the word ("nexus") that shut down the sky-orbs. I was already sick to death of the interference of these so-called "superior" beings, and their condescending attitude towards those of the "lesser" races. I considered abandoning the project altogether, but I couldn't do that to Niobë, and I simply would not kowtow to the Overseers—not now and not ever, not while I yet drew breath. There had to be some way of fighting them.

Clearly, I needed to find out more information about… well, about everything. I had to understand how the Overseers controlled the æthernet, and see if I could find a way to turn that knowledge against them, to break their monopoly on non-accidental inter-world and inter-Circle travel. I had to find someone who understood the principles involved.

I again wondered if Melanchthon Malitiosus was still alive somewhere "out there," for he seemed to me the kind of person who would be willing to stand up to almost anyone—or at least be able to provide me with the knowledge that I needed. Perhaps his wherret would know, and Grit apparently wanted to see us.

Magicians can live, in theory, for hundreds of years, although we are as subject to accident, murder, and misadventure as any normal man. Doctor Scarabbaios, I knew, had survived the better part of three centuries, at the least. But there were rumors and stories of other mages, very shadowy figures such as Master Mathurin, who'd extended their time on this sphere to a millennium or more. Many of these tales were likely apocryphal, but perhaps there was a kernel of truth somewhere in the mix. How long, in theory, could drugs, spells, and sheer will keep us going?

I had no idea. I looked younger than I was, of course—we all did. But Scarabbaios *appeared* old to me, at least in form—was that also an affectation, or was it real? I speculated then, just in passing, on how old the Lady was. She could have been anything—and in any event, she very carefully always kept part of her face enshrouded. Why?

So many doubts, so few answers. It made me weary just to consider such questions. But someone had to.

I reopened the link with the Lady, and quickly shot her a compressed set of images that related our trip to the Overworld and our dealings with Doctor Scarabbaios. Then, before Mistress Zalmanna could interfere again, I abruptly closed the opening in the æthernet. Niobë would get back to me, I was sure, when she'd had a chance to examine the material I'd sent her.

Now, however, Grit marked the next step on our journey—Grit…and just possibly his Master, Melanchthon Malitiosus!

CHAPTER FIVE
"YOU MUST BE GRIT"

I was sitting in the garden the next morning, reading *Sub Ægypto*, the classic account by Marcus Menvillius the Mad Monk of his wanderings through the Psairothi brothels of Alexandria, where he converted all of the workers back into virgins—a truly wondrous feat remarked upon at the time by Count Karnigian the Cruel as equivalent to Hercules swishing out the Augean stables—when I was awakened by Scooter climbing on my shoulder.

"I was, uh, contemplating the wisdom of the great mendicant," I said.

"Ah, Sir, that must have been what the buzzing noise was all about," came the whisper in my right ear—a whisper that I did *not* recognize.

I sat up straight and dropped the book on a flower bed, crushing a few of them. I'd have to pay amends to the gardener later.

The wherret jumped into my lap. It was larger than Scooter, and coal black on top (instead of brown and white), with flashing red eyes.

"You must be Grit," I said. I called Scooter to join us.

"And you must be Master Morpheús," came the retort, "the young human mage who wants to travel through the Otherworlds. Hi ho, hi ho, another reckless, feckless idiot. You all want to go somewhere else. What's wrong with *this* world, eh?"

Then Scooter appeared, and I saw an expression on its face

that I'd never encountered before: jealousy. After all, Grit was resting in *my* lap—and Scooter wasn't!

The lighter-colored wherret hissed something at its countryman, and the larger creature hissed right back. I suppose that this was some kind of wherret-speech, but I couldn't make out any words as such. Finally Grit dismounted from its perch, and allowed its "brother" to take its place.

"We were surprised to hear from you," I finally said, trying to calm both savage beasts, without actually having to break into song.

"Why?"

"I guess because your last historical record showed you were departing this place for the Overworld."

"Yes, well, my Master had got himself into a bit of trouble with the Overseers, and when they discovered where he was living, they came for him. Simple as that, one, two, three."

"And where's your Master now?" Scooter asked.

"Lost! That's why I need your help," Grit said.

"You need *our* help?" I said. "We also need yours."

"I know that, and I'll trade you what I know for your assistance in retrieving Master Melanchthon. You'll find that our paths coincide in any case."

"Indeed. How so?" I asked.

"My Master was a Wildsider, a native of a world that lies on the border between the First and Second Circles. This place is also one of the nodes enhanced by the Overseers to facilitate their travel to and from the Overworld to the outer limits of the Fifth Sphere. They converted this planet into a way station staffed primarily by its natives, and enlisted some of the Wildsiders into serving as, well, underlings to the Overseers, working as bodyguards and technicians and builders and facilitators. A few of the brighter individuals were educated and even allowed transit eventually to the Overworld.

"Melanchthon was one of these students, and a very able one he became—so able, in fact, that he began designing enhancements to some of their more sophisticated equipment. I met him on the Overworld during this period. You must understand that Wherreton, our homeworld in the Fifth Circle, is another Overseer node, one of a chain of such major transit-stations, and wherrets are common travelers with and companions to the Overseers in the higher Circles—but rarely in the First Circle. We're too *outré* for most humans.

"But I was ultimately brought to the Overworld, whose real name is Tyrotarichos, to represent my people there. The Tyros have a very condescending attitude towards any race but their own. They regard themselves as the First People, both in terms of creation and in importance. Their intelligence predates any others that are known.

"Melanchthon and I and many others have tried to push back against such notions, and to create a more representative style of governance, in which all of the travelers through the æthernet would have equal (or at least somewhat greater) importance before their Council.

"But the High Master Ponnyshonn, with Masters Phenneïlonn and Ontonnionn, blocked our efforts, leaving us with few options. We didn't have the means to force the issue on the Overworld. I decided to return home to report to my people, and Melanchthon asked to accompany me, having never traveled to the Fifth Circle before.

"When we reached Rockville on my planet, my Master asked the station manager for permission to examine the equipment there. You see, every world has its own vibration, and the æther varies slightly from place to place—and much more greatly from Circle to Circle. So the transit-devices employed in one Circle will often not work in another—or will produce unexpected results.

"When he'd finished his examination of the station, he came to me one night and said: 'There's something you ought to know. The configuration of the machines on your world suggests a counterbalance at work somewhere "out there." I don't have any idea what it is, but it has to exist. Without the balance evening out the æther flow, none of these devices would work in *any*

Circle, even at the base—on the Overworld.'

"'But don't the Overseers know this?' I asked.

"'Not from what I can tell,' he said. 'Their ethnocentricity blinds them to the reality of the situation. They consider themselves the center of the universe, when in reality they just represent one of two equal poles.'

"'Where *is* this…this great counterweight?'

"'It has to lie beyond the Fifth Circle. If it were destroyed or removed or damaged in any way, the entire transit system would collapse almost immediately, reducing the power of the Overseers to nothing. Perhaps the influence of whoever else is out there would then rise to fill the vacuum. I have no way of knowing exactly what would happen, or how long it would take. The vacuum *would* be filled eventually, of that I'm sure.

"'And there's another corollary inevitably flowing from the first. If both poles are equally balanced, as they appear to be now, that balance can be governed or affected or influenced by a third device or object, something that most likely also lies within the chaos surrounding the Fifth Circle.'

"'But how did such things come into existence?' I asked, for it seemed to me impossible that they could have been created accidentally.

"'I'll leave such questions to the philosophers,' he said. 'Of course, I have no hard evidence of their reality, but I believe if we search for it, we'll find it.'

"And we *did* search, and my Master eventually came to believe that he was drawing close to an answer. But then the Overseers somehow grew suspicious of our activities, and we were arrested and brought back to Tyrotarichos, where we were closely questioned by the High Master. However, we said nothing of our theories.

"Still, they knew somehow that we were hiding something, and that it had to do with the transit-system. My Master had a younger brother named Markosian whom he hadn't seen in many years, and one day he encountered him near the main station on the Overworld.

"'I've been given a major chance,' his brother said. 'They say I'll be a keeper in the Great Zoölogion within a decade. Isn't that wonderful?'

"But Melanchthon knew that he was being subtly threatened with the disgrace or death of his sibling. The next time we met with High Master Ponnyshonn, that old man looked at us as if we were beetles infesting his fruit, some vermin that he could exterminate by just stepping on them.

"'We want you to do something for us,' he said. And then he told us about The Fourth Elephant's Egg."

"Aphlak!" I said. "That's what they wanted *us* to retrieve."

"And many others, so many others," Grit said. "Many have been sent by the Tyros to the outer limits of the Fifth Circle to find this object, whatever it is, but few have returned, and none have ever been successful. We were not the first, and you won't be the last, I fear.

"But we did try. We were sent first to Kallimine, and then to Ásteri, and then to Berdoo, but nowhere did we find The Fourth Elephant's Egg. We heard…rumors sometimes, and stories, and tales, but none of them made sense, and none of them coincided with each other either. And never, ever could we determine upon a location for the thing, whatever it was.

"Finally we tried transiting through a strange mirror on Redland to another world named Highland, but something went wrong, and we wound up instead on Nova Europa. This place was so far off the transit routes that we thought we could grab some rest and relaxation for a few months before resuming our quest—but the months became years, and the years decades, and we never did anything further until we were forced to save Julianople.

"When we thus revealed ourselves to the Overseers, we were taken back to Tyrotarichos, and Melanchthon was forced to return to the outskirts of the Fifth Circle, to a world called Verdugo, to complete his quest, while I was held prisoner on the Overworld. But then his disk went silent, and as the years went by, the Tyros finally wrote him off as another lost cause. They began looking for the next unwary traveler to trap into their quest."

"Why don't they go themselves?" Scooter asked.

"Perhaps they have, but I think that they now lack the courage to venture into the void on their own. They're not an imaginative people, but a very conservative one that strives to hold onto their edge, as they perceive it, over all the other races in the universe. They honestly don't know what the Egg represents—and frankly, neither do I. Perhaps it's the third object that Melanchthon believed existed, or maybe it's just a pachydermal ovum. There are some very strange creatures out there. But who cares, really?

"I just want to find out what happened to my friend, and to save him if I can. I don't give a wherret's turd about the rest. Let the cosmos sink or swim on its own accord, if it dare."

I pondered everything the creature had said, but I could make no real sense of it. The answer still lay "beyond beyond," as they say, somewhere out near the border of the Fifth and Sixth Circles. If we ventured there, the chances were good that we'd never come back. And what would happen to the Lady then?

So many questions, so few answers.

"Do you wish to join our quest?" I asked Grit.

"Of course. Why do you think I'm here?" it said.

CHAPTER SIX
"IN THE END, HE JUST DISAPPEARS"

I needed someone's perspective other than my own: I needed to talk to Niobë at length, about these and other issues. But I didn't want Mistress Zalmanna to listen in or to interfere again, so Scooter and I spent a few hours rigging a "whistler," a feedback loop keyed to the frequency of the Overworld (which we knew, since we'd visited there). When Madame Z. tried to eavesdrop on us again, all she'd get back is a blast of high, screeching noise through the æthernet, much like the shriek of a banshee. It should set fire to her nerves!—and was almost impossible to contravene.

Then I contacted Niobë again, and had no trouble building a strong link this time. I started by telling her of my conversation with Grit, and asked her what she thought of our situation, now that she'd had the time to review the summary that I'd sent her the previous day.

"I've been mulling this over a great deal since talking to you last, and I believe that we should part company immediately," she said.

I must admit to being taken aback by this statement. "What? *Why?*" I asked.

"The Overseers are using you for their own ends. They're sending you on a risky mission with no expectation of return—and even if you're ultimately successful, they can fulfill their part of the bargain without difficulty. It costs them nothing.

It's an unfair contract in every respect. It's not an agreement of equals."

"All of which is true, but so what? I made a promise to free you from your prison, and I simply don't have the means to reach you without the assistance of the Tyros. I do have *The Necropompeion*, and that may contain power of a sort—but I don't know how to use it, direct it, or channel it in a way that will take me from here to there—or even close."

"My confinement is my own burden, Morpheús. Most of my ills are self-generated by my bitter loneliness and neglect. Well, perhaps that's my own fault as well. I can't honestly bring you into this Hell without feeling guilty about it. We've never met, except at arm's length, so to speak. We don't really know each other. How can you possibly…?"

"I've made my commitment," I repeated, "and I won't alter it. What I've promised to do, I *will* do, or die trying. My life here has become irretrievably stale to me, and I need to try something different.

"Moreover, there's something awry within the very structure of the spheres, something that's causing the underlying framework of the cosmos to fracture. I can see it everywhere I go, even during my brief sojourn on the Overworld. The more I look, the more it becomes obvious to me.

"You came to me at a time in my life when I was ready to make a change. You've given me a reason to believe that change is actually possible. You've also handed me something to help redefine myself. So, with all respect, let's forgo such notions. I'll come to you if I can—and if I fail in my journey, so mote it be."

"So mote it be," she finally agreed, sighing out loud. "Ultimately, I haven't any choice but to accept your charity, you know that. But I have to say that I'm glad for it as well. My confined existence here is gradually wearing my spirit away, and I can't survive more than another few years of this horrible isolation. Knowing that you're out there, that you're trying to transit to Naprimér, also gives *me* hope for the first time in a decade. And maybe the Volúcris can be defeated after all.

"From what you've indicated, it was Doctor Scarabbaios who gave the bird-men the means that they needed to invade our world. You need to bring him with you to the Fifth Circle, both because of the knowledge that he contains, but also to pay the price for his crimes against my world."

"I'll do so," I said. "My intent is to assemble the same team that I used in Indushia, plus a few others, and to depart within a week or two. Do you have any idea where your world lies in relationship to Yelloweyen, where the Overseers propose to send us first?"

"I've never heard of the place," she said. "What you call the Fifth Circle is an immensity of chaos, consisting of innumerable suns, planets, and planetoids, many of them uninhabitable. We know only of those in our immediate vicinity, except for a few cases where we've established contact through the zip-ports—and the initial off-world connections were all the result of accidents.

"What I don't understand is this: if Master Melanchthon was correct, and the entire system of transit-devices and worlds is stabilized through two opposing poles, where's the second one? The picture that you've drawn of circular spheres of worlds overlaying each other suggests that each 'layer' is larger and more diverse than the lesser one. So how can there be a 'pole' beyond the Fifth Circle?"

"I don't know," I said. "None of it makes much sense to me. Perhaps it's more of a counterbalance, something that offsets the mass or energy (or both) that are concentrated on the Overworld. And the third element?—that could be a kind of slide that could be manipulated up and down the connecting strings of æther. Move it nearer the upper level, and it produces one effect; move it down, and it produces another. According to Melanchthon, the answer, if there is one, lies somewhere beyond the Fifth Circle. Maybe the 'Egg' has something to do with it."

"Or maybe not," the Lady said. "How are you going to find that which may not exist?"

"Again, I don't know, but I have to try. If I learn enough

about the process while exploring, perhaps I can find some way to reach you without returning to the core again. You want to overthrow the bird-men—I want to destroy the power of the Overseers."

"Morpheús, I apologize for my lack of faith in you. You're a good man at heart, I can see that now, and I know that you'll search for me if you can. Have you given any thought as to what comes afterwards?"

I laughed slightly under my breath—but she heard.

"Yes," she said, "That's a hard place to imagine, isn't it? For both of us, I think. Will you help me in my struggle against the Volúcris?"

"I will," I said, "if you'll aid me in my crusade against the Tyros."

"Of course. But what then, assuming we survive our various trials?"

"I honestly don't know, Milady. I think we'll have to wait and see. The improbability that both of us will live through the next few years is sufficiently high that I'm not going to spend a great deal of time worrying about it. Whatever comes, comes.

"All I can say for sure is that I relish the challenge. For the first time in many years, I feel young again."

"I do too," she said. "By the way, I've given some thought to the problem of the continuity between our two worlds—and I think it may have something to do with the 'counterbalance' you mentioned. I think time may vary when this psychic weight touches upon this region of the Fifth Circle. I don't know if that helps or not."

"At least it gives me something else to consider. I need to find some way of communicating with you once I start my quest. I missed you when I was in Indushia—and I need your constant advice in any case. See if you can imagine some method to use a single sky-orb to link with your shining pool."

"I'll do that," she said.

"Now, what do you think of this story of Melanchthon?" I asked.

"I find it...inconsistent. He appears from nowhere, and quickly establishes himself as a major experimenter with long-range transit devices. Where did he gain such expertise? Where did he originate? I didn't believe that story about his background."

"Nor do I," I said. "It sounds too straightforward to me."

"Also, this is a man who knows things that he shouldn't know, and has skills that no one else does. And then, in the end, he just disappears. I suspect that if you ask the Overseers about him, they won't be able to tell you anything more about his present location or ultimate fate than you already know. He reminds me of Matrin in some ways."

"Do you think the two men could be the same?"

"Possibly. I just wish we knew more about both individuals. The other day, I requested a copy of an old history that I knew contained all the major myths about Matrin. After much hemming and hawing, my captors couldn't find anything in the volume that I could use to break out of here, and so I was granted supervised access—they brought the book to me, and I had to read it under the constant gaze of a mute Magus who wouldn't even respond to my greeting of 'Good morrow!' He just sat there like a fat old feline fluffed out in front of a fire, frowning whenever I had the temerity actually to look at or speak to him. What a horrid little humbug!

"But...about that biography—it's really not a biography in the sense that we usually think of one. *The Matrinology* is a collection of sometimes fanciful (at least I *think* they're fanciful) tales about a larger-than-life wizard who comes to Naprimér from the Otherworlds, during a time of chaos not dissimilar to what we're both experiencing now on our own worlds. He works wonders and helps the helpless, and causes the rich and powerful barons to trip themselves in various ways, often in a humorous fashion.

"In some respects he's almost a religious figure, akin to the Great Lady that we honor. He had no trouble speaking our language from the very beginning—not in the way that you and

I do, via our minds channeled through the converter, but actually *speaking* it—the tales emphasize this ability, and marvel at it. It's a sign of his special nature that he can talk with the people—all of the people, of whatever race or nationality—with the fluency of a native.

"I was reading through this book last week when I came to the penultimate piece, and I was so struck by the words and images that I requested a copy be made of the story, because I wanted to read it to you. It's not so very long."

"I would be delighted," I said.

And this is what she said:

CHAPTER SEVEN
"THE TALE OF THE DANDY LION"

"The Tale of the Dandy Lion," the Lady Niobë said, quoting the story title from *The Matrinology.*

"'In those days the Great Teacher'—for this is what Master Matrin is often called in these fables—'came to the aid of the village of Caribbë in the Province of Tontontoquë, for he had heard that the inhabitants thereof were sorely beset by a great beast, and that the mage resident in the district, Master Fessus, could not find a means of stopping the destruction of their crops and livestock.

"'Every spell that Fessus cast, every potion that he mixed, every power that he invoked, either failed to do what he intended, or rebounded on him and on the poor people that he was trying to defend. Finally, he gathered his courage in both hands, and went forth to battle the creature directly, for he could see no other way to turn it back.

"'But when he came to the place where the lion was said to be active, it wasn't there, but had moved its range to an area some three leagues on the opposite side of the village; and when he went to this new location, it had moved again; and so on. He could never actually find the beast himself.

"'Finally, his sense of rage and frustration reached the point where he did something very foolish indeed. He made a spell of "calling," and planted his staff of office on the outskirts of the last house in Caribbë. "Come to me!" he said, and placed a bit of himself in the working.

"'And so the lion came at his command, and the villagers all fled from their homes, for they knew that such a creature could not be fought by any ordinary means. But Fessus remained standing alone by the symbol of his office, for he had faith in his ability and training.

"'"Stop!" he yelled at the creature. The thing was as tall as he, tawny in color, standing erect on its hind legs like a human, with four others armed with great fangs, and four enormous teeth that pushed beyond the limits of its mouth, overhanging its lips.

"'Still the mage held fast, for he had found the last remnant of his bravery tucked away in a small corner of his tattered soul, and had carefully pulled it out and unfolded this bit of steadfastness on account of this very rare event. So he stood his ground, when he probably would not have remained standing on the day before or the day after, and moved not an inch from the approach of this awful marauder.

"'"Stop!" he shouted again, "or I will kill you where you stand. Do not doubt my ability, o heinous one."

"'So the creature stopped, and lowered its face to the dust of the ground; and when it raised its head up again, its visage had taken on the semblance of Fessus himself.

"'"Kill me if you can," the lion told the man, "but if you do, o mage, know that you murder yourself as well. Whatever thou art, I am—but I am the greater of the twain."

"'Then the lion with the man's face continued its advance, and ate the magician before he could react further, for the creature was marvelously hungry that day, and the man was not.

"'Now the village was defenseless, but Master Matrin heard of its plight, and strode across the Archipelago of Pomusa in less than a day, skipping from island to island like a stone cast sideways upon the waters; for the Teacher was such a one as knew the secrets of traveling through the æther, and could jump great distances in a single bound.

"'When the residents of Caribbë saw him emerge from the Nothingness into the heart of the town's square, they exclaimed with delight, "Our savior has come!"—for they knew of this gentle man's reputation as a champion of the innocent.

"'Again Master Matrin called the beast to the village, just as his predecessor had done, and again he awaited him just beyond the furthest cottage that marked the uttermost boundary of Caribbë, and again he confronted the creature that appeared there.

"'And when the lion showed the mage his own face back again, and threatened to kill the man if it was killed in turn, the Teacher just laughed, and said, "I have lived a very long time, o Dandy Lion, but not nearly as long as thee, Liar of Liars, and I know that thou regardest thy life with more care than I. So I believe you not!"

"'Then the beast put its face in the dust once more, and showed the mage an image of the visage of the woman he cared about the most, saying, "If you take my life, human, you steal also the life of this female who makes your insides weep."

"'The Teacher sighed and said, "I have not been home for a long, long time, Perverted of Persuasion, and while I miss my wife, and would miss her even more were she gone from these spheres, I believe that I shall see her again in the afterlife. That threat will not stay my hand."

"'But the great feline tried a third time, showing the Master the image of his first-born son, now a man grown unto himself, saying, "Kill me, sir—and kill thy offspring as well."

"'Now the villagers, hiding in their homes, had overhead the entire conversation, and were becoming increasingly angry that their champion was being ill-used in such a way. So they gathered up their hoes and brooms and arrows and sticks and knives, and they poured from their dwelling-places into the square, and marched up the one real street in the town, until they came up behind the Teacher, and flanked him on either side.

"'As they gradually encircled the beast, the lion became more and more nervous, and lost its human face, reverting to the ugly, dangerous creature that it was. But the townspeople had lost their fear, now that the thing had been revealed for what it was, and they slowly closed their circle of sharps, until the Dandy Lion screamed out its terror and its pain, and expired amidst the rising and falling of the scythes of time.

"""You see," Master Matrin said, when the deed had been done, "You had this result within your power all along. All you had to do was realize the fact, and act accordingly."

"'Then he turned, and with his right hand traced a circle in the air, and when it opened a door into the æthernet, moved towards it.

"""Where are you going, Sir?" the girl named S'rënë asked. She was the only surviving offspring of the mage Fessus.

"""To teach the others out there the lesson that you have already learned," he said. He reached down and touched the child on the center of her forehead with the end of his index finger. "Receive my knowledge, Little One, that you may follow in my footsteps here, and lead your people to peace and righteousness."

"'Then she fainted, but when she awoke from her dream, the Teacher was gone, and he only appeared once more in Naprimér—but that is another story, o reader of tales, for another day.'"

CHAPTER EIGHT
"DRAWING A CIRCLE IN THE AIR"

"What happened in the final tale of *The Matrinology*?" I asked.

"Matrin was absent, according to the story," the Lady Niobë said, "For about fifteen years. When he returned to Naprimér, he sought out the Lady S'rënë, my ancestress, who had now come into her ability, she being a hypatomancer, and brought her here to Mirabö. The two of them joined their powers together and began remaking the social order, starting first on this Southern Archipelago, and then continuing elsewhere. Once the process was started, he left our world for good.

"At about that time, men were permanently displaced from the ruling, magical, and priestly classes, which had the effect of ending the incessant warring that was commonplace in our early history. Of course, all of that's changed with the advent of the Bird-Men, who have once again restored men to the seats of power within society."

"You indicate that this Matrin was able to transit through the æther by drawing a circle in the air, and then opening a 'door' into the void. How's that possible?"

"I have no idea," she said. "But it's mentioned on several different occasions in the volume, and it's always described in similar terms, so I think it must have happened—if, of course, we assume that there's some underlying truth to these tales. It must have been some kind of advanced form of travel though the spheres—something that we've lost in the interim, because there's no tradition of that kind of magic on this world any longer."

"Nor on mine," I said. "Does the final story relate how the Lady S'rënë merged her abilities with his?"

"No," she said, "Only that she did, and that they were stronger working together than separately. The main purpose of the book was obviously to tell the reader, particularly the young reader, how our culture came to be—and why—and while Matrin is mentioned throughout the text, very few specifics are given about his background. He is a shadowy worker of wonders, a mage with a very kind soul.

"No, this is all that I could glean about the man, except this: he carried with him a set of implements! One of these was an irregularly-shaped, partially-clear stone that glowed in yellow and orange; that's what he used to make his circles in the air. Another was a covered container of glowbugs; he tells a villager on one occasion that the glowlight helps 'illuminate his way through the emptiness.' And he also owns several books that he stores in his very plain living quarters, 'tomes of power,' as *The Matrinology* refers to them, that he sometimes takes with him on his travels. All of these things vanished when he left our world, and have never been seen again."

"What about pachyderms? Are these mentioned anywhere?"

"I don't know that word—it doesn't come through our link as anything except gibberish. Can you form a mental picture of them?" she asked.

I made an image in my mind of the great, hairy, ivory-tusked beasts that roamed the northern tundra of Nova Europa, stomping through the snow and ice, and terrorizing the hunters of elk and seals.

"We have nothing like that here," the Lady said.

"So you don't know what the Elephant Eggs might be?"

"No."

"Rats!" I said.

"Those we do have, Morpheús, in great numbers!"

"I suspect they're universal, rather like roaches and pigeons."

CHAPTER NINE
"THERE IS NO 'BEYOND'"

Our council of war assembled in Hawk's studio in Paltyrrha. We were thirteen in all: myself; Hawk (also known as Sergeant Strook); his surviving men, Warbler, Gull, Bird, Roc, Raven, and Eagle; a new recruit, Brén the Single-Minded, my former classmate and a rock-climber (as the late Sparrow had been); Shah'rah, who insisted on not being left behind; the two wherrets, Grit and Scooter; and Doctor Scarabbaios, the only truly reluctant participant, who was trussed to a chair with a rag stuffed in his mouth to keep him from screaming out loud.

"Um-mm-mm," the mage said, trying to topple his seat to one side.

"I agree," I said, "But if you continue rocking that back and forth that way, you're liable to succeed, and the floor, right there where you'd smack it with your head, is very, very hard."

That shut him up!

"Doctor S. is here to help us with his knowledge of inter-Circle transit. This mission, gentlemen and lady and wherrets, if you choose to accept it, will be even more dangerous than your last. We're talking about traveling interdimensionally to a very far destination indeed. You'll see creatures and magic that you won't believe possible. Some of you probably won't return. I can promise you unspeakable horror—which is why I'm not saying anything about it—and unremitting terror—which may never leave your dreams. The terms will be the same as before. Which of you wishes to bow out?"

"Um-mm-mm," the mage said. His was the only voice.

"That sounds like a 'no' to me," I said. "So it's unanimous. We'll transit in about a week to the Overworld, and they'll send us, perhaps in stages, to a place called Yelloweyen. I know nothing at all about the conditions there. Perhaps the good Doctor can contribute something?"

I nodded to Scooter, who jumped up on the old man's shoulder and pulled his gag down slightly.

"Hellfire and damnation!" Scarabbaios yelled. "Let me loose right now, or you'll pay for this—the Overseers will make sure of that!"

"Actually," I said, "I've sent a message to the Tyros indicating that you've volunteered to join us, and they've told me that they approve. So you're going, like it or not. What can you tell us about our destination?"

"I won't do this," he said.

"Tell that to High Master Phenneïlonn, not to me. I don't think he has much of a sense of humor, though. I repeat: what do you know about Yelloweyen?"

There was a long silence. His bushy white sideburns pointed down towards his chest, targeting his round tummy. Then he sighed, long and loud.

"It's a small planet used as a way-station by the Overseers in the Fifth Circle, out near its further edge. The natives include intelligent canines on the one land continent that straddles the globe, and semi-intelligent, whale-like creatures in the two oceans. Its double-star casts a yellowish light over the landscape—hence its name."

"Now, that wasn't so hard, was it?" I said. "What's beyond this world in the station-chain?"

"There is no 'beyond,'" he said. "So far as I know, it's the last official transit-station sanctioned by the Tyros. There are, of course, transit destinations to other places from there, including some, I believe, lying within the so-called 'Sixth Circle' itself— but I'm not familiar with any of them. I've never actually traveled to this particular sector."

"Who else do you know who might provide some answers about these places?"

He thought for a moment before responding: "There might be some Overseer servants on Tyrotarichos who've traveled to this region, but I don't know any of their names, if they exist. However"—and he smiled when he continued—"I know that Mistress Zalmanna has been there."

"Indeed." I smiled too. "Then we'll need to have another discussion with the High Master. Grit, will you be able to translate for us?"

"Oh, yes, Sir," it said. "I know thirty-three languages, including Tyrosian. I can make him understand the situation."

"Good. When we transit there next week, we'll be sure to pay him a visit.

"In the meantime, all of you need to gather together two packs, one of clothing and other essential personal items, and another carrying whatever weapons or implements you think might prove useful on our expedition. I don't know how long we're going to be gone, but we'll improvise for anything else. Each of you will be given a money belt containing Tyrosian gold and silver pieces. I want you to return here a week from today. Understood?"

"Yes, Sir," Hawk said. "Am I to run the military bits once again?"

"You will," I said. "I'll handle the magical devices and the overall planning, but your men will report directly to you for most things. Shah'rah, I want you to bring along several of your dancing outfits. They might prove useful."

"I've contributed all I can," Doctor Scarabbaios said. "I'd like to be allowed to go home now."

"No," I said. "You're coming with us, Doctor S., all the way to the Fifth Circle. And if you try to evade me or escape in any way, I'll sic the Overseers on you."

"You're a cruel man, Master Morpheús."

"So I've been told. Just remember that if you try to run away, Hawk here will look after you for the next week."

Then I dismissed them, and took Shah'rah and the two wherrets back to the main station. After transiting them to my home in the south, I headed to the University at Julianople to meet with Doctor Árbogast. He had something to tell me, and I was curious to know what it was.

CHAPTER TEN
"A WILLINGNESS
TO INFLICT PAIN"

Doctor Remírdas Árbogast had been the terror of my undergraduate years at the University. His courses were the most difficult that I ever took—but I also learned more from his hard-nosed, logical mind than from most of my other instructors combined. He was one of the few professors with whom I still maintained active contact, and he always seemed to be genuinely interested in following what I was doing.

I found him in the Arboretum, one of his favorite spots, reading one of Plato's accounts of Socrates.

"It's interesting," he said. "I find Plato to have a lesser critical faculty than many of the other ancient philosophers, yet I enjoy reading him more. His portrait of his old mentor is one of the more endearing relationships in all of Greek literature. And when Socrates chooses to die as a matter of principle, when he could easily have fled, I'm still moved to tears. He was a fool, to be sure, but a fool that one must admire.

"So tell me, dear boy: what have you learned about the Otherworlds?"

I told him, and when I'd finished, he sat there for perhaps ten minutes without saying a word, just gazing off into the distance. I knew from previous experience *not* to interrupt, but to wait until he was ready to give his opinion—an opinion, I might add, that was always valuable.

"You have quite a stew going on here, haven't you?" he

finally said. "I wonder who's lying and who's telling the truth. Or perhaps the real truth is that no one actually knows anything for certain. You seem to me to have several issues that need to be resolved.

"Firstly, what exactly are these Elephant Eggs? Right now they're just a conundrum wrapped in a mystery encloaked in uncertainty. The chances are fairly good, I think, that something actually exists out there to correspond to the nomenclature, but until you know the reality of what they are, you'll find it very difficult to make a decision on what to do about them. I'm presuming, perhaps unwisely, that you'll eventually reach the place or places where the artifacts are housed, and find some answers to my questions in the process.

"Secondly, how do you handle the obvious manipulations of the Overseers? Thus far, they seem to be controlling most of the variables, and with their superior knowledge of the situation, they're able to use you for their own ends without you easily being able to stop them. Somehow you have to find a way to turn the tables, if that's possible—but to do that, you need to understand far more about the situation than you do now.

"Thirdly, how do you reach Naprimér and your Lady, and resolve her conundrum to the satisfaction of both of you? This may be the trickiest problem of all, because emotions are rarely predictable and are often ungovernable, particularly with the female sex."

"She does not strike me as that type," I said, a bit irritated at his blatant condescension. His commentary was becoming rather too personal for my taste.

"Nonetheless, there are real differences between the sexes, and you ignore them at your peril," the philosopher said. "Also, you don't know, really, *what* she is—human or something else, female or something else, hypatomancer or something else. Finally, you have remarkably little information about her true place in society, past or present, other than that she was perhaps part of the ruling class there.

"Fourthly, what do you do and where do you go afterwards—

and with whom—and also, how do you get there? Such questions are rarely posed in advance, but to leave them unconsidered is to flirt with potential disaster. You need to have some notion of where you want to be when your adventure is finally resolved. Again, I'm presuming that it *will* be resolved, and that that resolution will benefit you and/or the others. If you're killed, that ends all speculation right there.

"Just as a 'for instance,' what if you do succeed in turning the tables on the Overseers? Their natural reaction, from what you've told me, will be revenge, and you can see this in their unrelenting pursuit of Master Melanchthon. Even though more than a century had passed from the time that he initially escaped their control, they neither forgot nor forgave. As soon as they'd located him, they reeled him back in. How do you mitigate this? You need to give yourself a future that's relatively untroubled by retaliation."

"I seem to spend much of my time," I said, "Asking a great many questions for which I have no answers."

"And that is the essential condition of life, my boy," he said, chuckling at the notion. "We all do that. You obviously think that because I've been at the University all of these years, and have taught all of these courses, and have read all of these learned men"—he held up the small volume of ancient philosophy—"that somehow I know the answers to everything. Well, let me disabuse you of that notion. The older I get, the less I seem to know.

"What I *do* know is that I enjoy sitting here among the trees on a warm day, and I enjoy reading Plato, and I enjoy our conversations—and perhaps in the end there isn't anything more to existence than finding some small pleasure out of such relatively ordinary things. For me, that's enough at this stage of my life.

"But I see that you still carry within you an intense dissatisfaction with your present life. That's something that only you can resolve. Maybe this coming adventure of yours will provide the context to give you a new way of looking at things. I do hope so. I've always thought that you were a good man and an intelligent man and a caring man, one who has always tried to do the right thing in his life. Follow that precept, Morpheús, and you can't go very far wrong.

"Ah, I can see by the waning light that it's almost time for my next class. Those empty schoolboy minds are waiting—not too impatiently!—to be filled by something other than nubile girls, greasy food, and gambling at the races. I have to live up to my image, after all, as a tyrant of the tyros! I remember that you called the Overseers by that name. Remember: Tyros may indeed be tyrants, but they can always be foiled by a stern resolution, real knowledge—and a willingness to inflict pain! If nothing else, 'pain' always works.

"Good luck to you, my boy. Come back again and tell me the outcome."

He left me then under the swaying limbs of the trees, and I realized suddenly that I enjoyed the garden there as much as he. It seemed to me like Paradise enow, just for a moment, and I felt this pang within my heart—of such sweetness, of such purity, that my spirit was filled briefly to the brim.

All of it receded, of course, a bit at a time, but I still had the memory to take with me when I returned home to Barstölný.

CHAPTER ELEVEN
"DON'T TRUST
HER FOR A MINUTE!"

Grit the wherret accompanied me a week later when I appeared before the High Council of Tyrotarichos—only because I needed its services as a translator. I didn't want to be forced into using one of "them" again, when so much was at stake. It was time to be more proactive.

The High Master Phenneïlonn was seated at the center of the long dais, one of perhaps twenty or twenty-five "Masters" there. Mistress Zalmanna was positioned to his right, presumably to convey my words to him.

"Per your instructions," I began, "I've assembled a number of assistants who will help me locate and secure The Fourth Elephant's Egg, wherever it exists. They're waiting for me in our rooms. However, I need some additional help in order to maximize the chances that our mission will succeed. I'm aware that several other very accomplished individuals have been sent on this quest in the past, and that none have returned. That suggests that the artifact is both well hidden and well protected."

"What else do you require?" the Tyrosian leader asked, the translation being whispered in my ear by the wherret.

"I want a much more sophisticated and powerful sky-orb through which to communicate with this world from great distances—even, if necessary, from the Sixth Circle. I presume you have such devices."

Phenneïlonn discussed this intently with the man seated to

his immediate left, and then looked up again. "We can do this," he finally said.

"You have given me this black-gold medallion"—I casually open my shirt so he could see it attached to my breastbone—"to enable me to activate transit-mirrors here and elsewhere, but I need something that will also work on Fifth Circle worlds. As you're aware, some parts of the æther there seem to work on very different principles, and some of their machines employ very odd methods to transit from one place to another. We need to be able to move rapidly through the region without hindrance."

Again the High Master spoke to the mage to his left, this time for over a minute, before finally saying: "We can do this."

"We'll be facing many dangers, both known and unknown, out near the boundary of the Fifth and Sixth Circles. I'm taking with me a number of well-trained soldiers, but our weapons are relatively primitive compared to some of which I've heard. I need to provide our security team with greater firepower, something that will stop a man, a beast, even a group of enemies."

Once more there was a buzz-buzz-buzz of quiet discussion, this time among several of the Masters. Then an argument broke out between two members on one side of the dais, and several seated on the other side of the chairman. They shouted back and forth for several minutes.

Finally Phenneïlonn said: "We have such things, but are reluctant to give them to you."

"It seems to me," I said, "that if you really want our expedition to find and retrieve the Egg, you need to provide us with the proper support. Obviously, what you've done in the past, whatever that is, has been insufficient. Your agents have *never* succeeded. None of them save one has ever returned, and when he was dispatched again to the Fifth Circle, he disappeared once again, this time for good."

There was no discussion on the panel after my comments, just a long pause. Finally, Phenneïlonn exchanged several remarks with the group of two to his left. "We can do this," the mage said at last.

"Also," I said, "we need the advice and support of someone who's familiar with this region, and who can help communicate with the natives. I understand that Mistress Zalmanna has traveled to Yelloweyen. I want her to accompany us."

The woman immediately sat up and said: "No!"

"We do not dispatch our own people on such risky missions," the High Master said. "That is a matter of accepted Council policy."

"Nonetheless," I said, "that is my final condition for making this trip. She must join our group, and in matters of overall decision-making and security, she must defer either to me or to my second-in-command, Sergeant Hawk."

The buzzing and loud comments continued for ten or fifteen minutes this time, but at last Phenneïlonn said: "We will do this: Mistress Zalmanna shall be part of your expedition, under the terms you have stated."

Zalmanna herself had gone completely white, and was obviously very upset or even outraged at the Council's decision. But she'd been outvoted, and would be forced to do exactly as ordered.

I was quite satisfied, and told my companions so when I returned to our quarters. Grit was already regaling the group with the details of my exchange, laughing all the while.

"You'd best be careful," Doctor Scarabbaios said. "I know Zalmanna from previous experience, and she's exactly the kind of person who'll stab you in the back when you're not looking. Don't trust her for a minute!"

"But she *has* been to the Fifth Circle," I said.

"Oh, yes, and she has more experience on Yelloweyen and in the Gorgias Sector generally than anyone else I know. She was supervisor of the main transit-station there for many years. She'll know how to reach the Sixth Circle, for example. But—if she tells you to rely on anyone else, be very, very careful. She wants the Egg, I'm sure, as badly as the High Master, but for her own purposes. It might be just what she needs to displace Phenneïlonn. She'll be happy to allow you to assume the risks necessary to locate and retrieve the object, but she'll immediately try to bring it under her direct control, particularly if she finds out what it is and what it'll do."

"You'll be there to advise me," I said, "Although, come to think of it, I can't really trust you either, can I, Doctor S.?"

"Harrumph," was all he could say.

"Harrumph," both of the wherrets said.

I could see we were going to have an harrumphing good time!

CHAPTER TWELVE
"AN EARWORM SAVED IS A PEONY URNED"

There are occasions in life when one knows that a crossroads has been reached. Go one way, and your life develops along a certain path, possibly going nowhere; go another, and perhaps you die or become rich or gain great power or meet the beautiful princess. You never know for sure. This was one of those times, and I realized it immediately when we stepped into the control room.

We didn't use any of the main transit-stations on Tyrotarichos. I don't think that the High Master wanted us to be seen by anyone else, but I also suspected that special equipment was required, because the device itself was unlike any I'd ever seen.

Like the small, round *atraurum* mirror owned by Doctor Scarabbaios (and given to him by the Overseers), this construct was fashioned from black-gold metal, an unusual alloy of aurum, obsidian, and something else I couldn't identify. The difference lay in its size: the Tyros had built a shiny, shimmery thing at least fifteen feet in diameter, forming an ovoid slightly taller than wide, with wires projecting off each side.

A technician sat at a console on the right-hand side of the room, touching spots on another, much smaller mirror, fashioned of what appeared to be *purpuraurum*, a magical metal that had been postulated, but never actually achieved on Nova Europa (the closest that we'd come had been a dark alloy of *cærulaurum* [blue-gold]). The technology on display was incredible: it made the rest of us look like the stupid barbarians that we must have seemed to the Tyros.

Already I could hear a humming sound in the walls as the power levels gradually increased. The giant mirror spat sparks at us as it slowly gained the energy needed to transit us across the immensity of ætherspace. This went on for at least ten or fifteen minutes.

"How do we access the leys?" I yelled over the din.

"We do not," Zalmanna said. She was dressed more demurely than I'd seen her last time, in a practical set of pantaloons that hugged her form quite closely. "Olmosetter will do it for us." She nodded at the man seated at the purple-gold mirror.

Almost as if he was responding to her, the technician looked at that moment and said, "We're ready, Mistress."

She handed each of us ear- and nose-plugs and masks to tie over our eyes. "We need to protect ourselves from the hazards of the long-void," she said, leading us as a group to the small platform in front of the great shining mirror, now pulsing with dark-energy, and showing us how to affix the covers over each orifice.

"Link your limbs together," she said. "Breathe in deeply just before we step into the æther, and then keep your mouths tightly shut until I send you a mental signal that it is safe to unmask. Are you ready?"

Each of us murmured our acquiescence.

"Then draw a deep breath and step forward!"

I almost fell down when we touched the surface of the *atraurum*, it was so electrifying. I could feel every part of my body tingling with energy as we fell through a seemingly endless emptiness. I don't know how long we were in there, but I've never experienced such an extended transit before. I desperately wanted to breathe, but I controlled myself until— quite suddenly!—we found ourselves staggering, even falling, out the other side of the gateway.

"Clear!" her voice screamed in my mind, and I staggered once again as I drew strangely-scented gasps of fresh air into my depleted lungs. Slowly I took stock, and then carefully removed the mask and plugs. I felt like I could sleep for a week, and almost fell on my face.

I looked around the room: we were at one end of a giant transit-station. Our section was partially partitioned off from the main traffic zones, and we were surrounded by security forces. Our guards were huge men seven to eight feet tall armed with oddly-shaped crossbows; each of them sported a mop of bright yellow hair that dangled down their backs in one solid braid several feet long.

"Where are we?" I asked our guide.

"This is Avalone," Zalmanna said. "It is a Second Circle world inhabited by the Tamallis. The ones who work in the station speak Tyrosian, which is a language, by the way, that you need to learn if you want to travel our network. We can facilitate that process.

"Transits of such a huge distance are a great shock to our biological systems. We must rest in between the major jumps, and so we will remain here for two days to restore our vitality."

When she saw me about to protest, she added: "If we do not do this, Morpheús, some of us could become ill—or even die—from the cumulated effects. You have never made this kind of leap before. Believe me when I tell you that large transits are not to be taken lightly."

We had no choice but to follow her lead.

During that first evening of our enforced stay on this world of giants, Zalmanna brought me something after dinner. It looked like a bug of some kind, housed in a small glass vial. It was long and slender and brown, almost like a living twig. I'd never seen anything like it.

"What is it?" I asked.

"An earworm," she said. "You put it in your ear at night, and over a period of weeks, it psychically transfers a block of knowledge to your soul. This one has been treated to teach you the essentials of our tongue, so that you can better communicate with the Masters and technicians who run our transit-stations.

In the morning, you put it back in its container again. You must also feed it with the nutrients from this jar"—she handed me a small clay pot containing the pungent, dried leaves of some plant I couldn't readily identify (a peony, perhaps?)—"otherwise, it will die before it completes its task."

Scooter, who was sitting on my right shoulder, hunched over to sniff the vial, and said: "It's just as she relates, Master. I've heard of these things before."

But after she departed, the wherret added: "However, this one will also implant a compulsion in you to obey her commands whenever she speaks the words, 'Zalmanna-hannah.'"

The creature opened the small glass container with his paw, and popped the insect into its mouth. It squirmed in an effort to get away, but Scooter knew what it was doing. After a moment, it reached up, pulled the brown bug off its tongue, and plunked it back into its small carrier. It held up a bristle in triumph.

"That's it!" my familiar said. "The rest of what it has to offer is legitimate, but this little bit can be safely disposed of"—the wherret dropped it in the flame of a nearby candle, and it sizzled briefly as it burned.

"Thank you," I said. "I never would have found that myself."

"An earworm saved is a peony urned."

I forgot to mention that wherrets can move very quickly indeed when you try to swat them.

CHAPTER THIRTEEN
"UH, OH, YOU TRIED
THE *BOZOBIGUWËRRA*"

Earworms can be quite efficacious in accelerating the learning process—by the next morning, after moving and shaking all night in an ecstasy of assimilation, I'd picked up a number of basic phrases in the Tyrosian tongue:

"Where's the garde-robe?"
"Who's in charge here?"
"The High Master will be displeased."
"Do you know the way to Pompom Bay?"
"Do you have anything to declare?"

and so forth and so on. At this rate it would take me weeks to put together a meaningful sentence!

Shah'rah wanted to see the sights of this strange new world and new civilization, so I boldly went where no hypatomancer had gone before, and agreed to act as her guide in this enterprise of exploration. But everywhere the pair of us went, we felt dwarfed by the gigantic humans on this way station of a world.

We found an eating establishment near the transit-station, and entered the front door, expecting to be served or at least seated. On Nova Europa, such places typically featured long wooden benches on which the patrons would sit, crowded in amongst each other, while whatever was on the menu (there was never any choice) was ladled out into rough bowls. Sometimes it was edible—sometimes not!

On Avalone, however, you were expected to choose from a list of dishes chalked onto a board, and since I didn't ken either the local lingo or Tyrosian (at least not yet to the degree necessary), I had no idea what any of it meant. Finally I pointed at something, and got a very strange look in return, but then the server just shrugged, said something to the effect of "__ furriner," and walked away.

We were toying with our drinks, a local brew that had a sour aftertaste to it, when he finally returned, bearing a huge platter with something laid out upon it. The first thing I noticed was that it was still moving! Shah'rah screamed when it sat up and clicked a claw at her. Our waiter just frowned in disgust at this cowardly display of *faux-pas*-ery, pulled out a fork at least a foot long, and stabbed it right down into the thing's slimy body, stopping it quite dead in its tracks.

I examined the beastie more closely: it was some kind of giant, segmented arthropod with a slick red sheen. It was still quivering when the attendant carved two sections of it onto different plates, and plopped the mess down in front of each of us. He then muttered some local equivalent to *"bon appétit"* and left, leaving us to figure out how (or if) the thing could (or should) be consumed!

"What...I...do?" Shah'rah said, reverting back to the Andalusian patois that she'd had when I first met her.

I took the sharp knife next to my plate, held down the twitching segment, and sliced right through the cartilage. Then I pried the covering back away from the flesh on either side, revealing the pink interior. I managed to tickle a piece away from the inside, and popped it into my mouth. It tasted a bit like roasted fowl, with a dash of pungent spice added.

"Not bad," I said, and meant it.

The former dancer followed my example, and soon we were enjoying our meal. In fact, we had a *very* good time, laughing and talking and, well, I'm not really sure! I suddenly found Shah'rah much more captivating as a companion than I'd ever imagined before, and the feeling seemed to be quite mutual, from what I could tell. She kept smiling, and reaching over and touching me on the arm to emphasize her remarkably witty and prescient remarks.

We'd just about finished with lunch when Mistress Zalmanna made her appearance.

"Uh, oh," she said, looking down at our repast. "You tried the *bozobiguwërra*. You mean, nobody told you?"

"Told us what?" I asked.

"Well," she said, "of course, there is nothing inherently wrong with eating *bozo*—it is perfectly safe, as are all the items on the menu (we make very certain of that)—but this one is usually served only on special occasions."

"What *kind* of occasion?"

"Uh, yes, celebrations of different kinds. Yes, uh, weddings and engagement parties, and, uh, other things like that."

"Really?" Shah'rah said.

"Yes. Under Avalonean law, you just became man and wife."

I started laughing. "You're joking, of course."

But then I noticed the delegation that was approaching our table. It was led by a particularly tall Avaloner wearing a funny-looking green-striped hat that bent forward in a half-crescent from his forehead.

He bowed to us, handed me a document and quill, and pointed to a blank space at the top of the page.

"The Chief Magistratus wants you to sign right there," Zalmanna said, indicating the empty spot.

"Why?" I asked. "What's this for exactly?"

"This is your acknowledgment of your obligations for the meal you have just consumed."

"Obligations?" I repeated.

"Yes. You agree to pay the charges for the food you just ate, and to cherish and assume all financial and legal responsibility for the woman you have just married."

"What?" both Shah'rah and I said simultaneously.

The official smiled and rattled something off to Zalmanna.

"He says that he can already see a bonding developing between you two. Even though you are dirty, uncouth, wretchedly small foreign peoples, you might have a few redeeming qualities in you after all. Just sign the form, please, he says, or he will have to arrest you for illegally digesting the sacred *bozo*. I strongly suggest that you do this, because you do not want to spend the next ten years waiting for an open trial date before an Avalonean court."

I gulped, grabbed the pen, and affixed my name to the document.

"Does Shah'rah also have to sign?" I asked.

"No, her acquiescence is assumed," the Tyrosian Mistress said. "Congratulations to you both. You will be expected to consummate your union prior to your departure to the next station."

I started to say "You're kidding" once again, and then I saw the look on Zalmanna's face. She did *not* have a sense of humor. I don't think any of the Tyros did.

"Oh, my," I said, looking over at my new wife.

I wasn't quite sure *what* her expression meant exactly—but it certainly wasn't good!

CHAPTER FOURTEEN
"THEY HAVE TO WATCH"

"They have to watch," Zalmanna told me.

"Why, that…that's completely uncivilized," I said. "I can't, uh, perform before an audience."

"Nonetheless, those are the rules here. You should have inquired further before attempting the *bozobiguwërra*."

All we'd done, Shah'rah and I, had been to venture out that morning to a local eatery—and now we were suddenly married under Avalonean law, and we'd been told we had to "seal" the bond, so to speak, before departing this world.

"Look at it this way," Mistress Z. said. "They do not really regard any of us as human. To them, you are just a couple of foreign animals, really. None of them care *how* you 'perform'— but perform you must, Master Morpheús, or into jail you will promptly go, together with your bride. That is how things work here. You must never assume that you understand the customs of a place that you have never visited before."

This was one lesson that I was learning all too quickly. How stupid I'd been to venture into town without some basic grounding first. But stupid or not, the deed had been done, and now I'd have to find a way of rectifying the situation.

"Can we get a divorce?" I asked.

"Only after you have been married for a short period of time," she said.

"How short?"

"About five years."

"Turds and curds!" I almost shouted. "Bits of shits!"

I stewed about the problem all day. Scooter and Grit, of course, thought that my predicament was utterly hilarious. They gabbled on endlessly about human sexual mores, and how uproariously funny all of it was.

"That's easy for you to say," I said to Scooter. "You don't have to do it!"

"But I *could*, Sir," the wherret said. "Grit and I would be happy to demonstrate…."

"No…thank…you!" I said, emphasizing every word. "What you do in that box of yours is bad enough. Besides, I thought that neither of you was a sexual being."

"We're not, Sir. But we both have the capability of, well, it's difficult to explain: it just comes naturally to us."

"Great!" I said, sighing. "Oh, what the hell am I going to do?"

"Well, Sir, have the Avaloners ever seen humans 'do' it?" Grit asked.

Suddenly I smiled. "I don't know," I said, but I was determined to find out. I sought out Zalmanna again, and posed the same question to her.

"Probably not, and if they have, they likely paid very little attention to the details. As I said, they regard all other humans except possibly my own people (and even then I wonder) as substandard."

"Then *that* is my solution," I said, and went to find my new spouse.

That evening Shah'rah donned one of her belly-dancing outfits, and began the routine known in the trade (as she informed me in advance) as the "swan-arm," in which the performer swoops up and down, her hands formed into the shape of a bird's head. I made some appropriate noises in return, whooping and screeching like a great swan overcome with pleasure and pain, and hunching my shoulders every few seconds.

Around and around me she swirled, her nearly transparent costume caressing my upper torso. Actually, I was beginning to have some difficulty in controlling my response to her increasingly erotic moves.

I whooped some more, this time more closely achieving some semblance of reality in my not-so-feigned agony of response, and she responded by dipping her barely covered breasts right down in front of my eyes, where I very nearly fell into the valley of the dolls, so to speak. I was having considerable trouble keeping my breath (and other things) in check.

Then she gave one loud shriek of simulated ecstasy, straightened up, and swooned her arms in a cross right over my head, coming to rest pressed tightly against me. I could feel her heavy breathing against my chest, the sweat of her body permeating my shirt, the points of her...well, never mind! At that moment, I would have gladly continued the ceremony right up to its final consummation, irrespective of the audience, but she abruptly undraped herself from me, and bowed to the Magistratus observing our final act of union.

He bowed back, and quickly departed the scene, no doubt utterly disgusted at the prurient display of small-human sexual mores.

"So, Master, or do I, uh, say, uh, *esposo*, do you enjoy my dance?" Shah'rah said to me, as she covered herself in more demure attire. She'd regained her composure enough to clean up her accent a bit.

"Uh, actually, um, yes I did," I admitted. "I found myself greatly, uh, moved by the, uh, performance."

"Yes, I, uh, I can tell, Sir," she said, casting down her dark eyes and smiling slightly. "I be happy to, uh, dance *por usted*, in more, uh, better place? *Usted y yo*, just we the two? What you think of that?"

"I, uh...." But I didn't know what to say.

"*¡Sí!* That's what I think," the belly dancer said.

CHAPTER FIFTEEN
"DO *NOT* STARE AT THEM"

In the morning we gathered at the transit-station on Avalone to begin the next segment of our journey. Once again we carefully covered our orifices with masks and plugs, and for a second time experienced that "dropping-away" feeling that was so unsettling, as we transited through enormous lengths of the æthersphere. When we emerged on the other side, we collapsed as a group to the soft floor, which had obviously been designed for that very purpose.

Attendants immediately rushed over to us, stripping away our covers, and giving us quick sips of an energy drink to restore our vital fluids.

"I never imagined that travel through the æther could be so debilitating," I told our guide.

"It is ever such," she said. "This is why we do not send our people out to the Fifth Circle very often. The body can only stand so much strain, and too many trips have a tendency to result in a marked deterioration in one's health—and even, on occasion, death. We discovered this over many years of trial and error."

"What is this place?" I asked.

"Tohubohu in the Third Circle," Zalmanna said. "The people here have yellow, hairy skins and wear no clothes. Do *not* stare at them—they find such attention personally offensive, and are allowed to strike you or have you arrested if you peer at them too closely."

All of the Tyrosian transit-stations shared similar features with each other, but each also displayed some unique aspects. The Tohubohuns had decorated their facility with colorful images of giant plants and flowers climbing up the inside walls of the great domed building. I realized after examining them more closely that the work was fashioned completely from minute pieces of tile.

"Extraordinary!" I said.

"They are well known for their craftsmanship," she said. Then she led the way to our new quarters, where we'd remain for the better part of a week, gradually recovering our strength again.

And I *was* noticeably weaker this time, I realized. I went to bed earlier than usual, and slept very soundly until sometime in the early morning hours.

I abruptly awoke with a sharp pain in my left calf. It felt as if someone had stuck a knife right through my leg, and was twisting it back and forth every few seconds. I screamed out loud in agony, and Shah'rah was immediately there to help. She took my poor limb in her hands, and rubbed it vigorously up and down until finally the muscles relaxed.

I briefly wondered if some other mage had ensorcelled me, but then I realized that such things can occur all too frequently from natural causes, particularly when fatigue is involved—and I knew that the dancer was undoubtedly very familiar with such deep-muscle aches. She'd probably suffered from them herself on occasion.

I thanked her and sent her back to her bed, and then lay awake for a long time, thinking about what had transpired in recent days. I didn't really want to be married, particularly to someone I barely knew. On the other hand, I wasn't sure either whether I wanted to pursue any kind of romantic relationship with the Lady of Naprimér. I'd lived alone for a *very* long time, and was used to my own company—and now also to Scooter's. How would I adapt to anyone else? Or they to me, more to the point?

I wondered, and not for the first time, whether I was rushing into an adventure that would ultimately wind up enmeshing me in something that I wouldn't be able to abide.

But of course, that was the true excitement of the thing—I was doing something wholly unlike my previous life. I was trying to alter the damnable dullness that had slowly crept into my existence over the decades, and in the process to make some real difference in the world at large. So perhaps I just ought to let things run their course, and see where my road would take me. I was musing on this when I fell asleep again.

The next day, I asked Mistress Zalmanna again about my "marriage."

"As I told you," she said, "You have to be married for five Avalonean years before you can file for a divorce."

"But we're no longer on that world!"

"We operate our transit-system according to certain guidelines. By treaty, the main stations and the barracks of the personnel needed to operate them are considered Tyrosian territory—and our laws apply there. However, the local rules and regulations of the member worlds apply to everything else, and we honor these up and down the line. So if someone should commit a murder, for example, in an Avalonean pub, and is charged and convicted of the crime, even *in absentia*, then he is liable for it on Tyrotarichos or on any of the other transit worlds, and can and must be arrested and returned to Avalone for punishment.

"So we regard your marriage as valid if the Avaloners do. You participated in a wedding feast. You and your 'bride' were both single persons eligible for matrimony, I believe. You have the financial means to support a family. You signed the official document ratifying the agreement. And you consummated the union…."

"Wait!" I said, "no, we *didn't* consummate it, and you know it. We just pretended to do so."

"Nonetheless, you told the appropriate official observer that you had solemnized the marriage, and he signed a document to that effect. If you now say that you lied, you thereby diminish his stature, and under Avalonean law, you can be challenged to a duel to the death, with the offended party having the choice of weapons. Believe me when I tell you that you do not want to do this!

"No, Morpheús, you are officially married to Shah'rah, whether you like it or not!"

Humbugs and fiddlesticks! Then I thought of something else. "How long is an Avalonean year?" I asked.

"Three Tyrosian years correspond roughly to one Avalonean year."

"How does your calendar match with that of Nova Europa?"

"One Tyrosian year is about two of your years."

"Oh, no!" I said. "That means that one Avalonean year is equal to six Nova Europan years. I'd have to wait through thirty of our years before I could do anything." I felt like crawling in a hole somewhere and pulling the cover over my head.

"Something like that," she said.

"Maybe I'd do better disappearing into the void," I muttered to myself.

"By the way," she said. "If you leave your quarters, the local customs require that you either copy the natives by dispensing with your clothing, or that you cover yourself completely up to the neckline. Leaving any part of your body bare while you are clothed is considered obscene under Tohubohun law, since you are thereby attempting to put that particular part on display, and drawing unseemly attention to it. You could be arrested and jailed. Do *not* do this! Warn your companions, please."

I went to breakfast with a downcast heart, but I dutifully repeated the instructions Zalmanna had given me.

"We'd probably best remain within the compound," I said. "I don't want to see any of us get into local trouble."

Everyone agreed, but by the third day, we were starting to get on each other's nerves, and it was clear that we could not stay confined there for another four days without losing control.

And so, when Shah'rah asked me to take her around to some

of the local shops, I reluctantly agreed.

"Meet me in the lobby in an hour," I said.

I made very sure that my clothes completely covered my arms, torso, and legs. I did *not* want to violate any Tohubohun customs.

I was sitting on a stool near the entryway to our compound when I heard a step behind me, and turned to greet my fellow-traveler. I nearly passed out: she was completely nude!

"What are you *doing*?" I asked, trying to avoid staring at her, her, well, parts.

"Just following the local custom," she said, smiling sweetly at me. "And, after all, we are married, aren't we, husband?"

"I'm not *your husband!"* I hissed, trying to keep my voice down so no one would hear.

"That's not what Mistress Zalmanna says."

She extended me the marble perfection of her arm, obviously wanting to link it with mine. I was so flustered that I didn't know what to do.

"Shall we go?" she said, pushing open the door, grabbing my limb and pulling me right after her.

The next couple of hours I passed in utter agony. I wasn't supposed to stare—at anyone!—but I constantly had to find some way of keeping my eyes from drifting southwards, if you know what I mean. Tohubohu was, in a word, *hot*—hot and humid and very unpleasant to someone buttoned to the gills in stiff clothing. No wonder the natives dispensed with such things.

We looked at hats, we looked at jewelry, we looked at shoes, we wandered through a bazaar of the bizarre, all the while pursued by peddlers who wanted to sell us this or that, or just to beg alms from us. The din was overwhelming, and I soon was sporting a royal-sized headache.

We tried the various local delicacies offered by the street vendors, some of them at least interesting, and others outright disgusting; my stomach, alas, didn't find the local cuisine agreeable, and I was starting to get a distinctly uncomfortable feeling deep down within my "gulliver," in addition to everything else.

Finally, I said, for the seventh time: "Can we go back now?"

"Oh, just a few minutes more," Shah'rah said, leading me to a pottery stand. I was *not* enjoying married life!

Then it started to rain.

The Great Turtle in the Sky (according to Tohubohun myth) began to piss all over us, just adding to our discomfort, because there was nothing in that deluge to cool us down. It simply made things even steamier than before.

I grabbed a cloth from a nearby stall, and draped it over Shah'rah's head to protect her from the storm. Suddenly I heard the loud clang of a bell somewhere overhead, and we were abruptly grabbed and roughly hustled out of the marketplace.

"What's going on?" I yelled, but of course they didn't understand a word I said.

I tried again in rough Tyrosian, which was all I'd assimilated at this point: "Uh, what…go…to?"

One of them rattled off a quick sentence, but I only understand a few words: "You…arrest…jail."

"What?"

In my attempt to preserve my "bride"'s comfort, I'd apparently violated the local laws—again!

When we reached the municipal building, I was shoved into a room with about thirty other misfits, all of them Tohubohuns. Of course, I couldn't make myself understood with any of the natives, and when I tried to talk to one of them, he beat me up (obviously because I was staring at his ugly, hairy, yellow mug). Soon they'd stripped me—not only of my clothes, but all my money, implements, and dignity. I finally sat down on a bench and waited—and waited—and waited.

No one came for me until the next morning, when an official finally fetched me from my hellhole. Both Zalmanna and Shah'rah—*sans* any covering—were waiting for me out front. I tried to avoid staring at them—I really did—but without much success, I'm sorry to say.

"They robbed me!" I said. I truly felt violated—and utterly

defenseless while standing naked in the public eye.

Zalmanna handed me my magical pouch.

"No one wanted this," she said. "And I will restore your cash belt when we get back to the compound. You have been freed on probation under my supervision. Try not to get into any more trouble, Master Morpheús, if you please. Now, take your wife home."

"She's *not* my wife," I said, "really!"

"Oh yes, she is," the Tyro said.

My spouse just smiled, linked her bare arm in mine once again, and yanked me down the street, with me stumbling along in my effort to keep up with her. The stones hurt my feet. More bruised than my toes, however, was my ego. I was *not* enjoying married life!

That night, when I told Scooter and Grit about my adventures in Tohubohun society, they just laughed.

"You humans!" was all they could say.

So much for the understanding of my friends.

CHAPTER SIXTEEN
"WHY WEREN'T YOU EXECUTED?"

On the seventh day, we were back in the transit-station again, this time heading to a Fourth Circle world called Quidni. Curiously, the transit itself didn't seem nearly as jarring this time. Perhaps we were getting used to this kind of travel, or maybe there was some other reason that I didn't understand. My reaction was confirmed by Mistress Zalmanna.

"We will be staying here for three days," she said, as we gathered around her in the stallway in front of the great mirror.

"Are there any cultural issues that we ought to be aware of?" I asked.

"You will not want to venture outside," she said. "There are plenty of amusements available in your quarters. Remain there, please."

Then she led us to our dormitory: we each had a private cubicle in which to sleep, arranged around several common rooms intended for use by the entire group.

When we'd settled, I sought out our guide once again: "What do you mean that we won't want to go outside?"

She led me across the room to a small round window of thick glass, and motioned for me to look. The exterior landscape was a white blur of mounds covered with snow and ice. I realized after staring at them for several moments that these were the buildings of the town, but I couldn't make out any details through the ongoing blizzard.

"The natives eschew any contact with offworlders, including

we Tyros, except when absolutely necessary," she said. "They are xenophobic in the extreme. If you attempt to interact with them, you are likely to be attacked or even killed without warning. All such contacts have to be preceded by a series of messages forwarded through a sky-orb, under a particular protocol."

"Then why do they allow your station to remain open?"

"For the money, I presume."

Our conversation reminded me that I had yet to employ the communications device that Zalmanna had given me on her homeworld, and for which I'd received some small amount of training before our departure.

Back in my cubicle, I closed the door and removed the orb from my pack. It was smaller in size than one of our Nova Europan crystals, and was indented slightly at top and bottom. I focused my energy on a point of light, and spoke a word of activation, "*Coniunge*." Suddenly the æther opened before me.

I manipulated the leys to the signature that would lead me to Naprimér. "Niobë!" I whispered.

I heard a faint reply, "Morpheús?"—and then another, stronger response as she moved nearer the cup she was employing as a receptacle. "Is that you?"

The link did seem to me to be stronger and steadier, but whether this was due to our increased proximity or to the higher energy level of the sky-orb, I really didn't know.

I brought the Lady up-to-date on our adventures since leaving Nova Europa.

"Married?" She abruptly started laughing. "How did *that* happen?"

I told her, and then explained my legal difficulties.

"Well, that would only apply on worlds controlled by the Tyros," she said. "I certainly wouldn't worry about it other-wise—unless…."

"Unless what?"

"Well, unless you and the, uh, dancer regard this as a serious union."

"We have *not* had a union," I said, with some vehemence.

"We pretended for the Avalonean official, that's all."

"But you must find her attractive," Niobë said. "She's presumably young and beautiful."

"If you like that sort of thing. I find her shallow and uneducated," I said. "I want a divorce."

"Well, you have another, what, thirty years to go?" She laughed again. "Maybe if you get a good interceder...."

I just growled.

Then I changed the subject. "Niobë, when I was skrying the future of Sadokéy Drugánis, your captor, I saw something that I didn't understand. Sadokéy was standing over the body of an older gentleman, maybe in his mid-sixties, who'd obviously been struck down recently. You were standing off to one side. Who was this man, and what does this mean?"

"I, uh...." Then nothing but static for several moments. "That man," she finally said, "was Lord Sadokéy's father, Lord Drugán Yevnikiánis. When the Volúcris originally came, they at first tried to convince me to collaborate with them, but I refused.

"I was then serving as the elected Regent of the Grand Council of Mirabö, a body consisting of thirty women appointed from various segments of our society. Mirabö is the main country of the Southern Archipelago of Naprimér; another, much smaller neighboring state is the mountainous Queendom of Caffardö.

"None of us would cooperate with the Bird-Men, so they went instead to one of the husbands of a Councilor, and persuaded him that our religion had it all wrong, that men were intended to rule, as the males did on Volucripimpant, their homeworld. When I learned of this, I had him arrested before any of the invaders could interfere, and he was tried and executed for treason.

"But his son was also a collaborator, and he took his father's place before the Volúcris. With their assistance, he seized me and the rest of the Council. My colleagues were confined to their homes, but I was illegally tried and condemned to perpetual confinement in this place, part of my former residence."

"Why weren't you executed as well?" I asked. None of this

made any sense to me.

She sighed and finally said: "My son did not have the same fortitude as his mother."

It took me a moment to assimilate what she'd said. *"Drugán was your husband?"* I asked, stunned by this revelation.

"Yes. I did what was necessary to help preserve the state, but it wasn't enough, Morpheús: I couldn't stop them."

"But you must have known that before you tried him," I said. I was suddenly seeing the Lady in an entirely different light, as a hardnosed politico.

"Of course I did, Morpheús. Do you think I *enjoyed* having my life-partner killed? We do what we have to do, and then live with the consequences. It was *my* responsibility, and *my* fault for failing to recognize the character flaws within him. I knew when I allowed him to marry me that he was weak-willed and vain, but he was very handsome, and I was young and foolish back then. And this was the price that I eventually paid for picking someone not my equal.

"Under our laws, had he applied them in concert with his beliefs, I should have been executed for what I did. Of course, our system actually requires the leadership of women; men are too easily swayed by emotion to be allowed to rule—as was amply demonstrated in this case."

"But you would have been killed," I said. "Surely...."

"Don't judge what you haven't experienced yourself," Niobë said. "It's like your marriage: I didn't condemn you outright for making the mistake of getting entangled with some local customs on a foreign world. It's meaningless without the meaning, if you understand what I'm saying.

"Our laws have evolved to suit our society and our culture— and, I might say, our particular nature. Whether I'm wrong or right doesn't really matter. Drugán violated our marriage vows, in which he committed himself to obeying *me*, as well as the laws of our country that prohibited him from assuming the supreme power. More to the point, he actively worked with a foreign invader to subvert our nation, and no ruler can allow that to happen. I *had* to have him executed, just because I was Regent. *No* one is above the law: not me, and certainly not him."

"That's very cold," I said.

"Yes," she said. "But you become hard when you have to make life-or-death decisions on behalf of your countrywomen. I did the best I could. It obviously wasn't good enough, because my beautiful Mirabö is still enslaved, and I'm still a captive of the Bird-Men. And until I'm free and they're free, I can never rest again. You're my only hope, Morpheús. Perhaps I've placed too much faith in you, but there it is."

I didn't know what to say. Again I had this very unsettling feeling that I had no understanding whatsoever of this woman and her situation—or of any women really—and that I was missing key information on which to base any kind of decision about my (or about our) future. Still, I'd given her my word, and the word of a scion of the House of Parakôdês has always been good. But I didn't have to be happy about it.

"I have to think on this," was all I could finally say, in my limp and completely inadequate response. "I'll talk to you again tomorrow."

"Then goodnight, dear hypatomancer," came the faint reply before she terminated the contact.

I sighed and stared off into the distance, before lying back down on my hard bed. This was a cold cot on which I rested this evening, in a cold world placed within a colder universe. It seemed to me that I was getting in deeper and deeper—with everything!—but understanding less and less. What the bloody Hades was I doing here, anyway?

More than anything else, I feared making of myself a spectacle, of being a fool, of *being* fooled. Was I being played by the Lady? Was I being played by the Tyros? Was I being played by Shah'rah? Was I being played by someone or something else?

I honestly didn't know.

CHAPTER SEVENTEEN
"SORRY, MISTRESS, FOR TROUBLES"

I was prodded out of a sound sleep by the bleat-bleat-bleat of a horn. Suddenly the door to my cubicle was flung open by Zalmanna with a loud bang.

"Get your people together, Morpheús! Quickly!"

"What's happening?" I asked, rolling out of my cot.

"The Quidnis are attacking. I do not know anything else. Go, if you value your life!"

I gathered our group at the center of the common room, made sure the "birds" had their new weapons at the ready, that everyone had their packs packed and in place, and that we were all wearing heavy coats, in case we were forced outside. Then I waited for Zalmanna to return.

I could hear shouts and crashing sounds and sharp retorts off in the distance, so muffled that I couldn't really make out what was happening. The two wherrets were huddled on my shoulders, and Shah'rah and Doctor Scarabbaios were hovering right behind me, their hands touching my back for comfort. I wasn't all that comforted in return!

Suddenly the door to the rest of the compound burst open, and Zalmanna came rushing back inside.

"They have most of the transit-station," she yelled. "They are wrecking the equipment and mirrors, and killing anyone they can find. We cannot hold them much longer. Follow me!"

Then she led the way through a back exit, almost running,

and we rushed to keep up, with Hawk's men covering our rear. The Tyro pushed through a door marked "Emergency" and told us to "link arms" as we surged outside into the cold.

The blast of frigid air was almost stupefying in its intensity. The temperature must have been well below freezing, and the steady wind from the north robbed any bare skin of its warmth almost immediately. It hurt even to breathe. I pulled my living furs close around my neck to protect my ears, and grabbed onto Zalmanna's hand, reaching back with my other for Shah'rah. Doctor S. could fend for himself, as far as I was concerned. I had no idea where we were going, but our guide seemed to know what she was doing. I could smell smoke behind us, but could see almost nothing through the icy haze.

My fingers were beginning to go numb when Zalmanna abruptly stopped in front of a small building, and pounded out a pattern of rat-a-tat-tats on a side door. It popped open with a gush of warm, fragrant air, and she pulled me inside after her, the others trailing behind.

"Is everyone safe?" I asked, when the entrance shut again.

We sounded off, and all of our party was accounted for, thank the Lord.

I turned to Zalmanna, and thrust my face down close to hers. "What the bloody Hades is going on?"

"I do not know, Morpheús." She pulled out a small orb, and held it up to her lips, speaking a word into the device. I heard nothing but static. She tried again, and once more got no response, and finally pocketed the æther-speaker.

"I have to assume that our personnel are either dead or captured or are simply too busy defending themselves to respond. We are now on our own. Fortunately, this place has a backup transit-mirror, albeit one with a limited range.

"Káthaper!" she said, and a small man shrouded in furs emerged from the shadows. Then I looked more closely, and realized that much of the hair was actually his.

"Sorry, Mistress, for troubles," he hissed. "Some o' this tribe, they not 'appy 'bout strange menfolk."

"Where's the mirror?" she asked.

"Come! I display to you."

In a small storeroom in the back of the house or the business or whatever it was, the little creature pointed one of his four fingers at a wall full of shelves. Zalmanna felt around the edge of the emplacement until I heard a "click," and then she swung the entire section of shelving away from its backdrop. Embedded in the alcove thus revealed was a grimy, square, metal mirror about three feet across. She touched it briefly, then nodded her head and turned around and handed Káthaper something. He waddled away, babbling happily to himself: "Joy, o joy, o joy!"

She placed one hand flat on the *rubraurum* to activate it, and tried to find a link in the æthernet. While she was working, her hand-held sky-orb came alive, and she brought it to her face again. Someone said something that I couldn't hear, then she muttered a word in return, and shut the thing off.

"No help there," she said. "The station has fallen, the personnel are dead or fleeing. We have to find refuge somewhere else. Morpheús, help me, please."

I scrunched up beside her, and placed my hand next to hers on the cold metal surface. This was a fairly primitive device, even by Nova Europan standards—I couldn't imagine what she thought of it.

"None of the places I know are responding," she said. "Try probing the æther."

"Scooter and Grit, I need your strength," I whispered, and the two wherrets nipped my ears and joined in the link. Then I reached out into the void, looking for any refuge that I could find. Suddenly I found a possible receptacle—but it had a very odd feel to it. We were so far out among the Circles that transit-devices were morphing into rather unusual configurations.

Well, "any port in a storm," as they say. I reached out and twisted the leys, and the connection gelled. A reverse psychic wind almost pulled me through to the other side.

"Let's go!" I yelled, and stepped through the aperture. Zalmanna remained behind to make sure that everyone came through the rather narrow opening safely, and then closed the link after she transited through herself.

The huge wave of sound almost overwhelmed me. I looked up and took stock of our situation for the first time. We were standing at the very bottom of a large, bowl-shaped arena lined with stone benches, and every seat in the house was filled with what looked like large monkeys.

And we had suddenly become the prime entertainment!

CHAPTER EIGHTEEN
"YOU REALLY OUGHT
TO TRY THE BUGS"

"What *is* this place?" I whispered to Zalmanna.

"I do not know," she said, also keeping her voice low. "I have absolutely no knowledge of its existence."

"Where's the mirror?" I asked, again looking around me. The stadium floor was curved slightly at the bottom, but I saw no evidence anywhere of a traditional transit-device. How could that be possible?

Sometimes, I knew, transits could only be made in one direction, either because the receiving mirrors had been jimmied in such a way that they would only work as receptors, or because the æther there wasn't conducive to outbound traffic, or because… well, there were an infinite number of possible reasons. But if I couldn't find or make some kind of transit-station, then we'd be trapped on this world until we died. That was not a prospect that thrilled me. And there was no mirror evident here.

And who were these monkey-people? The answer to that question was about to be revealed, because a gate on the far side of the arena had opened, and what appeared to be an official (he wore a fancy harness) was moving towards us.

"Gobble, gobble, gobble," he said to us, and I shook my head to indicate my lack of understanding.

He tried some other gobbledygook then, but that didn't work either. Zalmanna spoke a line in her own language, but he didn't understand her any better than we understood him.

"Master Morpheús," Grit whispered in my left ear. "I think I recognize a few words of this tongue. If you will permit…."

I gave my permission, and then the wherret said something to the official. The ape-creature canted his head to one side in puzzlement, and then gobbled something in return. This went on for about ten minutes, before Grit finally said: "I think I have enough of their vocabulary now to conduct a primitive conversation. The Mouchards—that's what they call themselves—want to know where we come from."

"Ask them if they have heard about the Tyros," Zalmanna said.

When the message was passed along, the official spewed forth a long series of comments, punctuated by gestures with his arms and hands, mostly in the direction of Zalmanna.

"Yes, Ma'am, they've encountered the Tyrosians," Grit finally said. "I assume that the words he was using to describe them were his equivalent of obscenities. Apparently, they didn't get along too well with your people."

"Ah, then tell him we're fleeing the Tyros," I said, "and would appreciate his help in getting off this world and escaping from their evil clutches. This one"—I pointed to Zalmanna—"she's our prisoner!"

Our guide looked daggers at me.

But Grit dutifully translated my message, and then gave us the response: "He doesn't know how to get off Mouch—their name for this world. He said that when the Tyros came, they appeared out of the air exactly like you did—and then went back into the air when they left. They were obviously great magicians, but they were also liars and thieves and evil ones, and the Mouchards want nothing more to do with them."

"We are *not* liars and thieves," Zalmanna hissed to me. "We always treat native peoples honorably."

"Just like you did on Quidni, eh?" I said. "That must be why they were so fond of you there."

"That was a simple misunderstanding," she said. "They…."

"Never mind," I said. "Grit, ask him if they can provide us

with food and shelter for a few days, until we can figure out what to do."

The old wherret exchanged a few more sentences with the ape-creature, and then said: "They can do this, but you have to pay."

"Well, I have plenty of cash...."

"No, you don't understand, Master. They want to be paid through entertainment."

"Entertainment?"

"Yes, Sir, they enjoy public spectacle—hence this arena. You must provide them with one good afternoon's display of something they haven't seen before, something unique that they'll relish."

Cripes, another *quid pro quo*. "Very well," I finally said, "we'll come up with something. In the meantime, I want us to be watered and fed and coddled like *very* significant guests. Make him understand that, please."

"They'll do it," Grit finally said, after exchanging several "gobbles" with our hosts.

But, of course, the Mouchards' idea of Class Five lodging was something very different from ours. We were taken through the city to a hostel of some kind. The cots were all arranged barracks-style in large communal rooms, and they were all short!—just like the ape-creatures.

"This won't do," I had Grit tell the overseer. "We can't possibly sleep on these Procrustean beds. Have them spread some mattresses on the floor, please. At least then we'll be able to stretch our legs."

Our first meal wasn't much better. Nothing was cooked, and some of the grubs were still moving!

"Yech!" Shah'rah said, looking down at her bowl with disgust. "I...not eat this."

I demanded something more appetizing, so they brought out several large platters filled with fruits and vegetables of various kinds, none of which I recognized.

"How do we know these are edible?" I asked Zalmanna. "I

don't want to poison anyone."

Grit and Scooter offered to help. Although they preferred live flesh—like the grubs!—they could also digest just about anything that we could. So they tried small sample bites of all the victuals that'd been served to us.

"I'd put this one aside, Master," the younger wherret said, pointing to a purple tuber. "It contains chemicals that would give you humans gas and indigestion. Also, that three-pronged pink fruit over there, while passable in minor quantities, could be toxic at some higher level—better just to avoid it altogether. The rest are fine.

"You really ought to try the bugs, though—they're very tasty, and so full of protein!"

I picked up one long, white, squirming larva, and was about to bite into it when I swear I heard this little voice squeak, "Help me! Help me!"

I looked around the table, but no one was paying any attention to my situation at all. So I tried again. "Help me! Help me!" I heard.

I stared down at the grub, and sure enough, its wee mouth was working to produce the sounds.

"They're not really intelligent, Sir," Scooter said from my elbow. It reached out a paw to my hand and popped the wiggling thing into its mouth, crunching down hard. "But they do have some nascent psychic abilities, and they can mimic sounds very easily. They're picking the words right out of your brain. It's just a defense mechanism. Um, that's *sooo* good!"

But I decided I didn't want my food talking back to me, and I passed on any further attempts to enrich my protein. I was enriched enough as it was!

The fresh food wasn't all that filling—I missed the possibility of a good roast—but it was probably more nutritious in the end, although I experienced plenty of gas that night, even without the purple thingies.

Fart, fart, fart! I tooted all the night long, and I noticed that my fellow travelers were producing their own chorus of hoots and hollers in accompaniment. The ape-creatures could have powered their entire planet from a room full of digesting humans—if they'd only known!

CHAPTER NINETEEN
"OUTRIGHT BUFFOONERY MIGHT WORK"

"The question is," I said, "What do the Mouchards consider to be appropriate entertainment?"

Grit had spent some additional time talking to one of the local officials earlier that morning, and said: "The language barrier is a real problem. We can't produce any of the plays or comedies or other standard fare that we know they'd enjoy, because only I can speak their language—and not very well at that.

"However, I had the impression that outright buffoonery might work—something loud and energetic."

I looked at Doctor Scarabbaios and Mistress Zalmanna and Shah'rah the dancer and the two wherrets and my not-so-merry men, and everyone just shrugged back. Obviously, it was going to up to me once again to rescue our sorry asses from this predicament.

So I asked for something to write on—and to write *with*—and had to make do with dried leaves (they looked a bit like palm fronds) and what appeared to be carrot juice; and then I squatted down on the floor next to one of the low tables, and started jotting down some notes.

After several hours of hard work, I called everyone together, and briefed them on what I'd imagined.

"Do you think that's really going to work?" Doctor Scarabbaios asked.

"It had better," I said, "because I'm fresh out of any other ideas. Now, Doctor, tell me where the transit-device is located."

"I've been thinking about that," he said. "It's impossible to move through the æther from one point to another without a receptacle at the far end to focus the energy and reconstitute the physical components being transited. So the thing has to be exactly where we appeared. It's either invisible, which I don't believe (they're using the facility constantly for entertainment), or...."

"...It is located underneath the floor of the arena," Zalmanna said.

"Yes, it has to be so. There are undoubtedly rooms down below to house animals and performers and costumes and other such paraphernalia. One of these contains the mirror, possibly as part of its ceiling. I don't know whether we can activate the device from above or not."

"I may be able to help with that," I said. "Before I left Tyrotarichos, I requested and received a medallion that would supposedly aid me in employing Fifth Circle transit-machines. I was given some basic training in its use, but I haven't employed it as yet. Perhaps now's the appropriate time."

"Such things are rare," Zalmanna said. "Even I do not possess one. Are you sure it is genuine?"

I opened my shirt and showed her the two metal orbs attached to the skin of my chest, one black and one yellow. I took her right index finger, and led it to the center of the large gold circle. I could feel her body stiffen at the moment of impact.

"Yes," she finally acknowledged. "It is real." Then she looked down at the floor. I knew what was going through her mind: the High Master Phenneïlonn had trusted me, a stranger, with the implement—and not her. *Why?* She was asking herself.

"Are we agreed? We'll put on this performance tomorrow afternoon, and then we'll decamp if we possibly can. But where shall we go?"

The Tyro looked up again. "The answer to that question depends to some degree on where we are, and how powerful the transit-mirror is. I think we must be in the Fifth Circle—this world is too *outré* to be otherwise—but how far this place is from the big station at Yelloweyen, I have no idea."

"Do you people have any other emplacements on this Circle?" I asked.

"Oh, of course, there are a great many. But I repeat: we need to know specifically which signature to access in order to make the transit. I do not have anything with me that will tell me that, and I do not believe that you do either."

"But you do have a sophisticated sky-orb, just as I do," I said. "Surely, they can be used to probe the æther for possible receptacles. After all, your people have been here before—the Mouchards have already indicated that."

"We do not have much power available, though."

"Yes, but I have the two wherrets to help me—and you have Doctor Scarabbaios to assist you. Together we can pool our energies and cover a much greater area."

So we got right down to work, and spent the rest of the day skrying the heavens for possible Tyrosian transit-stations, breaking only for our evening meal. We finally found a possibility when I got a "ping" from a probe at the six hundred and fortieth tier of the Quietus.

"Try this one," I said to Zalmanna.

"There is definitely something out there," she finally indicated, after manipulating the controls, "but I cannot as yet get a response from the outpost, if that is what it is. Some of our smaller stations are only manned part of the time."

"Keep pushing," I said. "It's our best bet yet. Have you captured its signature?"

"Yes, but we would be fools to transit there blindly. Look what happened with this world."

"We have no choice, Mistress. In any case, I'm going to call it a night."

Before I lay down, however, I went outside in the cool night air and tried contacting Niobë, but had no luck whatsoever. Overhead two of the three Mouchardian moons were grinning down at me. A good sign—or a bad? I had no way of knowing, and I didn't hold with such things anyway. I was tempted to try peeking around the corner into the future, but I knew that any such experiment would be futile, since it involved my own fate.

So I went back to my furs-on-the-floor bedroll, and tried to get comfortable. But it was a long time before I finally fell asleep.

CHAPTER TWENTY
"YOU GRUB-EATING, VEGGIE-FARTING REPROBATE!"

There was standing room only, and from every row and even the bleachers I could see avid ape-faces peering down it us, shouting and laughing and eating bugs and veggies while observing these tall interlopers down on the arena floor. The stench was…memorable.

"Are you ready?" I yelled to our group.

"Yes," they yelled back at me.

Then I grabbed one of our makeshift props and seemed to bang Hawk right over the head with it. "You grub-eating, veggie-farting reprobate!" I screamed to make myself heard above the constant racket of the crowd.

Hawk cried out in pain and rolled backward into the dust, then came up fighting, rushing at me with a club of his own. "You monkey-lovin', ape shit-eatin' mage!" he shouted to the stadium. Before he could hit me with the thing, I pantomimed twisting his nose with fingers.

"Owww!" he yelled—and the crowd roared. "Yikes!"

And they loved it!

Back and forth we went, men and women alike, pretending to hit and fall, hurt and be hurt, run and fight, all the while emoting like banshees. I'm sure that Marco Figaro, the Italian stallion, would have found our unprofessional pantomime and panjandrummery outrageously…well, bad—but these folks had never seen anything like it, and they thought that we were the funniest things to appear in their arena in a great many years. They were hooting and hollering and holding their heads, and throwing their feces at us (a compliment, I was told, although it certainly didn't help the atmosphere).

So we managed to stagger through our two-hour performance, and after several brief encores, assured the crowd that we would be very happy to do this again—sometime real soon.

The Mouchard official kept jabbering away at us.

"He says we've made him a ton of, of…feces, I think," Grit said, "and he's very happy about that. He'll give us anything we want in return."

"Tell him that I'd like to return here this evening, when the stadium is empty, so that I can consult my muse."

"I don't know how to translate 'muse' to him, Sir," the wherret said.

"Tell him that it's a ritual that we have to go through after each performance to cleanse our souls and to prepare for our next entertainment. It's essential to help keep things fresh."

"Ah, that he understands. Yes, 'Of course,' he says."

So about the time the suns went down, we gathered again at the now-quiet arena—quiet, that is, except for the crew cleaning the garbage out of the stands—and began our preparations.

"Any luck in making contact with the station?" I asked Zalmanna.

"No. I cannot get a response from them."

"Very well. We'll just have to chance it then."

I put my hand over the gold medallion on my breastbone, and felt through the sand and ceiling of the room below until I found the mirror. It had a very odd feeling to it, but I ascribed that to its presence in the Fifth Circle. Still, I somehow managed to energize the device, and sensed its power growing beneath us.

"Gather 'round, people," I said, and they all crowded as close to me as possible. "Be seein' you!" I added.

The ape-official was watching the proceedings with great excitement. "To actually see artists at work," he was probably thinking, "to be present at the creation of a new entertainment, why, that was something special indeed."

The only problem was, as it turned out, that he was standing just a tad too close to the center of the action; because when the transit-mirror finally activated, casting us once again helter-skelter through the æther, old Yé-Yé-Za-Zou was swept up right along with the rest of us.

Who could've imagined it!

CHAPTER TWENTY-ONE
"GLOWLIGHTS, ANYONE?"

We emerged into a small room whose only light was provided by a faint glow emanating from the structure's lone window. I extended my senses around me, as did Zalmanna, Doctor Scarabbaios, and the wherrets, but none of us detected any psychic energy or active devices remaining inside.

"Fiat lux!" the old mage said, and upheld his third finger, which sprouted a small, cold flame. It was enough to show us the dust that layered the few pieces of furniture—and also the floor. This place had been abandoned for quite some time.

"No one," Zalmanna moaned. "There is no one left."

I tried the main door, but it was locked tight with Bind-All, and the sole window was sealed in the same way. The outer surface of the building was probably covered with a fine sifting of Avert-All as well, although the uniformity of the protection that remained depended to some degree on the weather of this world, and also on the amount of time that had elapsed since the station had been vacated.

The ape-creature had gone completely…well, ape since transiting through the void, an experience that was obviously unique in his repertoire. He gobbled at the old wherret, who gobbled something back at him, and then he just looked absolutely terrified at what he was being told.

However, I knew we'd be safe until the sun came up, so I urged everyone to just find the most comfortable place to slump to the floor. And then we waited. And waited some more. And waited still further. Finally I decided that it wasn't going to get any lighter than it already was, so we'd better make the best of things.

"Glowlights, anyone?" I asked our group. With several lighted fingers and palms raised high to assist us, we managed to locate a couple of fixtures that responded to our magical prodding. Then we could finally see what we were facing.

The small transit-station was part of a complex of four inter-connected rooms, including sleeping quarters, a kitchen-*cum*-dining facility, and several garde-robes. The bedroom area contained four cots, each in their own cubicle, indicating the maximum possible staff—but I suspected from the configuration that one or two of these were reserved for occasional guests. Basic supplies still lined the storage cabinets and closets.

Zalmanna was already looking through whatever records she could find.

"I have never heard of this station," she finally said. "It was constructed 359 years ago, and the last entry in the logbook is dated sixteen years ago. It states quite simply:

"'Pr. Ord. H.M., facility closed.'"

"Why was it abandoned?"

"I do not know. Normally, we do not leave such structures intact on those few occasions when we withdraw from a world, the common practice being to destroy anything not worth carrying away. Everything about this place is highly irregular and contrary to established procedure.

"Moreover, I *should* have known of this emplacement, even after it was vacated, when I was supervising the station at Yelloweyen. We are required to be aware of all possible facilities available to us within each Circle, in case of emergency. This one was *not* on the list."

"And yet the transit-mirror is still active," Doctor Scarabbaios said. "How very odd! It's as if they'd planned to return someday, and then were forestalled by other events. What's the name of this world?"

"Festuca," she said. "It's supposed to have a large population of some kind, and was serving as a granary for the rest of this sector."

"If what we've seen through the window is typical of the light that this planet regularly receives," I said, "That just wouldn't be possible."

"Well, it was at one time. They took the original hunter-gatherer natives, and made them into civilized farmers, importing seeds from the homeworld, and exporting some of what they grew to support our facilities all throughout this part of the Fifth Circle. This was once (and not so very long ago) a very prosperous place, according to the records I have seen."

"It doesn't appear that way now," I said. "However, we need to get outside to see for ourselves. Do any of you know how to get this door open?"

"If they followed usual procedures," Zalmanna said, "There should be a counter-agent somewhere in the station that will deactivate the Bind-All spell that sealed the door and windows."

"Then let's look for it," I said.

The two wherrets quickly located a container with the appropriate chemical. As soon as we applied it to the entrance, we were able to pry the door open with a loud squeal.

The monkey-creature promptly ran full-tilt through the exit, and despite our entreaties was soon lost to sight, and would not return. We never learned more of him than his name.

Outside the air was cold and damp, filled with a light mist, and I could see just well enough to realize that a thick band of clouds obscured all of the heavens. The nearby ground was covered with scattered yellow ferns and dank fungi; the few trees that I could spy consisted of bare, dead sticks reaching futilely into the sky, as if seeking supplication from the gods.

"What a godawful place!" Gull said. "Master, there's nothing here."

He was right: I saw no evidence of anything moving. I'm sure there must have been some insect life, if I'd looked more closely, but not much else was evident.

"What's happened to this world?" I asked.

"Some great catastrophe," Scooter said, "some ecological collapse caused by an internal or external agent."

"Could someone have attacked this place?"

"In theory," Mistress Zalmanna said, "one can travel the æther by building giant, air-tight craft to sail the stars; but in actuality, the distances between worlds are usually so great that no one bothers, not when there are other, easier means available. The station itself shows no signs of tampering—it was completely secure when abandoned. No, everything indicates that this was an accident of some kind, and that the agents located here systematically and carefully left the place intact when ordered to do so."

"But what about the natives?" Shah'rah asked.

"Undoubtedly they perished," she said. "You could not ferry the entire population of a planet off-world without years of preparation and dozens of transit-devices, and there is no indication of that anywhere. The logs that I examined simply say that the 'incident,' whatever it was, took place five and one-half months prior to abandonment. There were several notes in the records that the station was under siege for some weeks prior to that time by the natives. If the food supply abruptly failed, the population would quickly starve, and there would be no way to save them, internally or externally. All the large animals would die very quickly—including man. The only ones that would survive would be small rodents or birds or insects—creatures like that that require very little food to live, and can sometimes adapt to radical changes in the environment. No, this is mostly a dead world now."

We finally went back into the station and resealed the door—just in case.

"Zalmanna, see if you can find out what happened here," I said. "In the meantime, let's take an inventory of the foodstuffs still available."

But there were plenty of supplies stored on the shelves—the

stuff normally lasted for centuries if the cans remained intact—and we were able to put together a veritable feast for our group of adventurers, although no one cracked a smile throughout the long evening, and very few of our party actually finished their meals.

"Not hungry," Shah'rah said.

Finally the Tyro Mistress reported back to us. "I still do not know exactly what occurred," she said, "But I found a reference to a forthcoming visit by several of the Masters from home-world—I recognize their names. They were arriving within a few days after the log entry to witness the 'great experiment'—whatever that was.

"Several days later, when they had been settled in the external quarters that had been especially erected for them, a log entry records that Stationmaster Bonosuvan personally flew them to the site of the test, and walked them through the procedure.

"On the day that the event itself was scheduled, something apparently went seriously wrong, because I found a notation that the two Masters and their entourage had abruptly returned to Tyrotarichos, several days in advance of their departure date.

"I gather from successive entries during the ensuing five and one-half months that the situation outside deteriorated very rapidly thereafter, although nothing very explicit was actually written down—which is odd in itself. There were just passing references to civil unrest and the conservation of food stocks and things like that.

"Then came the abrupt order to evacuate."

"And you couldn't find out what they were actually doing?" I asked.

"No. That fact was either expunged from the records, or it was never written down—I suspect the former.

"I also suspect that the station was left intact so they could periodically return to monitor the aftermath of the holocaust."

Then I thought of something. "Does the transit-mirror contain a log of its final transmissions?"

She went over to the device and placed her hand on the cold

metal surface. She manipulated her fingers up and down for a few moments, almost as if tapping out a melody on a musical instrument, before finally turning back to us: "Yes, I know now where they went. I have the signature, and the receptacle is still active as a station."

"Then I suggest that we go there next," I said, "unless one of you has a better idea."

But no one did. We stayed overnight, however—all of us badly needed rest, although I didn't sleep very well myself—and then quickly tidied up the next morning, gathering our few belongings together. None of us wanted to remain on this dead world any longer than possible, but we would leave the station as we'd found it.

Zalmanna activated the transit-mirror, and as soon as its energy levels reached maximum, she said "Now," and we all stepped forward, one by one, into the void.

Behind us we left an empty place, hollow and hallowed with the dark memories of a dead race whose faces, even unseen, yet appear in the night to haunt my direst dreams.

CHAPTER TWENTY-TWO
"ANYWHERE, AS LONG AS IT'S NOT CREPUNDIA"

Crepundia Station was another backwater facility manned by just two attendants, neither of them natives of the Overworld. They were suitably impressed by Zalmanna's credentials and by my medallions, which served the same purpose.

"We want to get to Yelloweyen," I said in Tyrosian. My skills in that language had much improved, thanks to the nocturnal ministrations of my earworm.

"Dunno that one, Sir," the supervisor said. He went to a shelf in the back of the main room, and pulled down a large volume. It took him quite a while to report back to us: "It's way the hell on the other side of the Fifth. Can't get there from here."

"Well, then, where *can* we go?" I asked.

"Uh, Biggberr, Arrohidd, Eiddelweld, Bunnin, Bohmunt, Lommalind, Grantirrace, Kristlind, Muskoi, Muskatt, Divórr, Brisquette, Heilind, Kassamaya, Millkrick, and many others besides. But we're just a local service, Sir."

"Great. Can you put us up for the night?"

"We have no room here, Sir, but there's an inn in the village."

"What's the name of the inn?"

"It's just 'The Inn,' Sir. There're only two of them, after all."

I was getting more and more frustrated with this bumpkin.

"Then what do they call the *other* inn?" I asked.

"What other inn?"

"You said there were two of them."

"Yes, Sir."

"What's the *other* one?"

"Which other one?"

I was about ready to strangle him.

"How do we find either of these damnable inns?"

"Well, there's no need to take *that* tone of voice with me, Sir, or to use that kind of language. I was just trying to help, after all. It's in the village."

"Which village? I just want some information."

"We only have one, Sir."

"Which is number one?"

"That would be telling, Sir. You won't find it on your own."

"Never mind," I said. "We will—by hook or by crook, we will!"

"Very well, Sir."

I led the way out the door and down the dusty lane into the nearby community. But I didn't see any obvious tavern or hostelry.

"Excuse me," I said to a passerby whom I thought was a child.

"Huh?" The native shook his head in the universal sign of incomprehension. He was about three feet tall, and was obviously, on close inspection, an adult.

"Now we have to deal with the little people," I said to no one in particular.

Then I led the way back to the station.

"Can you show us the way to the inn?" I asked the manager.

"I can't leave my post, Sir, without violating regulations."

"What about your junior?" I said, pointing to his second-in-command, who was lounging in a chair on the other side of the room, his head tilted back, eyes closed.

"Yes, Sir, what about him?"

"Well, can *he* take us there?"

"He's on his break, Sir. He's entitled to his break according to the agreement that we signed with the Tyrosian government, and I can't order him to give up his break without violating regulations."

"I'm sure Mistress Zalmanna can set you straight," I said, motioning to our guide to step forward.

"With all respect, Sir, Mistress Zalmanna is not my superior officer, and while I acknowledge her wisdom and excellent education, I have to follow the chain of authority. This book"—he held up a small red manual—"tells me what I can and cannot do, and I follow it to the letter. I've been told that if I fail to do so, I could be dismissed without notice. Then what would my wives and children do to survive back on Blottsburgh? They rely on me to bring home the baksheesh."

"I suggest we move on," Zalmanna said. "This man is impossible."

"That reminds me," the official said. "You made an illegal entry onto this world, and I need to know who you are and what you're doing here, so I can file my report, and also…."

I nodded to Hawk, who pulled out a long-knife.

"You see this weapon?" I asked the little man.

"Uh, yes."

"That gives me all the authority I need. Activate the transit-mirror."

"I, uh, can't do that, Sir."

"Zalmanna!" I said—but she was already working at the device.

"Hey, stop that…," the manager said, halting his own speech abruptly when Hawk caressed the edge of his knife along the man's throat. The second attendant snorted, awoke, and then made a move as if to rise, but Eagle promptly went over and tied him to his chair.

"Where do you want to go?" the Tyro asked.

"Anywhere, as long as it's not Crepundia."

And so we flew the coop, so to speak, and transited to the next station on the chain! I thought about bringing the agent with us, but decided that that would also be a futile exercise. You can lead a horse to water—but you can't make it think.

CHAPTER TWENTY-THREE
"IT'S THE ITCH I CAN'T SCRATCH"

For three weeks we bumped from Bumpusville to Backwater, and galloped from Godforsaken to Nowhereworld, until finally we reached a major transit-node in the Tyrosian station chain. None of the local stations we'd visited had had the power to send us further than the next place up the line, and so we found ourselves having to take frequent breaks to replenish our energy. Transiting through the void was far more tiring than I'd ever imagined back on Nova Europa.

But when we came to Brannyboy in the Corsy Sector, I knew that we'd finally reached a point where we could make some progress again. This was a busy, bustling station that reminded me of the best that the Tyrosians had to offer.

The station management also recognized Mistress Zalmanna immediately, and gave our party its due deference as a result. We were sent to the finest lodgings in town, and given special chits to use at the local eateries, all of which were accustomed to serving foreigners.

It was good just to get a hot bath again.

That evening, when I reached the privacy of my own room (a luxury in itself), I tried contacting Lady Niobë again, since I hadn't followed up with her as I'd promised during our previous communication. My first attempt failed, but on the second go-around, I finally heard her voice responding faintly at the other end, and could see her image through the ætherhaze.

"Where are you, Morpheús?" she asked. "It's been a week."

Once again the time scale had shifted 'twixt here and there.

"Well, at least we're in the Fifth Circle now," I said, and I brought her up-to-date on our series of adventures.

"I don't know that Brannyboy. Perhaps you should try asking the station-master if he can locate Naprimér in his records."

"I'll do that," I said, "but this Circle is such a large expanse that I wonder if your world will even be listed. In any case, I wanted to talk to you about our last conversation."

She sighed, long and loud. "You must realize that the events of which I told you took place a decade or two ago, not long after the Bird-Men invaded our world. I've had years to consider what happened afterwards, and I regret that I acted so precipitously, although at the time I didn't really have any other choice—except, perhaps to resign my position. Maybe that's what I ought to have done: I shouldn't have allowed myself in any case to become involved with the judgment of someone so close to me.

"But I was juggling several personal crises at the same time, and I briefly lost my way, I think."

"Several crises?"

"Yes, there was another," the Lady said, "but it had nothing to do with this. The problem was that I was enamored more with my position and the power it gave me than with my family. I realize this now, but I can't change what happened. It's part of my history."

"But you killed your husband."

"Have you never been close to someone, and then drifted away over the years? We were still married, but in name only. And yet, his death affected me more than I can say, more than I ever thought possible. There are nights even now when I cry for him, and for the love that we once shared. But it's all gone, all of it, and I'm just a shell of what I was back then. I want to see my people free again, of course, but I have no desire to lead them anymore."

"I never married," I admitted. "I had...um, several possibilities, but they never seemed to materialize. I was working or having fun or whatever excuse I used at the time. The truth was, I never really wanted to assume the responsibility. I was frightened of being tied to someone else on an exclusive basis."

"So what happened?" she asked.

"I finally became bored with my unchallenged existence. I looked in the mirror one day, and I realized how stale my life had become. I'm not…as young anymore, and I want something else. I'm not even sure what *that* is. It's the itch I can't scratch."

"Yes, I know that feeling as well. I've had plenty of time here to contemplate what I *would* do if I *could* do what I *ought* to— although whether or not I'd actually fulfill any of those fantasies if I were free again, I can't honestly tell you. I still have obligations, even if I don't want them. I'm not so feckless that I'd just run away from them and leave my people in chains. And there's something else I have to do as well, but that's something I can't share with you, because of a promise I made. You know about promises, don't you, Morphy?"

She laughed slightly.

"Yes," I said, "I know all about promises. I made one to you, Lady, as I recall, and I intend to keep it."

"Why do you call me 'Lady'?"

"I don't know. It seems fitting somehow."

"That puts me in my place, doesn't it? My family calls me 'Nobie,' and you're welcome to use that if you choose."

"I don't think I know you well enough to employ a nickname," I said, and then realizing what I'd just uttered, quickly added: "And that's not intended, please, as a put-down or an insult. It's just how I am."

"I understand." She sighed again. "I too am no longer young. It's harder to adjust oneself to the demands of others as one gets older, I think."

Then she said: "What? What's that?"

I perceived the whisper of an animal voice: "Mistress! The Lord Regent Sadokéy approaches."

In the background I could hear a door being pushed open

with a loud squeal, and then footsteps approaching the Lady.

"Close picture!" she hissed, and the image went blank, although the audio link continued—and something abruptly squealed in the background.

"I don't like that creature, Mother," the man said, "and I never have."

Now I could hear Sable shrieking in fear.

"If you harm her or take her away from me, I'll curse you," Niobë said. "I'll condemn you to the seventh Hell, which is the Hell that coexists with this place—and you know that I can do it, too."

"Then keep your damned plaything!" he said. "What am I to do with you, Mother? I've given you every possible comfort here."

"Everything except company, and the freedom to come and go as I please."

"You know I can't do that. All I want in return is some respect—and a foretelling."

"I've told you all that I can," she said, "And I've explained to you why it's impossible for me to read your future accurately."

"The Volúcris think you're not giving me the whole truth. Ssissever believes that your talent has the capability of providing at least a partial forecast of events. Things are coming to a boil in the æther, they tell me, and they want to know why. Ever since that foreign mage gave them their knowledge, they've been expanding their magical horizons."

"You don't want to see the truth, Sado," the Lady said. "The Bird-Men are your masters, not your partners, and they'll destroy you in the end, one way or the other. You've made a pact with the Devil himself, my son, and I fear for your life and your soul. Turn away from this path while yet you can."

"Pah!" Sadokéy said. "You speak as if you were still running that council of hoary old spinsters. Well, they're all dead or imprisoned now, aren't they? At least the Birdies understand the true relationship between men and women. It'll take decades to put things right here, but when we do, the Volúcris will return to their world, and we'll be in charge."

"They'll never leave of their own free will," the Lady said. "Never! You're just fooling yourself, Sado."

"We'll see," he said. "Gad, I'm thirsty." Then he reached down, lifted up the cup, and took a sip, before I could close the thing off. "What *is* that?" he said, and began coughing.

Without even thinking, I surged through the link and into his mind, seizing control of his consciousness against his will, and driving myself to the furthest limits of his awareness.

"Aaaaaah!" came the man's long scream, and I heard Niobë yelling "No!" in the background.

But I paid her no heed, and I sifted over and through his thoughts at lightning speed, looking for whatever I could find that might prove useful. Before I could finish, the pottery shattered in Sadokéy's grasp, taking the link along with it. He would be unconscious for some time afterwards, I knew.

I pocketed the copies of his key memories in a corner of my mind, leaving them to be organized more fully when I had the time. The Lady wasn't the only one who could be ruthless when necessary.

CHAPTER TWENTY-FOUR
"YOU SHOULD REALLY
TRY THE BROWN BONE"

Tyro Onzaïnn, the stationmaster at Brannyboy, couldn't find any mention of Naprimér in the Tyrosian master atlas, but indicated that specific localities within the huge expanse of the Fifth Circle often could only be referenced locally. In other words, some other transit-station located closer to the site might be able to provide us with more information—if only we could pick the right one!

The straight-line distance from Brannyboy to Yelloweyen, which was located on the exact opposite side of the Sphere, was twice as great as that which we'd traveled to arrive here in the first place—and the casual voyager can see this for himself if he should plot our route out on a graph—and so once again we were required to make major transit jumps from node to node with extensive rest periods in between. In fact, we'd have to travel in a broad curve through the æthernet on a trip that would take us many weeks.

We spent another two days at Brannyboy, and then arrived on the morning of the fourth day at the main transit-terminal there, once again covering our eyes, ears, and other openings against potential damage from long-transit travel. And then zip-zip-zip, and we shuttled through to Rubesco—and thence to Branchage, Borgomill, Vivida, Rumpes, Augenblick, Douxy, Pittacus, Betancourt, Phæder, and finally Yelloweyen, with appropriate stops on each world to recover our energy.

After a while, our frequent breaks all tended to blur together in my memory. I'm sure that every place we visited had its unique features and glorious pursuits, but I was so bleary-eyed by the time we reached our destination that I was ready to collapse—and so were my comrades-in-arms, particularly old Doctor Scarabbaios.

"Oh," he kept moaning, "if only I could see my Rhenus again!"

I even began feeling sorry for him, always a bad sign. In the meantime, I hadn't tried to contact the Lady Niobë again. My guilt over my impetuous assumption of her son's consciousness during our last meeting prevented me from facing up to my potential miscreancies. Time enough to replay the music, as they say.

Yelloweyen in the Gorgias Sector, also called "Bug Eyes" by its staff members, was one of the last of the major Tyrosian outposts near the mythical boundary between the Fifth and Sixth Circles, having been named for the twin, pale yellow stars that provided its sustenance. The station was the oddest I'd encountered yet, filled with machinery and transit-devices of all shapes and configurations—some of which, I knew, connected to sites out in the Sixth Sphere, the place we wanted to go.

The workers consisted mostly of the four-foot-high, canine-like natives, with thick, muscular hind legs and tails on which they hopped around the floor, and long, thin forelegs that ended in a curved paws-'n'-claws arrangement that enabled them to grasp small implements—as well as the live prey that they consumed. Most of them also sported floppy ears. However, all of the supervisors were either Tyros or (more frequently) their human servants brought there from other worlds and Circles.

Mistress Zalmanna was well known here, having managed the facility for over a decade some years earlier—and we were treated like nobility as a result. Tyro Brentinna, the current Overseer, allotted us a suite of rooms in the best part of the Station apartments, and provided us with passes to the local entertainment and eating establishments.

"You should really try The Brown Bone," she said. "The cook there is, well, out of this world—ha, ha!"

Mostly, we just wanted to catch up on our lost sleep during those first few days, and so we ventured no further than the station itself.

On the third day, I called a meeting of our group, and ordered in some *hors d'oeuvres* from the "Bone" to provide refreshments.

"What *are* these?" Shah'rah wanted to know, picking up what looked like light brown, crunchy biscuits that had a meaty flavor to them.

"They are called 'tritts,'" Mistress Z. said. "The native Yowlers consume them as snacks. The ones that you want to avoid are the 'sitts'"—she pointed to the dark-colored cylinders.

I picked one up and sniffed—although firm, they smelled like, well, excrement of some kind. Grit snatched it out of my hand and started wolfing it down. "Great!" the wherret said, and then went looking for more.

After we were all feeling comfortable and full, I turned to the Tyrosian Councilmember and said: "Your people sent us here. So why did you pick this place? What else can you tell us now about The Fourth Elephant's Egg?"

Zalmanna brushed her hand back over the orange-colored strip of hair that ran down the center of her head. "Several years ago," she said, "We had a report that Master Melanchthon had been spotted on a Sixth Circle world called Erésvepe. Yelloweyen is the closest Tyrosian transit-facility to that world."

"Exactly when did this sighting take place?"

"We do not know for sure: it could have been quite some time ago. The report filtered back to one of our agents here thirty of our months ago. We have heard nothing from the mage in a great many years, and yet we believe that if anyone knows of the whereabouts of The Fourth Elephant's Egg, it has to be Melanchthon. *He* at least was certain of its existence, although why he thought that way is unknown. He never would justify his argument. But according to his reports, even he did not know what the Egg really is."

"And that's *all* you have?"

"That is all we have," she said, her face downcast.

"How do we get to this Erésvepe?"

"We transit from here to Baseline, a world beyond the boundary area, and thence to Brummér, and finally to Erésvepe. That is as far as our knowledge presently extends—but you must realize that the number of worlds known to exist within the Sixth Circle far exceeds that of the Fifth, and there are so many of them that no one has ever explored more than a fraction of those that can be visited by our kind. Also, many of these places have no transit-facilities."

"Well, I can see the possibility of reaching such planets, but getting back again…," I said.

"Yes, that is always a problem. However, even a glass mirror can be used as a passive transceiver both coming and going—and that is what your gold medallion is for, to make the necessary linkage in an emergency. Yelloweyen Station has a particularly powerful energy source, allowing us on occasion to retrieve travelers from halfway across the Sixth Circle."

"But what if the world on the other end has nothing that can be employed as even a passive transit-device?"

"Then we will all be trapped there for the rest of our lives," she said. "I believe that this is one of the reasons why none of the venturers we have sent into the Sixth Circle to retrieve the Fourth Elephant's Egg have ever returned."

"Great!" Scooter said. "I'll never see Wherreton again."

"Do you know of anyone on this station who's had experience in exploring the nearby worlds over there?"

"There are tradesmen and free spirits who wander among these places—we will encounter some of them in our travels. But I would suggest that we wait until we reach some of these worlds before seeking any assistance."

"Very well," I said. "How soon can we leave?"

"We must remain here another few days," Zalmanna said. "By then we will be completely fit to resume duty again; and the staff here will resupply our packs. In the meantime, enjoy the break. The gravity here is light, and the Yowlers are very congenial allies."

"No local customs or laws that we need worry about?" I asked.

"Do not stare the natives in the eyes—they might regard that as a challenge. They can be fierce when crossed. Do not conduct 'number one' or 'number two' on the sidewalks...."

"Number one or number two?" Grit repeated. "What's that?"

"...Do carry a packet of 'tritts' to use as bribes. Do not disturb a mother with her litter, even if the little ones run over to you looking for affection. The family group here is the 'pack'—so, when dealing with Yowlers, be sure to ask about the significant others in their lives. Most of the natives who regularly deal with foreigners speak Tyrosian. Master Morpheús is now proficient enough in the language to translate."

And so I was, thanks to the late and unlamented earworm, who'd finally become a dried-up husk when it'd finished imparting its precious knowledge in my head. (Although Grit had helpfully suggested to me that what actually had happened was that the little bugger had perished laying its eggs on my cerebellum, and that these would eventually hatch, leading me first to madness and then to imbecility as the larvae gradually consumed my brain. I suggested that if I did finally attain a state of utter craziness, that I'd lose all my inhibitions, and roast a large fat wherret on a stick over an open fire—*that* shut the creature up—for once!)

We ended our *fête* with a toast to the future and a nod once again to the memory of Sparrow, who'd perished on our expedition to Indushia. It was time to be moving on.

CHAPTER TWENTY-FIVE
"THE THIRD HOUR OF THE DOGDAY AFTERNOON"

The next day, Zalmanna treated me to lunch at the Den-Eye-er, a hole-in-the-wall establishment that she remembered from her years on Yelloweyen. There was someone there she wanted me to meet, she said—and who was I to deny her?

The Den was clearly a local Yowler hangout. We had to duck through a round doorway hole to get inside, and then sit in plush, padded seats embedded in the floor. The standard drink was water served in a common bowl on a central table.

"Their kibbles are not bad," the Tyro said. "They use bits of grain mixed with chunks of meat taken from an animal that is similar to your cow. Be sure, however, that you specify that you want the mix 'well done,' or it will be served almost raw by our standards."

I did so, and found, much to my surprise, that the resulting "stew" was actually quite tasty.

About halfway through the meal, a Yowler hopped over to us and asked if he could sit at the third station of our low, round table. Zalmanna motioned him to join us, and he partially lay down on his side.

"I am Arrgruffruff of the Yurrorro Pack in Oldbone," he said.

We introduced ourselves in turn, and then he ordered.

After he'd eaten, he licked his lips back and forth several times with his long red tongue, and said: "I smell the need for a 'Finderrerr'."

In Nova Europa the art of Finding was a valuable talent, and I'd occasionally employed such individuals in the past—as with Jécko the Mallet earlier in our quest. But I sensed that this type of Finding was somewhat different.

"We *are* looking for something," I said, "but out there in the Sixth Circle."

"I been therr," he said. "Harrd to know yourr way rround a place without some sniffin' at it firrst."

"It is indeed," I said.

"So mayb' I can help yourr findin' out therr," the Yowler said.

"Maybe. Depends on what you want in return." I didn't want to give the creature too much information yet.

"Pack-mate Durrdrruff missin' out therr. Many dangrr-rus places in Sixth Cirrcle. Betterr to go with pack, with yourr pack. Me help you out—you help me out."

"We're looking for a man named Melanchthon," I said.

"Yes. Have hearrd of this one—on Errésvepe. Mayb' three years 'go. He jumb' some otherr place from therr."

"Where!" I asked, almost yelling the word.

"Dunno. Can find out, you take me," the Yowler said.

I looked over at Zalmanna, and she nodded her head slightly. She obviously knew more about this "Finderer" and the talent that he represented than I did.

"Very well," I finally said. "We're departing on...."

"Dogday Sixteen," Zalmanna said. "Meet us at the transit-station at the Third Hour of the Dogday Afternoon."

"I be therr," the Yowler said. "Now go talk to pack about leave-takin'. Good huntin' to yourr pack."

Then he left.

"Interesting creatures," I said.

"Yes, but very dependable," the Tyro said. "They will do exactly as they say, so long as you treat them courteously and straightforwardly. This one will also follow your directions without question."

"I'm glad to hear it."

When we returned to our quarters, I called a meeting to let

the others know about our new recruit. Then Doctor Scarabbaios said, "I wish to remain here when you go."

"You know I can't allow that," I said.

"But I'm old and ailing, and I won't be able to add much to your expedition to the Sixth Circle."

"The minute we leave, you'd be gone," I said. "No, I need you there when we find Master Melanchthon."

"I don't want to see him again," the mage said.

"Now, why would that be? What did you do that might cause him to be angry with you? Did you betray him?"

"No! Of course not! It's just that we didn't always see eye to eye on certain things."

"And when he was gone, you moved into his place, didn't you?" I said.

"Well, I *was* next in line."

"So, did you tip off the Overseers about his presence on Nova Europa?"

"How could I have done that?" the old man said. "We had no transit connection between our world and theirs."

"Yes, but you had sky-orbs, and they can sometimes be jimmied to reach a very far distance indeed," I said. "Maybe Mistress Zalmanna can tell us."

"I was not on the Council at the time," she said. "I was just an acolyte back then, barely out of the Conlegium. I know Scarabbaios has been 'ours' for quite some time, but I do not have the circumstances by which he came to us originally."

"Well, Doctor S.," I said, "whether you like it or not, you *are* coming with us, and that's my final word on the subject. I simply don't trust you anywhere else except right under my own observation."

That night, I tried calling Niobë again, but instead of reaching her, I heard the voice of her companion, Sable. "Mistress, she is confined to infirmary, Master," the creature said. "Lord Sadokéy beat her when he retook his health, saying she'd attacked him. She was badly bruised and had one broken bone, although she'll recover within a few weeks. You should not have done what you did."

"It was necessary," I said. "I had to know more about her circumstances."

"That information, you will have to obtain it in the future from Mistress directly," Sable said. "This person cannot tell you anything herself, Master. You surely must realize this."

"I'm not asking you to betray her trust. But do send my sorrow that she suffered because of me, and my hope that she'll have a quick and complete recovery."

"This person will do so." And then she cut the link.

This brief conversation left me with very mixed emotions. On the one hand, I had no compunctions whatever about violating Lord Sadokéy's little mind. I needed the information, and it was obvious that the Lady was simply not going to talk about certain aspects of her past.

On the other hand—well, on the other I knew in my heart of hearts that what I'd done was wrong, in so many ways, and violated both ethical and moral codes, from Nova Europa to Naprimér itself (I presumed). But when does the necessity of saving someone also require harming that person? Does doing something for the right reasons justify an inherently evil act? The philosophers always offered a great many thoughts about *that* particular conundrum, but they rarely provided hard-and-fast answers. I knew what Doctor Árbogast would say, but then, Doctor A. wasn't here fighting the good fight, was he? It's surpassingly easier to win a war from behind a desk than out in the field, so to speak, where everything blurs from black and white into a mottled gray.

Sadokéy's memories might give me an edge in saving his mother from her imprisonment of body and soul, and also in saving his world—in spite of himself. I'd get no help from him, that was certain. In the end, Sadokéy would likely have to go the way of his father.

However, Barlévin's adage still applied. I would leave such considerations to the future, when they would have to be considered once more, and remeasured in the face of the realities that then appertained.

Oh, dear Morpheús, you've done it again!

CHAPTER TWENTY-SIX
"WE ARE CÁNEVAS CAFÁRDIS"

Baseline, the transit-facility on the semi-mythical border between the Fifth and Sixth Circles, was not operated by the Overseers, but by a company called Bluefly, owned in turn by a man named Cánevas Cafárdis. Every passenger, every piece of freight, that passed through this place was assessed a tax, depending on weight, distance, and risk. And those who couldn't pay had to work off their haulage in three-to-six-month stints.

The facility had been built on a small moon encircling a great, green planet in the Avoco Sector. Although it sported an atmosphere of sorts, it was insufficient to support life, and the gaseous world that it orbited had no land surface at all. Thus, the station itself was located within a large, clear-topped dome, and no one could venture outside without employing an air-mask of some sort. I thought the mechanical apparatus looked very clunky, and told Zalmanna so.

"We also have these kinds of machines," she said, "for use on worlds where we cannot breathe the air ourselves. But we prefer not to visit such places directly, and to send surrogates instead—or to deal with the natives through sky-orbs, whenever that is possible."

"How many worlds have you contacted?" I asked.

"No one knows. Certainly over one hundred thousand."

I was staggered by the number. That so many other civilizations existed in the void, filled with living, thinking beings—it was incomprehensible to me. And here we'd thought on Nova

Europa that we'd known so much about the universe. *We knew nothing!*

Baseline Station was filled with a myriad of complicated, incomprehensible machinery and mirrors. Sentient beings were coming and going from the transit sites at a constant rate. Many of them were obviously traders of one kind or another, although I also saw what appeared to be religious groups, military units (very tightly controlled, however), individual travelers, and many other folks whose nationality, purpose, function, or even form I did not recognize.

Some of the creatures that I saw were enormously large, one reaching more than twenty feet in height, but I also spied a group of small, bird-like creatures that reminded me of nothing more than a flock of sparrows, in both size and shape, save that they were completely dressed in a bright orange…something. Whatever it was, it certainly wasn't avian plumage, and I don't know to this day whether the "flock" was a composite intelligence of some kind, or if each of the minute critters was viable on its own.

I had to pay the passage-tax for my group, but my Overseer gold strips were perfectly acceptable to the functionary seated behind the table. "What's your destination?" the two-headed human asked in passable Tyrosian.

"Brummér," I said.

"The next transit-shuttle for that station departs in three Base-hours. Gate 22, over there." They pointed one of their three fingers across the dome to the other side. "That'll be another 3.2 units for each of you."

I handed over the amount.

One of the heads tilted slightly and smiled. "Have a nice day," he said. The other one just frowned. The official handed us a metal strip that served as our "ticket."

"I wonder what happens," I muttered to Zalmanna, "when they fundamentally disagree."

"I, uh, have seen that particular occurrence," she said, "and you would not want to be there, believe me."

"So you've been on this world before?"

"Twice. I came here with a team to track a criminal who had escaped our jurisdiction, and then returned the other way to bring her back again."

"The, uh, 'heads' didn't mind?" I asked.

"Ah, as to that, Cánevas was willing to pass us through, but Cafárdis objected, and the argument was almost a deal-breaker, because the crew of the station began to take sides—except that 'sides' in this case meant a schizoid division of each individual's mentality. We were very lucky that day."

"How did you get back?"

"While they were fighting amongst themselves, I walked over to the transit-terminal that connected with Yelloweyen, entered the coordinates, and took our people through. We paid the tax after the fact, plus a ten percent bonus to erase any 'hard feelings.' But this place still makes me nervous."

Just about then I heard this yell above the natural background din of the facility: "Tyro Zalmanna! You stop!"

A very large, two-headed man came waddling over in our direction.

"Oh, my gods!" she said. "Listen to what I say now very carefully, Morpheús: I am *not* Zalmanna, but her cousin, Bilmenna, and you, as the leader of this expedition, have no idea what he might be blathering about, since you have never visited this place before."

"Very well," I said. Then I turned and put both of my hands out in front of me, empty palms facing up. "Yes, Sir," I said, "can I help you, Sir?"

"This...this creature," they said, pointing their fat finger at the Overseer, "she is, uh, needed for multiple violation of law in this place. You turn her over to us immediately."

"Well, Sir," I said, "I know for a fact that she's never even visited Baseline before. None of us have. I'm Master Morpheús, leader of the Nova Europan Academy of Xeno-Archaeology and Hypatography, by the way. I'm very pleased to meet you."

"We are Cánevas Cafárdis, owner of station. We the law

here. You turn Tyro Zalmanna over to us."

"Zalmanna, Sir?" I said. "Who's that?"

"This female," they said.

"No, no, Sir, her name's Bilmenna. She's one of my aides on this expedition. We're, uh, investigating the dig on Dylldow. You know, the Palace of Pleasure of Plumppostimus?"

"Not heard of it. You sure about female's name?"

"Each member of our group had to be vetted by the Academy before they were allowed to come. All of her paperwork checked out."

"Let us see," Cánevas Cafárdis said.

"Well, obviously I can't carry all those documents with me," I said. "Look at how many attendants we have. But you could send a message back to Nova Europa, and I'm sure you would hear back again within, oh, five or ten years. But in any case, I do have a list of our members. Let me see. Uh, Scooter!"

"Yes, Sir, just a moment, Sir," the wherret said, and plucked a piece of parchment out of its pack. It was the message that Grit had sent him.

I handed it over. The manager passed it back and forth, and looked it up and down, and even turned it over—but they didn't want to admit that they couldn't read it. "Very well," Cánevas Cafárdis finally said, "You can take shuttle." Then they pocketed the document and wobbled slowly back across the room to their stall again.

"That was close," I said.

"But they took the note!" Scooter whispered. "What if they have it translated?"

"What if they do? We won't be here then."

Or at least, I certainly hoped we wouldn't.

CHAPTER TWENTY-SEVEN
"UNLESS, OF COURSE, YOU TOUCH THEM ON THEIR BELLIES"

There was no denying the beauty of Baseline Station, particularly with the emerald immensity of the motherworld hovering overhead, but we wanted to get away from this place right away, before the manager could change their minds; and so we immediately headed to Gate 22 on the other side of the facility.

Parked on a slot in front of the transit-area was a long metal cylinder open at the top, with single seats lined up one behind another inside the capsule. I'd never seen anything like it. The carriage was standing up before an open chute that seemed to go nowhere—except out of the dome itself.

"What *is* that?" I asked Zalmanna.

"Out in the Sixth Circle, the ætherspace is warped so badly that different kinds of machines have been developed to transit from one world to another. The standard *aurum* mirrors may or may not work in a predictable fashion—that is, one can certainly employ them, and they will indeed take you somewhere, but not always to the destination that you have in mind. *This* device"— she pointed to the shuttle—"will get us to the next station on the line, Brummér."

"You're certain of that?"

"Oh, yes, I have been there myself. It is a world perpetually enwrapt in fog. The natives are blind in the conventional sense, but use both physical and mental feelers to find their way around."

When the time came, we actually had to be loaded into two of the cylinders, since our party was so large. The two wherrets were allowed to rest on my lap, although they kept nudging each other for position, and I had to shush them several times to avoid creating a stir.

Then the bottom half of the capsule was rolled over my head and fastened down, and I could feel the entire carriage start to move forward into its chute. I was pressed back into my seat by the acceleration, and then we…transited, and I almost lost my lunch. Somehow the fact that I was confined in a small, cold, poorly lighted space made me both dizzy and nervous at the same time, and I was heartily glad to be finally released from my metal coffin at the other end.

As we moved ever further out into the Sixth Circle, we began to notice more and more "changes" in our environment. Brummér Station, for example, featured the same hustle and bustle as one of the emplacements operated by the Tyros, but the ambience was totally different. Here I saw an increasing number of intelligent non-humans, including a few wherretudes, Yowlers, Bruisers (ursine-like beings), several kinds of ape-folk, large rodents with buck teeth (Chewies), Mendips, and many others. Thus far, all of these creatures were obviously mammalian or avian in nature, but I had no doubt that if we traveled far enough, we'd encounter reptilian and amphibian intelligences as well.

The complex actually consisted of several adjoining "machine" rooms, filled with about thirty transit-devices of varying kinds, including a few of what appeared to be ordinary metal mirrors (I was assured by Zalmanna, however, that these were not at all similar to our standard issue).

The next service to Erésvepe wasn't scheduled for two days (another change from what I was used to), so we had to find lodgings in the nearby town, which was called Toc. The native Anis were humans with somewhat feline features, particularly in their faces, with long, bold, stiff whiskers that stuck straight out several feet from their cheeks and ears, like pins pushed into a cushion, and very large incisors. Although they sported large eyes and pupils, I was told that they could actually distinguish very little with them, other than various shades of light and darkness. They had some nascent psychic powers that allowed them to identify living creatures close to them, and also an ability to bounce very high-frequency sounds off inert structures.

"They are also quite docile," our Tyrosian guide informed us, "unless, of course, you touch them on their bellies, in which case you could lose a hand. But so long as you are careful, you should not have any trouble. They are used to serving foreigners."

Zalmanna's words were no comfort to me at all, given our previous experiences, but I assured her that the group would heed her directives. We rented a suite of rooms in a large lodge fronting on a small pond. To get there we had to follow a set of railings installed along the side of the street that led from the station, because the pervasive mist was so dense that you could not literally see any further than a hand held in front of your face—and sometimes not that!

There were gaps in the rails at the entrance to each building; these were bridged by light chains that one could latch or unlatch, as needed to enter or exit the facility. A post mounted before each opening had a metal sign with raised letters affixed, giving the name of the structure in both the Anisian and Tyrosian languages.

The Lollygaggle Lodge clearly catered to foreign visitors with human-like dimensions. The manager questioned the inclusion of the wherrets and the Yowler in our party, but I told him that if he wanted our business, it was all or nothing.

"Very welcoming, but you are firstly responsible," he said, in a soft, almost sensuous voice. "We don't make especial provisions for the likes of them."

The Yowler growled at him, but the Ani just hissed back.

After we were settled, I tried to contact the Lady again, but got no answer. So I spent a few hours reviewing in my mind what we wanted to do on Erésvepe, and then went to bed.

The next day, before I sought breakfast, I tried Niobë again, and this time got a response.

"I can't talk for very long," she said. "I'm still recovering from my injuries, but I think Sable told you that."

"I'm…truly sorry," I said. "I certainly didn't mean for you to be blamed for my actions, or to be punished for them. I did what I thought was necessary at the time."

"You surprised me, Morpheús. Just when I thought I had you framed within my mind, you suddenly altered the picture. I realize now that you have dimensions beyond my first impression of you. Perhaps that's a good thing, although I hope you'll consider the possible consequences of doing something like that again. My son tends to overreact to what he perceives to be challenges to his authority."

"I won't put you in jeopardy again—at least without good reason," I said.

"That is, uh, less of a comfort to me than it would have been earlier," the Lady said. Then she sighed. "Well, it matters not. If he kills me, it'll be a relief. And if he doesn't, then I'll still be here waiting for you."

A moment of silence passed between us.

"Are you there?" she finally said.

"Yes, Niobë. Could you do something for me?"

"What?"

"I'd like to see the face of the woman I'm supposed to rescue."

"Ahhh." There was an hourglass full of wisdom in that exhalation. After another pause, she said: "So you're a man after all."

"Did you ever doubt it?"

"Our worlds—nay, our lives—are so different that I've wondered what possible conjunction there could be between two satellites located in such different orbits. Would there be a head-on collision—or just a series of near-misses?

"I've told you before about our custom here—I'm shrouded because it's unseemly for an unmarried woman to be viewed in the face by an unmarried man."

"Yes, you explained that. Still…."

"Still…," she echoed. "Very well. Briefly, and just this once."

She reached up to her right ear with her good arm, unhooked a catch of some kind, and then slowly peeled the gauze away from right to left. The Lady had an old scar that zigzagged down the right side of her cheek. Her lower lip was puffy and dark where she'd been struck by Sadokéy, and her left eye was blackened around one side. And I could see the ivory tips of two upper incisors peaking out from between her lips.

I wouldn't have called her pretty under the best of circumstances. Her pointed chin had a faint cleft running down the middle, and I could see fine lines etched on either side of her mouth and eyes. Her cheeks were hollow—from hunger or from suffering, I wasn't sure. Her green eyes were large and the pupils almost cat-like in their configuration.

And then she smiled, and it was like the rising of the sun on a summer's morn. That simple act transformed her face from a rather plain vista riven with cares and years into something that shown with the light of a newfound day. It was a revelation, even to one as jaded as I.

"You…." But I could say no more, imbecile that I was, and I was left, like all inherently adolescent males, babbling in my beer again.

And then the smile dissipated, retreating into its hiding place once more; and very slowly, very carefully, she refastened the veil back in place. "You see the inevitable wreckage of the years," she said. "Sado's recent handiwork hasn't helped that any. I'm sorry that I have no more to offer, Morphy, but this is who I am."

Then she yawned involuntarily. "Oh. I must rest again, I think."

"I understand," I said. "I…."

"It's all right. You don't have to say anything else. Just free me from this damnable prison. Please!" She started to yawn again. "Must go now. Good night, Morpheús." Then she shut down the link.

I shook my head. I didn't understand women—never had—and was left wondering, not for the first time, whether these aliens who lived among us, and whom we shared as partners in our lives, were our masters or our mistresses—or indeed, whether any of that mattered.

Sometimes just having a warm body to snuggle up to in bed was quite sufficient, thank you. Perhaps the only wisdom that any man ever attained in his life was simply recognizing that one fact—and accepting it as one of God's great gifts.

CHAPTER TWENTY-EIGHT
"WATCH OUT FOR
THE L'IL BIRDIES"

"He's not here!" Grit screamed in my left ear. We'd just emerged from the small, wood-encased, cabinet-like structure that had served as our transit-mechanism from Brummér to Erésvepe.

I stepped back away from the door so that the rest of our group could finish their journey. There was a bright white flash that illuminated both the carrier and its surroundings, and then Hawk and several of his men emerged from the bowels of the thing.

"*Who's* not here?" I asked the old wherret.

"My Master Melanchthon," he said. "I'd sense him if he was present on this world, and he's not."

"Nonetheless," I said, "we still have to look for any traces he might have left. Perhaps they'll give us some clue as to his current whereabouts."

It took four transmissions in all to ferry our party from one planet to the next. I checked to make certain that everyone had come through intact, and then we headed out of the small facility onto the main street in Gettouttahir, the capital of the Republic of Marsi.

"What do you know of this place?" I asked Zalmanna.

"It consists of several hundred islands of varying sizes. Marsi comprises the second largest land mass on Erésvepe. It has an arid climate, but most of the populace live on or near the coasts.

Fishing and mining are the primary occupations."

"What do they mine?" Doctor Scarabbaios asked.

"Mostly guano—the islands are covered with birds—and they also dig for minerals in the interior, using imported labor. They export any precious gems they find, which are small and easy to transport. Gettouttahir has the only transit-link, so it controls all off-world traffic.

"The natives are human-like, but possess both lungs and gills, as well as webbed feet and hands, enabling them to swim quite readily."

We were standing on a hill, and I could see the sweep of the red-hued bay spread out below.

"Why the unusual color?" I asked our guide.

"Some kind of algae, I think," she said. "The report on this world says, 'Do not go near the water,' so I would suggest that you enjoy the vista, but forgo the pleasure of a dip."

We found an inn that catered to human travelers a short distance away. "Home Sweetie Home" the sign proclaimed in Tyrosian, which still seemed to be the *lingua franca* of the Avoco Sector, although the portrait of the purple cow flying over a stone wall was scarcely conducive to thoughts of domestic tranquility.

"How some many?" the proprietor wanted to know. He had a round, blubbery gray face, double chin, and long whiskers stuck to either side of his mouth.

I showed him (or her—I wasn't sure which) our mongrel party.

"Two golpecks," he said.

I looked back at Zalmanna.

"Three and one-half gold strips," the Tyro said.

I handed them over.

"Commodes extra," the innkeeper noted.

I gave him one more *aurum*.

"Meals at sixteen and nine," he said, "in common room. Have a good daytime!"

Then he squawked—I swear he sounded just like a seal back

on Nova Europa.

Our rooms were neat and clean, which is about the best that one can hope for, I've found, and the beds looked at least halfway comfortable. They were built up from the hardwood floor and covered with large feather cloaks. The problem was, though, there weren't enough facilities to accommodate all of our party, and when I went back and complained, the proprietor shrugged his jowls and said: "Full upper! So sorry!"

So I gathered the group together and explained the situation. "We're going to have to double-up," I said, "or some of us must sleep on the floor. We have four rooms and four beds."

We decided to put the ladies into one room, myself and Doctor S. in another, with the Yowler and the two wherrets on the floor, and Hawk's men dividing the remaining two facilities. I didn't relish sharing my bed with the mage, and I don't think he liked it any better himself.

"I'm getting too old for this," he complained—but then, he complained all the time anyway!

We went down to the evening meal at nine-ish, which was the Erésvepean equivalent of sunset, and joined a number of other travelers at common round tables that held ten or a dozen at a time. I found myself sitting next to a pretty woman with vaguely porcine features. She said that she derived from Popino, one of Erésvepe's trading partners, and was the equivalent of a peddler or sales agent.

"Don't you just love the warm weather here?" she burbled, stuffing her face with a crooked chunk of denormo fish (fish and fowl were the only "meat" they served here); it was dripping with some kind of sweet sauce, and smelled as if it'd been setting out in the sun *way* too long.

I allowed as how that was so, and tried munching on the crispy wing of some small bird—they called them bissons—but the gooey covering in this case was fiery hot, and I attempted to douse it with a blown-glass overflowing with a green liqueur— but that didn't help matters any.

The woman just started laughing, and then handed me a mug

of a beer-like brew that helped quench the roaring fire in my mouth and throat. "You have to watch out for the li'l birdies," she said. "They can sting ya!"

But I'd had quite enough of this repast—and the company—and politely excused myself. Back in my quarters, I gathered all of our people together, and briefed them on what we were looking for here.

"You got somethin' of his?" Arrgruffruff asked Grit.

The wherret reached into his small pack and pulled out a dark, blue-green, polished piece of turquoise set in silver.

The Finderer bent down and sniffed it—once, twice, thrice—with very deep breaths, and then said: "Have it now. If your masterr lived herre, I will locate him."

And then, although it was quite late, the Yowler left to pursue his new-found scent.

The rest of us headed off to a well-deserved bed—for again, although the distance we'd traveled had not been all that far as ætherspace was concerned, the transit had taken its toll upon everyone. We would function much better in the morning.

CHAPTER TWENTY-NINE
"THE SNIFFER HAS
YET TO RETURN"

But I had an uncomfortable bed-partner in Doctor Scarabbaios, who kept moaning and moving and mumbling in his sleep, occasionally kicking me, so much so that I was able to get very little rest of my own. Every time I would finally find some semblance of silence, the elderly mage would light up the æther with a massive exhalation of noxious fumes from his nether end. I worried that the coals still burning in the fireplace might light the fuse, so to speak, of the "*bombus magnus,*" thereby sending me straight to my eternal reward—whatever that might be! The words "old fart" had taken on a whole new meaning.

Finally, I arose just before dawn and wandered down to the garde-robe to use the facilities and splash some cold water on my face—although I wondered if it was tainted by the same red tide that had afflicted the seawater. Oh, well, just living from day to day is taking a great chance on life.

When I emerged in my shaggy night-shirt I was astonished to see Shah'rah standing there, waiting her turn.

"You too?" she said. "I couldn't sleep much, Master."

She had a large shawl or wrap pulled taut around her body, but not much else, I suspected. I could feel the radiant warmth emanating from her skin as she turned sideways and brushed by me—and a faint odor of, what?—femininity? It took my very breath away.

I shook the cobwebs out of my weary brain. Whatever was I thinking? I muddled back to my room and got dressed, recycling my clothes from several days earlier. Everything (and everyone) was getting a bit ripe, but I had none better to wear.

Doctor S. murmured something else about ifrits and golems and pestilent peasants, but that particular fruit was even riper than my own, so I went down to the common room, where at least it was quiet. The two wherrets were already there, of course.

"Greetings, Master," they both echoed.

"And a good morrow to you as well," I said. "What news?"

"The Sniffer has yet to return," Grit said. "I've tried extending my senses into the surrounding æther, but the result is more puzzling than enlightening. I detect the traces of only one passage by Master Melanchthon to this place, but none emanating from the opposite direction."

"Well, that's not terribly surprising, if he was on his way to a specific location. He may have traveled from here to somewhere else by conventional means."

"Perhaps."

One by one over the next hour the members of our party—and the other guests at the lodge—joined us, and precisely at "Sixteen," about an hour after sunrise, the Ani attendants began bringing us platters heaped with fruit, plants, and some dried fish.

Although some of the victuals had odd shapes and colors and odors and equally unusual tastes, all seemed at least passable to our palates, and I soon found a combination of flavors that sat well with me. Once again I was joined by the Popino trader, who was wearing a rather fetching, off-the-shoulder gown that displayed plenty of flesh—and she certainly had plenty to display! She kept reaching over and past me to grab some titillating morsel off the plate to my front and left, thereby ensuring that her ample bosoms would brush against my arm on each and every occasion. Ah, I strongly suspect that this did more for her than it ever did for me!

"So what are your plans for today?" she warbled in my right ear, casually pushing Scooter off my shoulder onto the floor. I thought the wherret might bite her, but I gave it a hard glance that proclaimed in no uncertain terms, "Stay away!"

"Oh, I am *so* sorry!" she said. "By the way, my name is Semela Akhidaya Denarro Pusilla Maffluye Bouboulierre. I am really, truly pleased to meet you!"

What sins had I committed to deserve—first, Doctor Scarabbaios and his scatter-bombus—and now, *La Belle Dame en Marsi*? *O tempora, o mores!* I nodded my head in acknowledgment of her immense fleshy pulchritude.

And then, wonder of wonders, I was rescued!

"Oh, husband!" I heard warbling from the next table over. I turned around to see Shah'rah beckoning to me.

"Alas, that I must leave you now," I told Semela of the Simpering Sigh.

"Thank you!" I whispered to my sometime wife, as I squeezed in next to her. "I was afraid that that godawful woman was going to engulf me in her unyielding embrace—right there on the table."

"Perhaps I should have let her," Shah'rah said. "After all, you've been ignoring *me*, my dear."

"I am *not* your 'dear,'" I said. "Now, try one of these." I popped a yellow string of what looked like seaweed into her dainty mouth, and watched as she oohed over the piquant flavor.

"I never would have guessed," she said.

"Obviously, I have much to teach you."

"Do you now! I suspect that the opposite might also be true, husband."

"I am *not* your spouse," I repeated. "Please do not call me that."

"Very well, Master." She burped slightly. "The food is a bit better than it was last night. Or, perhaps I just have a better guide this morning."

At that moment, Arrgruffruff entered the room, and spotting me, immediately hopped over on his two legs and tail. He sat up next to me and took an ort right out of my hand.

"Not bad," he said. Then: "Sirr, I have found him!"

CHAPTER THIRTY

"EDUCATION IS 'GUD' ENOUGH FOR ME"

"Not here!" I hissed at the Yowler, shushing him up. "We'll gather our people together after breakfast."

After we'd finished our repast, I led the group onto a terrace in the back of the inn that featured a fifteen-foot-high statue of the winged, empurpled bovine that had also been appeared on the establishment's business brand hanging out front.

"I never saw a purple cow," Scooter said, "Particularly one that could fly."

"I'd rather see one than be one," Grit said.

"I'm also curious: what *is* it?" I asked our guide.

"I have no idea," Zalmanna said. "They are not mentioned in the briefing book for this world. And the Erésvepeans certainly do not have creatures of this type living here."

Emblazoned on the base of the thing was a dual inscription in both Anisian and Tyrosian: "'Education Is Gud Enough for Me.'"

"Who can argue with that?" Hawk said.

"We shouldn't educate the peasants," Doctor Scarabbaios said. "Why, they're positively revolting."

"They're always revolting somewhere," Brén the Single-Minded said.

"Enough of this frippery!" I said. "Arrgruffruff, what do you have to report?"

"Masterr Melanchthon live in town called Gettalonnlittelldauggy on norruthrrrun coast."

"That is also where the University is located," Zalmanna said, "the only institution of higher learning on Marsi."

"How far?" I asked.

"We could easily sail there in a few hours," she said. "I can make the arrangements, if you wish."

"What about translators?"

"A number of the professors on campus will undoubtedly speak Tyrosian, since it is considered the language of the educated class. This is not a problem."

"Very well, then," I said. "I suggest that we go there this afternoon. Gather your belongings together, folks, and meet me in the lobby in an hour's time."

The Tyro was there before us, and after I checked us out—"so sadness to see you go," the innkeeper said—Zalmanna led the way down to the docks, where we boarded a vessel called *The Damsel Flyer*, captained by one Wherrarrugoyin Lilwon. I understood that his given name, in the usual Anisian fashion, was the second word in this linguistic menagerie.

I was doing fine until we rounded the headland of the bay that sheltered the capital city. Then the boom-boom-boom of the waves hitting the bow of our intrepid "flyer"—whatever it was—soon had me wishing that I hadn't sampled the seafood again that morning—and even sooner, my little fishies were joining their brethren in the deep, as I coughed up every last bit of breakfast—and then some—while hanging over the rail!

I was not alone in this utterly retching enterprise, for at least half of my fellow travelers joined me there in giving their all for the joy of exploration.

"Are you all right?" my wife asked, obviously not at all bothered by the ups and downs of seafaring existence. "Can I get you anything, dearest husband?"

Ohhh, even the mere thought of eating something again had me spewing my guts once more into the ruby-red ocean. Bless her, she grasped me around my waist and offered me whatever comfort she could provide—which was not all that much in reality.

It took us an eternity—actually about three hours—to make the voyage up the coast, and I'm certain that the vista of shore and beach must have been beautiful; but when I wasn't voiding my insides, I was curled up on a cot below decks, wishing—oh, ever so hard—that I was anywhere but Erésvepe.

Finally, though, the ordeal passed when we entered another cove that marked the entrance to the college town of Gettalonnlittelldauggy. The more infirm among us were helped onto the dock by the others, and then we secured passage on the bird-carts that provided transportation in all of the larger Marsian communities.

These strange vehicles consisted of wagons with padded seats (and sometimes top-coverings) hitched to a giant bird ten feet tall. The creature's wings had been clipped to prevent it from flying, and its forward-facing eyes shielded on either side with blinders to keep its vision focused on the road ahead. An Ani driver would sit in a little pot of water in front of the vehicle, and direct the avian taxi with squawks and clicks and pulls on a tether. It seemed to work.

Soon we entered the University of Marsippi compound, a jumble of buildings and narrow streets that spread out from the main entrance. They seemed strangely quiet to me. We stopped there at a small building that served as a checkpoint.

"Babble, babble," said the guard in Anisian.

"Can you speak Tyrosian?" I asked.

"Ah, yes-can, Sir," he said.

"We need lodgings for the night, and I'd like to talk to someone in charge, if that's possible."

"Uh, down street this to right to Madame Yessirrdattismaibebe. She have room plenty. School not here right now. Very still this days. Provost not on campus here. You see him later?"

"Sounds fine," I said. "We'll be back tomorrow. Would you leave him a message, please?"

"Yes-can, Sir."

So I jotted down a note for the missing administrator (in my experience they were often missing!), and left it to be delivered whenever he returned. Then we headed into town.

Madame Yessirrdattismaibebe Pallin's establishment was actually larger and better apportioned than The Violet Bovine had been, and I was able to secure private rooms for everyone— and at half the price too!

"I do cookie-pile for you," she said in broken Tyrosian. "You betcha!"

And even though she only had a few hours to prepare our evening repast, the matron was as good as her word. We were brought heaping plates full of boiled eggs and egg hash and baked eggs and a root-and-vegetable stew with chunks of tender, lightly seasoned fowl and what appeared to be roe and eggs, and several different salads comprised of sea plants and shellfish (and eggs!) covered in a pungent sauce that left one wanting more—and much, much else. My appetite was restored just by the fragrant odors alone.

"Good, eh?" the Madame asked.

"Good, indeed," I agreed.

And afterwards, she brought in her sons and daughters (if I understood her correctly) to entertain us with their pantomimes and songs and warblings, all seasoned with a sharp pale drink that packed a grand wallop at the end, and left us, each and every one, staggering off to our beds—although none of us, amazingly, suffered from any ill aftereffects, either from the food or the drink. We just slept surpassingly well—me particularly, since I didn't have to share my accommodations with old Doctor S.!

It was the best time that we'd had on the trip thus far.

CHAPTER THIRTY-ONE
"YOU KNOW THIS: PIECE OF FURNITURE IN WHICH ONE SITS"

The next morning I, Mistress Zalmanna, and Doctor Scarabbaios met with Provost Aillbieyagudboimomy in his office in the University.

"I'm, uh, sorry so that President Faransissanwillieyarbadbois is, uh, not-in-town visiting the hinterland," the educator said in passable Tyrosian. "He's, uh, doing search on immigration of unlettered children from one gradation to other."

"In the hinterlands?" I asked.

"Ah, yes. They, uh, tend to enflock there during, uh, break of academe, for strange reason do not understand it myself. It is science esoteric, methinks."

"We're looking for some trace of one of our colleagues," I said, "A mage named Master Melanchthon."

"Yes-can, do recall him," the Provost said. "He, uh, teach in Department of Biothaumaturgy for some year. Very, very popular with student-folk."

"What became of him?"

"Well, uh, he left, I think. Yes-can, fairly sure I am that he is gone now. Have not spy him on campus for long time passing."

"Where did he go?" I asked.

"I really, uh, I could not say. You have to talk to Chair."

"The Chairman of his Department?" I asked.

"No, no, course not—his *chair*, Master Morpheús, his chair. You know this: piece of furniture in which one sits."

"I'm familiar with the basic concept," I said. "Why <u>his</u> chair in particular?"

"Because, uh, he implant himself in it all the time?" the Provost said. "Do not know. Maybe Dean Ohwisselandaillkumtoyumyladd can help."

I was finding the multi-syllabic Marsian names very cumbersome indeed. "Where can I find this Dean?"

"In Deanery, of course—at College of Fish and Fowl, Citadel de River-Run, past Eve and Adam's, from swerve of shore to bend of bay."

"Which is where?"

"Down road perhaps," he said. "You, uh, you cannot miss it. It has dead fish on sign.

"Now, saddest to say, have appointment with podiatrist. Thank you and have nice stay!"

I realized after we left that he didn't really have feet as such—they more closely resembled flippers.

The Dean, when we finally located him, wasn't much more helpful, and I was beginning to get the idea that the people here didn't really *want* to talk about Master Melanchthon.

"Where was his office?" I finally asked the administrator.

"Biothaumaturgy Department located in Koondakjian Hall on main campus, very top of seventh hill. But he has not been there in long-years."

"*How* many years?" I pressed. I was getting tired of all the obvious obfuscation.

"Uh—few?"

So we went back up the road to the University of Marsippi again, and asked the entrance-keeper for help in finding the biothaumaturges. He gave us a map—"You, uh, never find 'em otherwiser."

"Do you know anything about Master Melanchthon?" I suddenly asked, just out of curiosity.

"Verrry nice man to me," the attendant said. "To everyone! Sorry when see him go."

"When did he leave?"

"Three year, six month. Big, big, uh, 'spearmint. He disappear—poof! Everyone so sorry."

"Who can tell me about this?"

"Try, uh, Master Efferitas. He know."

"He doesn't sound Erésvepean," I said.

"No—foreign man. But good friend for all."

"What's your name?"

"No name please, just work here. No need name. Thank you for many niceties."

Then we shook, uh, flipper-to-hands, and headed up the hill to the Biothaumaturgy Department. We had no trouble locating the facility, since it had a mushroom cloud emblem hanging over it. (I was forever perplexed and amazed by such devices, but we saw them everywhere on these worlds, often without any explanation of what they were or why they were important to the indigenous natives. Someday I would obviously have to pen a thesis about their symbolic significance.)

Master Efferitas, when we found him, was much more forthcoming about a man that he described as both friend and mentor, and was also fluent in High Tyrosian.

"He was trying to locate a biothaumaturgical object that he called the 'Egg.' I was never quite certain in my own mind what this was, but he seemed to have a clear concept of the thing—or rather, things, because he came to the conclusion near the end that there was more than one of them.

"'There are actually four, Ferry,' he said to me once, just a few months before he vanished. 'Four of them, and I've only found one or maybe two thus far. I need to go off-world to locate the others.'

"Then he showed me this small, crystalline ovoid with a faintly reddish tint to it. It seemed almost to pulse when he held it up to the light. 'That's The First Elephant's Egg,' he said. 'And when I have the others, my friend, oh, when I have the others, then I'll tell that Council where they can finally go!'"

"So what happened to him?"

"He built a special transit-mirror for use in the Sixth Circle," the teacher said.

"But I thought that the only such devices were located in Gettouttahir," Mistress Zalmanna said.

"That's not quite accurate," Efferitas said. "We have a number of experimental machines and mirrors located here at the University, but they're not for public use, and we don't have the energy in any case to transit anyone very far. Or at least we didn't, until Master Melanchthon appeared.

"He found a way to draw power directly from our sun, thereby greatly boosting our ability both to æther-travel and to troll the ætherspace for possible destination signatures. He started forging a mirror composed of gold and something he called augurite, which he himself had discovered in the remains of a huge meteorite on the island of Dolbi—about a thousand *bledstad* west of here.

"And then one day he powered up the device, activated it with the help of a control, and vanished through its eye—never to be seen again. Several of our graduate students also attempted to employ the mirror, but they too were lost in ætherspace. Wherever this, uh, invention had sent my mentor and these acolytes, they could not return on their own or be retrieved by our efforts."

"Did Master Melanchthon indicate where he thought he was being transited by the mirror?" Doctor Scarabbaios asked.

"He never named the specific destination to me," the instructor said. "Only that he was trying to find the Planet of the Pachyderms, whoever or whatever they are. I've never found anyone who knew of this race, or located any mention of them in the literature that we have in the Library. And I've never had the courage to essay the mirror myself."

"Could we see it?" Mistress Zalmanna asked.

"Yes, of course." Then Master Efferitas led the way down several corridors to a large open room that obviously served as a laboratory for the Department. I saw a number of different kinds of transit-devices lining the wall, some of them partially dismantled—and one being put back together by several young

Marsis.

"You'll pardon the mess," he said. "We always have various tests and practices in progress here. Master M.'s device is over here."

The mirror was a large, diamond-shaped instrument framed and resting on its point. It had a vaguely coppery tint to it, almost shimmery in effect. A number of what were obviously power cables were connected to the structure at its base, and a separate console was attached to one side.

"This machine requires an operator to monitor and control the flow of energy," the teacher said. "Otherwise the transitee could be scattered throughout the æther in a disassembled state, never to be reintegrated again."

"Melanchthon obviously made contact with something at the other end," Zalmanna said.

"Yes, but no one has been able to determine here exactly what that receptacle was—indeed, whether it was an active or passive link. If the link was passive, then there might not have been any easy way for him and the others to transit back again. At least, this is what we assume. They could also have been killed or disestablished, of course."

"Did he leave any research papers about the project?" Doctor Scarabbaios asked. "Anything that might tell us more details."

"I have all of his notes," Efferitas said, "or at least those that survive, and nothing in them seems to be of any specific use. Many, however, are encoded in a cipher that none of us can penetrate."

"Still, we'd like to view them," I said. "Also, do you have his chair?"

"His chair? Why would you want something like that?"

"I just do."

"Well, I can certainly get these together for you, if you want to come back tomorrow. Say, at the third hour of sunlight?"

I thanked him for his help, and we returned to the good Madame's cookery, which was certainly making up for some of our other misadventures on this long trip.

After a very satisfying meal of some kind of baked cuttlefish in a sweet-and-sour sauce, plus what tasted like cornbread, but was actually made from ground seaweed, I brought the group together to discuss the day's developments.

"Grit and Scooter," I said, "I'm going to need your expertise tomorrow. I assume that you know or can break the code to your Master's notes, Grit."

"I can probably read them," the old wherret said.

"We need to discover what it is about Melanchthon's chair that has significance," I continued. "Hawk, you and your men can help with that. Also, I want to examine that transit-mirror more closely. So I suggest that all of you get a good night's sleep. We're going to be busy tomorrow."

"What about me?" Shah'rah asked.

"Ha! You can serve me as my assistant," I said.

"Is that better than wife?"

CHAPTER THIRTY-TWO
"ALWAYS LOOKING FOR ANOTHER SOURCE OF FUNDING"

The next morning, when we returned to the Department of Biothaumaturgy, we were confronted by the Provost standing in the doorway of the main entrance.

"Understand you wish to examine documents that are private property of the University," he said in plausible Tyrosian. "Such research files are not open to view of general public."

"Perhaps the campus would accept a donation to its research fund," I said, "in exchange for which, you would grant us the right to peruse the papers of Master Melanchthon. After all, the gentleman himself has abandoned these records."

"How large this grant?" the administrator asked.

"Generous, Sir."

He squawked and smiled. "Of course, this institution can always make exception for *bona fide* investigators who are willing to advance investigative possibilities of faculty. Permission is granted."

"I'll stop at your office on the way out," I said, "to make the appropriate arrangements."

Then he bid us *adieu*, and we sought out Master Efferitas.

"I'm truly sorry about that," the instructor said. "The administration is always looking for another source of funding. It's embarrassing at times.

"However, I've managed to organize all of the Master's records into appropriate groups, at least to the extent that I can read them myself."

I turned these over to Zalmanna, Doctor Scarabbaios, and the wherrets, and then went to look at Melanchthon's chair. It seemed ordinary enough to me, just a padded piece of furniture, so I left Hawk and his men to examine it carefully for any hidden treasures.

Then Efferitas took me once again to the Department's laboratory, where I began a detailed survey of the transit-mirror that the old mage had constructed.

"You say the power source is ultimately your sun?" I asked.

"Yes, the Master found some way of capturing a portion of its energy through ætherial traps, and redirecting its power to collectors that funnel the current through these cables that you see at the base. As a result, this instrument has a capacity that surpasses any of the others here by a factor of ten or twenty."

"That much?" I was surprised.

"He was a clever man, and he had the ability to motivate our students to levels of enthusiasm I've never seen before. I wish I could have that kind of effect on my graduates. For him, they would cheerfully slave all hours of the night on the device, and then come back for more. They loved the Master, as did I. He was a great magus and a good friend."

"You say 'was'—do you think he's dead?"

"I don't know what to think. He promised to return to Erésvepe, but he hasn't been seen these three years, and I wonder now what's become of him. As I mentioned before, several of his students followed him into the void—and we've also heard nothing from them, not a message, not a whisper. All of them carried sky-orbs with them that should have been able to bridge the æther, even if a transit-machine wasn't available wherever they landed. We've had no communication from any of them, however. So I have to think the worst. Maybe the world 'over there' isn't habitable by our kind. Many such places exist, you know."

"So I'm told. You indicated that the machine has to be manipulated by a second person. Who was operating the instrument when he transited?"

Master Efferitas looked down. "I was the one in each case who assumed the responsibility for handling the controls. No mistakes were made: I followed Master Melanchthon's instructions to the letter. From every indication that I could see, each of the individuals who ventured into the void through this mirror transited safely to their ultimate destination, wherever that was.

"But I also must tell you that my understanding of the principles behind the operation of this particular mechanism is weak at best. My Master was doing things here that I've never seen done on any other of the implements housed in this room." He swept his hand around in a broad gesture behind us. "He would tell me things, to be sure, but I simply could not fathom the theoretical framework he was employing. I'm truly sorry."

"From all accounts," I said, "Master Melanchthon has lived for many centuries. He undoubtedly has amassed a depth of knowledge about ætherial travel that surpasses all of our comprehensions put together.

"And now, I'd like to examine his creation for myself, if I might. I'll find you back at your office again."

"Very well," he said, and left me to my musings. I spent some time checking the parameters on the diamond-shaped mirror, but it had such an odd feel to it that I couldn't make much sense of the thing.

After a while, one of the students working on rebuilding the machine across the room wandered over and said in Tyrosian: "An amazing piece of work, is it not? I was one of the fortunate few who helped the Master fashion this thing. I am Acolyte Coclis of Iokósos, if you please."

I introduced myself. "Not from this planet, then?"

"No, but this place has the only research facility of its type within easy transit-distance; many of us come here from off-world. It's not cheap, but we want to learn."

"What guided Master Melanchthon to build this device?"

"I do not know for certain, Master Morpheús, but I suspect that the discovery of the great meteorite in the Dolbi Sound a decade ago had something to do with it. Apparently, it had fallen there in prehistoric times. Its composition was unusual, to say the least: a stony covering over a metallic interior, and that metal was unlike anything ever analyzed here. It had unusually potent levels of conductivity.

"My teacher immediately saw the possibilities for its use as the base for a transit-mirror, and gained permission to melt most of it down for that purpose."

"But where did he get the design?" I asked.

"I am not at all certain, but I heard him in his office several times talking to someone about the philosophy of transit-travel—and yet I never saw this person enter or leave his room. And once, when I had to disturb him on an urgent personal matter, I knocked and opened his door before receiving permission, and saw him holding that crystalline object in his hand."

"The Egg?"

"Yes, that was it—the Egg. It was, well, changing color in a kind of a pulsing pattern of light. At least, that is what it looked like to me. It was the only time I ever saw the Master angry—he shooed me out of his office right away, and only allowed me to return again after he had put the crystal away. It was very odd. Normally, he was the most mild-mannered of men, kind and generous and open to one and all. This was very unlike him.

"He apologized for his outburst—imagine, a professor apologizing to a student!—and then asked me what I needed. We did not discuss the matter ever again, and thereafter, I noticed, he locked his door whenever he was sequestered."

"Do you know how to operate this machine?" I asked, nodding at the great diamond mirror.

"Not really. It requires a special kind of training to balance the high energy levels. He never let his students handle those kinds of advanced manipulations. It was always one of the instructors who worked the console, usually Master Efferitas."

"Where do you think he went?"

"A better place, I do hope," the student said. "He seemed very tired to me near the end. He said once that he was looking for the 'mate' of the crystal egg, and that he knew where one of them was located. That was where he was hoping to go. Perhaps he finally made it."

I thanked the young man for his help, and then went to find Master Efferitas again.

CHAPTER THIRTY-THREE
"TWO COPPER COINS OVER THE EYES OF THE RECENTLY DEAD"

That evening we gathered in the dining hall at Madame Y.'s establishment, and reviewed what we'd found.

"Anything new about Melanchthon's chair?" I asked Hawk.

"Well, Sir," he said, "we did find somethin', I wager, although I ain't so sure what it is. It was stuck a way down in the stuffin', but Eagle here, he spotted it. I think it's a coin of some sort, but it's not like any other I ever seen."

He placed the heavy object in my palm, and everyone gathered 'round in wonder, gaping at the shiny thing. It was so large that it completely spanned the area from the webbing of my thumb to the other side of my hand. The piece was fashioned from some kind of *aurum*, although I didn't recognize the species—it showed a darker hue than *flavaurum*, giving it an almost golden-red color. And it had serious bulk, being at least a quarter-inch thick—and heft, more than it should have had for the size.

The image on the obverse was that of a hooded man poling a small boat across a stream, a passenger seated in the rear. The inscription read: "TRANSITUS STYGE." The reverse displayed the great ouroboros mirror, with the following words marked around the rim: "TRANSITUS ÆTHERE." I could feel the pulse of power hiding somewhere deep down inside the heart of gold.

Wordlessly, I handed it over to Zalmanna, who examined it

closely and in turn passed it along to Doctor Scarabbaios.

"A thing of great potency and enormous beauty," the old mage finally said. "But why didn't he take it with him?"

"Perhaps he didn't need to," Grit said. "We've been looking through my Master's notes, Sir, and it's clear to us that he wasn't drawing his source of power from the local star."

"That would have been an extraordinarily difficult feat to accomplish in any case," Zalmanna said, "normally requiring many adepts and much machinery to avoid surges that would— perhaps—destroy the world on which the transit-device was located."

"Then what did he employ?" I asked.

"This coin refers to the River Styx, Sir," Scooter said. "In elden days, I've read, the Greeks would place two copper coins over the eyes of the recently dead to pay the fare to Charon, the ferryman who brought the souls of the deceased into Hades."

"But that was just a symbolic gesture," I said. "However, I can see where you're going with this. What if this coin, in tandem with something else, could provide the power to transit to worlds that have no receptacles as we know them? But— there would have to be a companion coin or device."

"Master, we have another artifact that originated in Hades," the wherret said.

"*The Necropompeion*—of course! The coin must work together with the book somehow. But that means that Master Melanchthon had to have owned a copy himself—and Jécko the Mallet told me that he thought that one or more of the missing volumes had migrated to the Otherworlds. One half of the equation, the part that provided the power to operate the mirror, would have remained here, while the other, the controller, would have transited with the traveler."

"What about the students who later employed the device?" the Tyro asked.

"They would have gone…somewhere," I said, "but without the book, they couldn't have transited to the place where Melanchthon went, not under any circumstance. They might have had their souls scattered to the æther." I shuddered at the thought—it would have been a horrible way to die, an eternity of dissolution.

"And the cables that are hooked onto the diamond-shaped mirror?" Zalmanna asked.

"All a sham," I said, "intended to turn away any real investigation of the thing. There might be something else out there that could power such an invention, but it would have to be brought, most likely, from off-world."

"But how did he intend to return?" Doctor Scarabbaios asked.

"I don't know. Whatever he thought or imagined, it obviously didn't work—or he went somewhere else from there. The question is: do we follow him through the æther? Do we dare to step into the unknown ourselves?

"And before you give me an answer, I'd like to say something else. Up to this point on our journey, our passage has been fairly straightforward—or utterly necessary for our survival. The next jump will be very dangerous. We have no idea where we're going, or what we'll find when we get there. In spite of the fact that some of you have made personal commitments to me, I now give you your freedom. I can't and won't hold you to any commitment beyond this point. If you join me, you do so as free beings. You'll still get paid, either way, those of you who signed on as mercenaries.

"So please think this over tonight, and give me an answer at breakfast tomorrow. That's all I have to say."

"Sir," Grit said.

"Yes."

"There was something else in my Master's papers." He pulled a note from his small pack, and handed it over to Doctor Scarabbaios.

The old man unfolded the thing, pulled out a monocle, and silently read the note from his mentor. Then he started to cry.

"What is it?" I asked.

"He forgives me," the mage said. "He *forgives* me! And I...I cannot forgive myself. Let me go home to die, Morpheús. I've lived too long already. I'm ready to die."

"Then I can do no better than Melanchthon," I said. "You're free to go."

And so we toddled off to our warm, waiting beds.

But the next morning, when Madame Y. banged on Doctor S.'s door and received no response, she found him lying stiff and cold underneath his covers. He would never see the River Rhenus again, but perhaps he traveled to a river of a different kind that night. Just in case, I slipped two copper coins over his eyes to pay his passage.

CHAPTER THIRTY-FOUR
"I'M A PRISONER OF SORTS"

"Master," Scooter whispered to me before breakfast. "We located a few other things of interest in Master Melanchthon's notes." We were sitting on the back porch of Madame Y.'s lodge, watching the fog bank recede just off the coast.

"Oh?" I said.

Then Grit handed me the letter.

It read:

> "To whomever finds these papers:
>
> > "Since no one but Grit is likely to be able to decipher my scribblings, I have to assume that he's present in some form. Greetings, my old friend and companion: I've missed you more than I ever thought possible, and I hope to see you again sometime soon.
> >
> > "The journey that I am about to undertake carries with it significant risks. I know that the place that I'm going, which I believe to be the Planet of the Pachyderms, has no transit-station or –receiver, at least of any configuration of which I'm aware. I've been able to determine this through a series of probes and experiments I've conducted over the past six months. I don't know why this is so: the possible reasons are infinite, of course.

"Therefore, even if I'm able to make the transit successfully—which means that I must find a focal point at the other end of the line that is sufficiently stable for a long enough period to reintegrate both body and soul—I may not be able to depart that world ever again. And yet, I feel that the possible significance of this place is sufficiently great that it's worth even the potential loss of my life or freedom.

"All my research points to the Pachyderms as the creators or protectors of the Elephant Eggs. I believe there to be four varieties or 'flavors' of these, of which I have certainly found the first (this one, I think, has multiple copies extant). I don't know their meaning as yet, but I think the answers must lie with the inhabitants of that world. This is what I've gleaned by interacting with the Egg that I possess.

"The fact that so little information is available about this planet tells me that very few individuals have transited to or from Pachydermia, my whimsical name for the place. So, I do have the sense that I'm a pioneer of sorts, as old and creaky as I am.

"If you decide to follow my trail into the æther, you must have a copy of *The Necropompeion* in order to generate sufficient power from the diamond-mirror to make the transit. I've left the passage-token that's the necessary key to unlocking the book's energy base buried deep within my office chair. The two implements can be employed in tandem in several different ways, but what I've chosen to do is to leave the coin on Erésvepe, and to take the book with me, in the hope that the resonance generated by the interaction of the two sympathetic devices will enable me to return back to the University again, even without a transmitter station on Pachydermia. If this does not work, then the other option is to transit with both implements, assuming, of course, that you can find another copy of the book itself.

"It is theoretically possible to power the diamond-mirror in other ways, but I know of no other source on Erésvepe that can do this—or I would have employed it myself.

"To activate *The Necropompeion*, you must turn to the section marked 'Quæstiones,' and ask out loud three questions: *'Quo vadis?'* ('Where are you going?'), *'Quo jure?'* ('By what right?'), and *'Quo pacto?'* ('By what means?')—while simultaneously holding the golden token in your less dominant hand. You do not have to be immediately proximate to the mirror in order to activate it.

"Once energized, the device will transit all of those who enter its window within a period of five or ten minutes—and then will automatically shut down several minutes after the last person steps through the aperture. But be warned: if the receiving medium at the other end is inherently unstable, then it must be calmed again before it can be reemployed; or those individuals traveling after the initial æther-surfer has passed through may arrive in a disassociated state. This is why I only allowed myself to make the first leap, and why I trained only my friend and colleague, Master Efferitas, to monitor the energy fluctuations. I warned him in the direst terms not to follow me, but I fear that some of my students who've worked on the construction of the machine may attempt to reactivate it. I don't know what will become of them if they succeed.

"The fact that you are reading this note, Master Mage, means that I never returned from Pachydermia, and may, in fact, be dead. I recommend that you destroy the diamond-mirror and these notes, and take the token with my thanks. Perhaps you can find some other use for it.

"But if you seek to follow me—if you have an adventurer's heart—then I wish you well with all your endeavors. And perhaps, just perhaps, we may yet share a meal together at some future date.

"*Ave utque vale*:

"Melanchthon Malitiosus"

"A remarkable man, your Master," I told Grit. "And a brave one, I think. I need to consider his words before we go into breakfast. Let me be, please, both of you."

After they'd gone, I watched the roiling clouds hugging the shore as they ebbed and flowed, along with the tide itself. Life itself was like that, I thought: full of ups and downs, of triumphs and disappointments, of good things and ill. I hoped for his sake that Master Melanchthon had succeeded finally in finding the Pachyderms.

Then I laughed out loud. One thing was for sure, though: I'd never been bored, not once, since starting this venture. And I *would* see it through—yes indeed! I would see it through all the way to the end! After all, am I not Morpheús, ex-Scanner Prime of the Kingdom of Kórynthia, hypatomancer and soothsayer extraordinaire, a scion of the House of Parakôdês, and a descendent of Mathurin? I will not disgrace my ancestors' names.

Most people live dull, predictable lives, the kind of life, actually, that I was so carefully building for myself back on Nova Europa. By leaving the place of my birth, by venturing into the void, by cutting my ties with the past, I'd changed the rules of the game. I felt better about myself now than I had in many years. At least I was living again. At least I was trying.

Besides…compared to the way most folks existed, the life of a magus was always intense!

I realized then that I was hungry. The fog was lifting from

the shore again. It was time to let the others decide what *their* lives would become.

CHAPTER THIRTY-FIVE
"TOUGH BIRD, BUT SEASONIN' HELP"

When I'd finished reading Master Melanchthon's missive to my comrades sitting around the breakfast table, I set it on the table, sipped a drink from the mug of fermented fruit juice my hostess had placed in front of me, and then put the cup down again.

Finally, I said: "I intend to follow Melanchthon into the æther, come what may. I'll take the usual precautions, of course, but still, you've just heard what he wrote, and it's a bald, bare fact that he's not returned. So the danger seems real enough, and I can't tell you what to expect out there. You have several choices: you can remain here, return home, travel somewhere else, or join me on Pachydermia. Tell me what you want to do."

Hawk spoke first: "Well, Sir, me and the boys have talked this over 'mongst ourselves, and you've played fair with us at each step of the way. Mostly, we're in for the full ride. I'll let the others speak for themselves."

My old classmate, Brén the Single-Minded, raised his hand and said: "This is more than I bargained for, Master Morpheús, so I think I'll head back, if it's all the same to you. I thought this'd be a bit of a lark, you know, and it was, but…it's getting too…serious for me."

"Can you arrange for his return, per our agreement?" I asked Mistress Zalmanna.

"Yes, the Tyros honor their bargains," she said. "Also, I have been directed by the High Council to remain with you until you obtain The Fourth Elephant's Egg, so I have no choice in the matter."

"My Master awaits me somewhere out there," Grit said. "I travel with you until we find him."

"Pack-mate Durrdruff still missin'. Must find him, sorrry," Arrgruffruff growled. "Cannot go with you."

"What about the Yowler?" I asked our guide.

"Since he was not part of our original agreement," Zalmanna said, "I cannot provide a voucher for his transit."

"Not necessarry," the Yowler said. "Pack will help."

Nonetheless, I gave him sufficient gold strips to pay for his transit back to his homeworld.

Then Scooter spoke up: "I'm bound to you for nine-and-forty years. Until my service is complete, I go with you, Master."

"I feel the same way, husband," Shah'rah said. "I walk wherever you walk."

"What about Doctor Scarabbaios?" I asked. "He hasn't joined us yet."

And that was when I sent Madame Yessirrdattismaibebe to rouse the elderly mage, and she discovered his untimely passing. After she reported his death to the rest of us, Scooter said: "Well, I guess he'll be staying behind then."

I batted the wherret on the nose for its ill-tempered remarks; but the truth was, no one much missed the old fart, whose stern, dyspeptic, and often disapproving visage had worn on all of us.

"Will Tyrotarichos transit his body back home?" I asked Zalmanna.

"Probably not," she said.

"Then we must make the appropriate arrangements here. Can you help?" I asked our innkeeper.

She gave me a rather strange look, but said: "Yessir, but only know local, uh, custom."

I looked around the table for anyone's opinion, but everyone deferred the decision, as usual, to *moi*. Sometimes I wish folks were more forthcoming.

"Very well," I said, "we'll do it the Marsian way."

"Need two day to fix," she said. "Down at Biddtaimfurbonzo Shrine on Pippirmin Bay. 'Kay?"

"We'll be there."

And so we were, each and every one, along with at least half of the local community, I think. Thousands of Marsians were crowded around a dozen great fire pits, singing and shouting and roasting all kinds of food.

"What is this?" I asked Master Efferitas, when I spotted him amongst the masses.

"It's called the Festival of Passing," the instructor said. "When folks around here die, all of the survivors have a smashing good time to celebrate the best of what the deceased said and did and was. They believe this honors the essence of the deadly departed in a way that they hope is pleasing to the gods of sea, sun, and land. This will ease their passage into the afterlife, they believe, and give them the best chance of living boisterously in their next existence.

"And so they tell stories, most of them fanciful, about the person, and they sing and laugh and have a good time. You might say they share the essence of the individual amongst themselves."

I thought on reflection that this was a very positive way indeed of conducting a requiem, and told him so; and then pressed forward to partake of some of the marvelous eats that were simmering in the baking holes that had been dug in the sand. I recognized the shellfish and real fish and vegetables that were heaped on my bowl, but others were new to me.

"This is very good," I told Madame Y., who was one of the cooks preparing this grand feast.

"Yes, goodie, goodie!" she agreed. "Tough bird, but seasonin' help."

"What kind of bird is that?" I asked, savoring a particularly spicy piece of meat. The juices ran down my chin.

"Uh, not know, uh, how to say," she finally said. "Goodie!"

"Yes, very, very tasty." I spotted Scooter and Grit perched on a small dune with the Yowler, and sat down beside them. Even they seemed to be enjoying themselves.

"You know, when I finally go, this is just what I want for myself," I said, "a few friends sharing a feast and having a good time. No tears or lamentations or anything like that."

"Are you sure, Master?" Scooter asked, grunting and gnawing at a small bone. "I mean, Doctor Scarabbaios was a bit over the top, but really…."

"What do you mean?" I asked.

"What Scooter means," Grit said, "is that he was a bit ripe for the feast, although the cooks did the best they could with him. You see, the natives here share *everything*."

I looked down at the dark gravy and pieces of meat swirling together in my pit of despair, and then upchucked the entire meal over my friends—who just thought that was another form of sharing, since they gratefully licked the half-digested bits of Doctor S. off their respective furs.

"Good!" Arrgruffruff said.

"Good!" the wherrets agreed.

"Oh, goodness gracious!" I said, and offered them another few orts.

CHAPTER THIRTY-SIX
"SOME SOFT MEDIUM AT THE OTHER END"

It took me several weeks of careful experimentation before I was comfortable operating Master Melanchthon's diamond transit machine in conjunction with *The Necropompeion*, which I had "borrowed" from the few belongings left by the late (and unlamented) Doctor Scarabbaios—after all, he wouldn't need it! With Master Efferitas's aid, I tried employing varying levels of control, and attempted to establish a link with the planet that Melanchthon had called "Pachydermia."

"There's some soft medium at the other end," I finally told him, "maybe liquid water or the like. That appears to be where Malitiosus ultimately landed."

"What about the graduate students who eventually followed him?" he asked.

"From the internal records of this device, I've been able to determine that they did travel somewhere—but where exactly, I have no idea. They weren't disassociated, thank the Lord."

"That's good news," he said.

"I want to invite you again to join our little group."

"Thank you kindly, but no," the teacher said. "My role in life is circumscribed by the walls of the university. I'm not an adventurer or explorer. I envy your passion for such things, truly I do, but I don't share it. I'm happy to assist you, if I can—and I'll have the stories to tell my grandchildren someday."

At that moment Zalmanna rushed in with Hawk and his men

in tow.

"Morpheus!" she yelled, "we must leave at once."

"What's happened?" I asked.

"I've just been informed by one of my contacts that the local magistrate has received instructions from the President of Marsi to seize the transit-device, the book, and the power-token. Apparently your old friend Brén got drunk one night in the capital and said too much, and they have arrested and questioned him.

"Now the government has decided that all of this research is really worth something. The town mayor is gathering together some of his gendarmes even as we speak, and will be here within the hour to confiscate everything that once belonged to Melanchthon—and also to sequester the members of our expedition, and all the transit machines at the University."

Scooter and Grit were already there working with me, but I knew that my "wife" was somewhere out in town.

"We need to find Shah'rah," I said.

"I go, find herr!" It was Arrgruffruff again—I thought he'd already departed several days earlier.

"Then go!" I ordered, and he scampered out the door, his claws making click-click noises on the tile (when he was running, he tended to employ all four legs).

Then I turned to Efferitas: "We need to fire up the diamond transit-mirror."

I fetched the book from its hiding-place in the æther, and turned to the page of "Quæstiones" halfway through the text. I iterated the three queries while holding the *aurum*-token in my dexter hand, and felt an immense power surge from *The Necropompeion* directly into the transit-device. As the immense yellow-gold capacitor slowly began to build its energy, I motioned to Master Efferitas to assume his position at the control-console. It would be his job to monitor and adjust the energy fluctuations that otherwise could destroy this building and this city, if allowed to go unchecked.

"How long do you think we've got?" I asked our Tyro guide.

"Perhaps three-quarters of an hour," she said.

"Hawk!" I shouted above the din.

"Yes, Sir," he said.

"Clear the building of any civilians. Then get your men arrayed around the main entrance, so you can control all traffic in and out."

The sergeant hurried away without speaking further to me, barking orders to each of his crew in turn. They were already pulling out the stubby weapons they'd been issued on Tyrotarichos, checking their ammunition. I'd heard them practicing with the things once or twice, and the loud banging noises that they made when activated would have frightened any natives that I'd ever encountered, that's for sure. I had no idea how they operated—I don't think Mistress Zalmanna did either.

I needed at least half an hour for the transit-machine to reach its maximum storage level to facilitate multiple jumps to Pachydermia. The process simply could not be hurried any faster.

"How's it coming?" I yelled at Efferitas, when I'd thought the appropriate time had passed.

"Almost there," he howled back at me. The background noise was getting ever louder as the device revved up—almost a buzzing that permeated the very soul.

Suddenly the Yowler appeared in the doorway with Shah'rah.

"Found herr!" he growled. "Me decide betterr go wit' you than stay."

Then I heard some loud, muffled explosions from the front of the building—and shouts of "Get back!"

"Time to go," Zalmanna said.

I activated the great glowing mirror, and twisted the leys, searching for the signature I needed. Then I ordered Master Efferitas, "Send the others through as soon as I've stabilized the receptacle."

He looked at me and said, "Good luck, Master Morpheús. It's been an honor to know you."

"And you," I said—and turned and stepped through the

opening in the ætherspace, plunging almost immediately up to my neck into an ice-cold bath of water. I illuminated my hand, and saw that the small pond was completely surrounded by rock—I was stuck in a cave!

I maneuvered myself onto the sandy beach surrounding the pool, and reached out and steadied the surface of the liquid. Then I helped Shah'rah come through—calming the waters once again afterwards—and in turn Grit, Scooter, Arrgruffruff, Eagle, Roc, Bird, Warbler, Hawk, and then a young man that I'd never seen before.

"Where's Gull?" I asked the sergeant, as I felt the link go dead.

"Wounded, Sir. Couldn't bring him. Efferitas hurt too"—and then I saw that Hawk'd been cut as well, low on his left thigh. "Not bad," he said, when he noted my concern. "Where are we, Sir?"

"Wherever Master Melanchthon went. Folks," I said, "welcome to Pachydermia!"

CHAPTER THIRTY-SEVEN
"DON'T WANT IT TO PUTREFY"

We were all very damp and cold, and needed to find some place soon where we could build a fire and dry out.

"Locate the entrance to the cave," I ordered the Yowler, who immediately started sniffing here and there, and then bounded off into the dark.

"I can feel my Master's presence on this world, Sir!" Grit said. "He lives!"

"I'm very glad to hear it," I said. "But before we can locate him, we need to get some warmth and shelter first."

Then I turned to our interloper: "Who are you?" I asked.

The clean-shaven boy couldn't have been more than eighteen or twenty in age. "My short name is Boupho, Sir," he said. "My teacher is Master Efferitas. I was part of the team of students that worked on the machine that sent us here, helping to keep it going. When I saw the way was open, I didn't even think, I just jumped. I want to see the universe, Sir. And I knew that I would never have a better chance than this. I'll do anything that you want me to do."

"Very well," I said, "You're here now, and I doubt that you— or we—are going anywhere else very soon. You'll report to Sergeant Hawk."

"Yes, Master," the lad said.

Arrgruffruff returned shortly thereafter, and said: "That way, Sirr"—and indeed, I could feel a very slight hint of a draft coming from the direction he pointed out with his nose.

"Follow me," I told the group.

The Yowler led the way, with me providing some faint illumination from my raised hand at the head of the column, and Mistress Zalmanna doing the same at the tail—just enough so that we avoided any obvious holes or rocks. Hawk's men assisted him with walking on his bad leg.

It was night when we emerged under the bright shining eyes peering at us from the heavens of that brave new world, but the air was clear and warm, and laced with a faint perfume of flowers blooming—or something very much like them. We found a small alcove near the entrance where we could huddle together until the sun came up again. The light breeze quickly dried our skins and clothes or furs, but even so, Shah'rah soon snuggled up close to me—for warmth, she said. I didn't try to move her away.

"Why won't tell me your real name?" I asked her, when her squirming against my side disturbed my sleep once again.

"Why you not tell me yours?" she said. She'd almost lost the heavy accent that she'd had when I first met her, and her diction was gradually improving as well. "It be fact that magi make false identities."

"We do so for valid reasons," I said. "Certain kinds of magick can be used to harm another mage, but only if the recipient's true identity is known. Otherwise, we are immune to most attacks of this type. Then too, a particular name can carry with it some inherent power of its own. But you don't have that excuse."

She wriggled again, trying to get closer.

"Are you cold?" I asked.

"Little," she said. "Master, I use name Shah'rah to hide me from *mi familia*. After-ward, it help keep the break clear that I make with my past. No more Andalusia. All that—lifetime ago to me. Can never go back. Truth—don't want to go back."

"Don't you want to see your parents again?"

"I...*mi madre* is *muerta*—she the only one who care for me. *Mi padre*, he is—how do you say?—*el patrón*, big man of small place. He own many *rancheros*. My two sisters, they married by him to others like him. My brothers, they *mucho* like my father: they drink and talk all-time about lands and *dineros* and *mujeres*. My uncle, he is Archquisitor in *La Inquisición*—his name is dear to Holy Roman Cæsar himself, *El Supremo Santidad* Leo Magnus II. My mother's father, he was councilor to *El Rey* Efraín IV. I had aunt who was sweet lady, but she live far away with husband, and I only see her once a year or maybe less. She may be *muerta* by now.

"So, husband, you see that no one miss me in Andalusia. Maybe Don Sebastián saw this in me when he take my soul."

I was silent for a long time, for, if I was being wholly honest with myself (and her), my own story was entirely dissimilar. But I still couldn't tell her very much of it, for obvious reasons.

"Do you sleep?" she finally asked, when I didn't speak.

"No. But you haven't yet told me your name."

She sighed very loudly. "Zuleica—Zuleica Odilia Luminosa de Magallanes. When I young, they call me Leica. I like Shah'rah better now, I think."

"Then Shah'rah it shall be," I said.

"And you?"

I sighed. "I can't tell you much about myself, because another mage could pry it out of you magically in such a way that you wouldn't even be aware of the intrusion.

"I was born on a blip of an island just off Asia Minor. I left there when young, and I have no idea what's become of my relatives. I try not to think about them, because I can never go back. To do so might potentially imperil them—and I won't allow that."

"Is world to you then so dangerous?" she asked.

"Sometimes. It's just better to be careful, Shah'rah. We're taught that in the Conlegium from an early age. 'Take care!' the masters say. 'A slip of the tongue can kill—or worse!' They were very dramatic about it, as I recall—it put the fear of God into all of us acolytes."

"Poor husband," she said. "Never much fun!"

"I didn't mean to give you that impression. Yes, we *were*

studious at times, but we could also be absolute hellions. We constituted a very smart and very talented group of young men.

"I remember one teacher of magical mathematics in particular. He was slightly deaf, so my friend Rufo trapped a sibilar in a small pot, and brought it to class. Whenever the instructor wasn't looking, he'd shake the container and the sibilar would screech in its high-pitched voice—so high, in fact, that the professor could just barely hear it, and couldn't tell whence it was emanating. He would walk up and down the rows of benches, looking for...he wasn't sure what. Just about drove him back to a monastery, I think.

"Then one day we came to class—and he just wasn't there. Finally one of the administrators wandered in and said that our teacher had 'gone on a sabbatical,' and that we'd have a new instructor with our next session."

"But that so cruel!" Shah'rah said.

"It happened. I'm not proud of what we did, but we were dealing with very hard-edged professors, for the most part. They kept an iron control over the classrooms, and you disobeyed or varied from the norm at your peril. They didn't hesitate to use the rod to maintain discipline. But we did learn, oh yes."

I noticed that the sky was starting to lighten, and so I roused our makeshift camp.

"How's the wound?" I asked Hawk.

"It burns," he said. "Don't want it to putrefy."

Scooter had a small flask of Purge-All in its pack, and the wherret sprinkled a drop of the liquid into the open wound, and then licked it with its tongue, which had curative properties.

"That should help," I said. "Get one of your men to tie it up for now."

And then over the horizon I saw two things that astonished me. A red sun peeked at us through a narrow band of clouds—and a yellow orb soon followed it—and a sharp, blue-white dot followed that. We were dealing with a rare triple star system!

Out of the center of the aura cast by the three suns fluttered a giant beast with eight legs and a wingspan of at least thirty or forty feet—and perched on a riding saddle over the front segment of this giant arthropod-like creature was a man in his prime. He blew a note on a great green horn that curled in upon itself—"Ta-ra," it said, "Ta-ra."

As the flying thing landed on the bluff in front of us, Grit jumped off my shoulder and ran at full tilt towards the dismounting rider.

"Master!" the creature shouted, "Master! You're alive!"

CHAPTER THIRTY-EIGHT
"THEY'RE NOT REALLY BUGS"

But there was something wrong here: if this was Master Melanchthon, who was supposed to be half a millennium or more in age, how could he appear so young, even with the enhancements that came so naturally to a mage? The handsome, even vigorous demi-god that strode into our campsite was the complete opposite of what I'd expected.

"Sorry to be so late," the visitor said. "I'm Melanchthon Malitiosus. You can call me Mellie. When I felt Grit's presence on this world, I knew that someone else had brought a copy of *The Necropompeion* to Erésvepe and activated the mirror. It was the only way that you could have come here. I had to rouse a libbéll from its torpidity—they'll don't normally travel at night—and force it to obey my will."

I introduced the others to him. "And I'm Master Morpheús," I said, "of Kórynthia on Nova Europa."

"Yes, I remember Paltyrrha very well," the "old" mage said. "Has much changed there?"

"Oh, they've put up a monument recently to Saint Katrina of the Holy Oak, but it's in a quasi-archaic style that I find inherently uninteresting."

"I, uh, don't seem to recall her."

"She married a Scottish laird from one of the Pictish principalities, and was martyred by a Ballantrae adept for chanting the same prayer over and over again: something about a sheep-shearer, I think. She was very popular among the masses for a time, but has now become largely *passé*."

"How interesting. However, I've come to bring you back to Verruwill."

"Is that the capital city?" Mistress Zalmanna asked.

"Ah, a Tyro, I see. I should have expected you. No, there are no capital cities here, or even any towns in the way that we would normally think of them. You would call it a village or a region. It's where I live now."

"Why didn't you return to Erésvepe?" I asked.

"I'll explain that later. Now, you need to gather together whatever belongings you have. The libbélli will be here soon to transport you."

"You, mean, those giant bugs?" Shah'rah said.

"They're not really bugs, Milady," Melanchthon said, "just gentle beasts of burden. You'll find them a quick and easy way to travel from place to place on this world. Ah, here they come now!"

We could hear the whine of their wings even before we could spy them. They came flying low over the landscape, and then soared hundreds of feet above us in sweeping circles of flight, moving sedately in interwoven patterns that made sense only to them. The suns' light splashed through the crystalline structure of their huge bodies as they crossed over and under each other.

"Magnificent, aren't they?" the mage said. "They're just one of the many beautiful things about this planet. I never cease being amazed at the myriad wonders here."

One of the creatures landed near the first, and Melanchthon showed us how to use the straps dangling over its side to mount the thing just in front of its wings, and then tie oneself onto the saddle there.

"You pull on this dark strip of leather to rise, and on this light-colored one to land"—he pointed them out where they emerged through holes in the seat. "They understand basic commands, but of course you don't know the language. However, they do recognize certain place names, and you only have to repeat the word 'Verruwill' to go there. In any case, they'll follow the lead of my steed, Vitesse. Just give them free reign once you're a-flight."

The great beasts were touching down all around us, and we found our way individually to our own mounts—except that Grit rode with its master, and Scooter with me. They shied away from the Yowler, apparently having never met his kind before, so he rode double with Melanchthon.

Then the mage was leading the way, his libbéll hopping from a nearby bluff into the air, with ours following suit—and I felt my heart briefly rise into my throat as the surface fell away beneath me. I crouched down, hugging the saddle so tightly that I almost lost my breath, until finally I became comfortable enough with the sensation of flight that I sat up straight and enjoyed the experience.

I don't suppose that we reached any higher than five hundred or a thousand feet above the land, but I could see further than I ever had before, save from Scarabbaios's mountaintop home—rivers and trees and plains and greenery tossed topsy-turvy everywhere, and some hills like the one from which we'd emerged, but nothing greater than that. Oh, it was gloriousness indeed, my friends.

When the libbélli were flying, as opposed to soaring, they flapped their wings to gain altitude and coasted for a time, and then repeated the process—although, as I discovered later, they could also move very fast when they wanted to, particularly when their backs were bare. I wondered what they ate.

Shah'rah seemed to be having a wonderful time, laughing out loud on occasion; but Mistress Zalmanna, I noticed, was almost white with tension and suppressed anxiety. The Tyros didn't much favor new experiences.

Our trip lasted several hours, but finally, about mid-morning judging from the position of the suns, we began to spiral down towards a large clearing carved out of the center of a ruby-tinted forest. As we neared the trees, I was able to resolve the reddish hue into individual large blossoms several feet in width poking their way up through the foliage. I also saw a few of the libbélli hovering over the flowers, sticking a long proboscis down into each stamen. They were obviously feeding on the nectar therein.

Then we landed, dismounted, and followed our host on a well-worn path that led beneath the shade of the trees.

"Where is the town?" Mistress Zalmanna asked, peering around at all the lush vegetation.

"This *is* Verruwill," Melanchthon said. "As I told you, it's not like any place you've ever visited before. The Pollýxerri don't believe in great buildings or monuments or things like that. They live simply. Everyone does here."

"The Pollýxerri?" she asked.

"What you would call the Pachyderms."

"They're the rulers of this world? How can we meet them?"

"There are no rulers here—or ruled either. They live peaceably with the other creatures that inhabit this place. And they'll come to you whenever they want to see you."

"I do not understand," the Tyro said.

"No, you don't, but you will. We have all the time in the world."

We came then to another clearing, this one perched on the bank of a minor river. I saw a green mound rising from a small hill near the water, and didn't recognize what it was until Melanchthon walked right through an opening that faced the stream.

"Welcome to my home," he said, bowing at us once.

CHAPTER THIRTY-NINE
"TRUST NO ONE"

I'd never been able to contact Niobë from Erésvepe, despite several attempts, and I didn't know whether it was because we'd moved further away from her into the flotsam and jetsam of the Sixth Circle, or just that she wasn't available at the times that I tried to reach her. This was often the case. We could never seem to determine any kind of synchronicity between her world and any other place that I visited.

Strangely enough, though, my first attempt at reaching her on Pachydermia or Pollýxerr succeeded immediately, producing a loud, clear link, one of the best that I'd ever had.

"Good evening, Lady," I said, when I saw her image appear in the sky-orb.

"And a good evening to you, Morpheús," she said. "Although it's actually about noon here. I have some news for you."

"And I for you," I said. "But tell me yours first, please."

"I was allowed outside yesterday, for the first time in at least a five-year. It was chilly and a little drizzly, but I thought it seemed like paradise. Of course, I was confined with Sable to a small garden surrounded by high walls, but still...."

"That's great! Why did...?"

"I don't know, Morphy, I really don't. Sadokéy ordered it for some hidden reason of his own. I'm sure he'll want something in return, though—he always does. I'm not going to question my good fortune in the meantime. They've told me that I can walk in the garden for an hour once a week. They've also said that the walls are warded in such a way that any attempt to leave, either by me or by Sable, will result in our instant death."

"But how do you get there?"

"I walk. They tie my hands behind my back, blindfold me, and then slowly guide me in the midst of a dozen guards down a long corridor lined with locked doors. We emerge outside somewhere, and then I'm untied and put through an iron gate that's locked and bolted behind me. Let me show you"—and then she squirted me a brief image of the place.

"Still, to be free and out in the open for just a few moments…," she said. "I never thought to see the sky here again. And I tell you, Morpheús, they don't know the half of what I can do. They don't understand my powers, not at all."

"Be very careful, Lady," I said. "They're probably watching you right now through some spy-hole in the wall, or by occult means."

"Oh, I count on that, my dear. I *want* them to watch. They'll watch me so closely that they won't see what actually happens. I can control what they see in this suite, because I helped remodel this room decades ago; and I aim to do the same thing in the garden, once I've taken its measure. These things can go both ways, you know.

"Now, do tell me what's been happening at *your* end. I always look forward to your accounts."

So I related our adventures on Erésvepe, and how we'd come to Pachydermia. "Although they don't call it that, of course. I haven't met any of the natives yet.

"This grand house of Master Melanchthon is a living construct, Niobë. I've never seen the like anywhere else. When we first entered, I realized that the 'door,' if you want to call it that, had widened itself to allow us admittance—and then closed behind us again! I've not seen one artificial creation on this world, not one! Even the 'saddle' on the libbéll I rode, I realized afterwards, was not fashioned of leather, as I'd thought, but grown from some kind of plant. I saw one remove itself from its beast by retreating into the soil beneath it.

"But this house—what a wonder it is! When I want to sleep, I have but to think the concept, and a bed grows right out of the floor and wall within minutes, complete with covering—although a covering really isn't needed in this ever-mild climate. And in the morning, it disappears again when it's no longer necessary. Amazing!

"All the food we eat derives from horticulture. Melanchthon told us that the consumption of animals is forbidden here. I asked what happened to the creatures that died, and he said that there were scavenger beasts and plants that removed the corpses and recycled them back into the ecosphere. All of nature on this world is perfectly balanced.

"He hasn't told me yet, however, why he never returned to Erésvepe or Nova Europa or anywhere else. It's a subject that's sensitive to him."

"I've wondered about that myself," she said. "I wonder too how he's able to maintain the youthful appearance you describe. Even the greatest of mages loses the ability to project youth past a certain point in her life. Doctor Scarabbaios was a perfect example of this, from what you've told me, and by all accounts, Master Melanchthon was far older than his *protégé*."

"He also hasn't discussed the Eggs yet, and I wonder why," I said. "I know he possesses one of them. He's just not the man whom I envisioned from the earlier accounts of his life. He's changed somehow."

"Then you need to be careful yourself, Morphy. Until you know why he's the way he is, and something about his current motivations, you can't trust him. Trust no one."

"Not even you?" I asked.

I heard her sigh through the orb.

"Not even me," she finally whispered. "Good night, Morpheús."

"Good night, dear Lady."

CHAPTER FORTY
"YOU'RE ALL DOOMED"

I again tried to broach the subject of this world and the mysterious Eggs with Master Melanchthon the next morning over breakfast, but he waved off my inquiries with a flighty "All will be revealed in time" remark.

My close examination of the man seated across the table from me revealed no traces of his true age, a source of continued wonderment. There should have been something. The tricks that we use to cover the tracks of time are well-known within the brethren, although they may seem miraculous to the *hoi polloi*. And although we may appear immortal to some, we most certainly are not, for sooner or later accident, mayhem, murder, or even suicide claims each and every one of us. We *are* immune to most diseases, and even those that we contract affect us less than ordinary men. I myself had seen…well, that's another story.

"How do you create such abodes as this?" I asked "Mellie," as he preferred to be called.

"All life on this world is symbiotic in nature. When the Pollýxerri wish to make a home, they implant special seeds on the chosen site, nurture the soil with their scat, and ask the vegetation to grow in a certain way."

"And it does this?" Mistress Zalmanna asked.

"Yes, always."

"But what if there's a tree there already?" I asked.

"They ask it to move."

"And it just moves?" the Tyro said. "How does it do that?"

"I have no idea, really," Melanchthon said, "but it creeps away, each and every time. They made this place for me according to my specifications, although in many ways it's very unlike their own dwellings. There was no clearing here originally, but all of the verdure occupying this site vanished within a week. It took them another month to grow this house."

"How do you get fed?" Shah'rah asked.

"Food appears from openings in the walls at certain times of the day—you tell the Pachyderms when you normally wish to eat at the time that your domicile is created. These can be altered for special occasions. Water is piped in through hard-shelled shafts grown for that purpose. The plates and utensils are also organic. It all works out quite well."

"Your appearance has changed, Master," Grit said from its perch on Mellie's shoulder.

"Remarkable, isn't it? I had the visage of an old man—well, I *was* an old man—when I came here, and now I look and feel no more than twenty and five. It has something to do, I'm told, with the effect of the vegetation here on one's biological system. As you ingest the nutrients from this world, you in effect become part of it, and over time it heals whatever ails you. If I ever left here, I would lose that edge very quickly."

"Are there many off-worlders here?" I asked.

"No. The Pollýxerri have deliberately shaded their world from casual inspection. Only something special, like *The Necropompeion*, has the ability to penetrate the fog in the æther that they've generated. You still have your copy, I suppose?"

"Of course," I said, "although it actually belonged to Doctor Scarabbaios." In point of fact, the thing was almost indestructible. Being immersed in the cold water of the cave pond had had no effect on it whatsoever.

"What about the pendant I left on Erésvepe?"

"I brought that as well," I said. "It was being misused by your students in their attempts to follow you here—which of course they couldn't without owning the book. I was able to determine that all of them landed somewhere, but where I couldn't say."

"Well, thank the gods for that, anyway. I'd thought I could use the token as a pendulum through which I could swing in the æther back again to Erésvepe, but my attempts utterly failed. Both elements had to be present to activate the link, and there's nothing here to abet the process."

"Nothing! Nothing at all?" Mistress Zalmanna said. Her face had gone white.

"No, nothing! This world is bereft of most metals. There's no way to fashion a transit-mirror. In any case, the Pollýxerri have no tradition or knowledge of technology. Even if I'd had the materials available, I'd have had great difficulty in creating a device. There's nothing you can use as a mold. It's just not possible. I couldn't even penetrate the void with my sky-orb. All I ever got back was static.

"No, you're all doomed—if you want to call living in paradise that—to spend the rest of your lives on Pachydermia. To the best of my knowledge, no off-worlder has ever left this place."

"What about the natives?" I asked.

"They have no desire to go anywhere else. Why should they?"

"Wouldn't the token and the two copies of *The Necropompeion* provide enough power to transit us somewhere else?" Scooter asked.

"It's certainly possible, but what would you use to concentrate the energy? The way you came here, through the pond in the cave, is a one-way shunt. The surface of the water there cannot be calmed sufficiently to focus on a point more distant than the local suns. You can't access the leys unless you can feel them.

"I spent much of my first year here trying to find a way 'out,' much to the amusement of the Pollýxerri, but nothing I attempted ever came close to working." The "old" mage sighed. "I wanted to continue my quest, I really did, gentlebeings, but here I am and here I'm likely to stay. Almost forever."

This was certainly disquieting news, if true. But I wasn't ready to accept his statement as verity just yet.

"Nonetheless," I said, "I'd like to explore the possibilities myself, if you don't mind."

"No, of course not. Take all the time in the world, Master Morpheús"—I thought he almost said my title in a slightly mocking tone—"You certainly have enough of it in front of you. In the meantime, you're welcome to stay here with me for as long as you want—or I can arrange for abodes to be created for you, individually or as a group. Just relate to me what you want."

"You haven't told us anything as yet about the Eggs," I said.

"Ah, the Eggs. Well, that's better done, I think, by the Pollýxerri themselves, since they imagined them in the first place."

"I thought you said that they weren't artisans."

"Actually, that's incorrect—I stated that they had no technology as we know it. They don't 'make' things like we do; they grow them. But you'll have an answer soon enough. I'm taking you to meet them this afternoon. Then you can hear them chant *The Song of the Elephant Eggs*."

"Song?" Mistress Zalmanna said.

"Yes. Much of their verbal expression consists of music. Their direct communications are mostly transmitted mentally. Since their songs have a psychic undertone, you'll be able to understand them instinctively. They have no language as we know the concept. They're actually quite a remarkable people."

"They seem to have made a positive impression on you," I said.

"I thought them very strange at first, and so might you; but I came to realize that they are a gentle and wise folk with a vast understanding of life, the universe, and everything."

"I've heard that one before," Scooter muttered.

"Another cynical wherret," Melanchthon said. "And what do *you* think, Grit?"

"I think I'll withhold my opinion until I see more of this place, Master."

"A wise decision, old friend. I hope you'll eventually come

to the same conclusions as I. But no matter. You're free to roam the house and grounds to your furthest content. Please don't venture too far away until you can recognize where you are—and how to return! It's very easy to get lost at first. If you do lose your way, yell or whistle, and one of us will find you.

"We'll leave here just after noon, again flying with the libbélli. Aren't they a wonder?"

"Everything thing's a wonder here," Scooter whispered in my ear. "I *wonder* how we got so lucky."

"Hush!" I said. "Mind your manners."

Then we went back to our room, and I told the wherret that I'd made contact with Niobë again.

"So your enhanced sky-orb works here, Sir," it said.

"Yes. And that means that other things might work here as well. I don't accept being stranded on this world, however pleasant it might be, for the rest of my days. I intend to leave this place, and as soon as possible, once we know where we can find the Eggs—and the Lady."

"Which is it: the Lady or the Tiger, Master?" the creature asked.

"That classic puzzle in logic. Well, I want both, Scoot."

"You humans are all the same, Sir: you always desire something you don't or can't have. Very well, then, how do we get them?"

"That's the real question," I said.

And one to which I didn't as yet have an answer.

CHAPTER FORTY-ONE
"WE KNOW THE OVERAWING OVA TO BE REAL"

I again marveled at the power of flight, and how it thrilled me in a way that I hadn't experienced in many years. The libbélli lifted off from the clearing where we'd disembarked the previous day—apparently there wasn't enough space around Melanchthon's home to allow a flock of them to land—and we headed across the great forest in a direction that took us further away from the place where we'd first entered this world.

Scooter clung to my shoulder with its little claws dug deeply into my tunic, hanging on as if its very life depended on the firmness of the grasp (perhaps it did). "I don't like this!" the wherret wailed in my right ear. "I don't like this at all!"

I noticed that Grit had a similar death-grip on its Master, and I attributed this to some basic instinctual fear of the unknown common to their species (height as such didn't seem to bother the wherrets, but the combination of being dangled a thousand feet over the landscape and trusting one's life to relatively unknown creatures seemed to be a bad combination for them).

We flew about twenty minutes before the great arthropods began circling again, patiently waiting one by one for a place to light as each creature settled in turn, disembarked its passenger, and then took off again.

There was a group of creatures waiting for us in front of the tallest structure that I'd yet seen on Pachydermia. The great green manse towered roughly five stories in height in several cascading tiers of interwoven and interlaced branches and vines. The place had the appearance of a piece of living art.

The Pollýxerri themselves were not what I expected, having very little of the appearance of the traditional elephant back on Nova Europa. True, they did sport long, narrow trunks at the front of their faces, but in pairs—and they could either be remain at rest, dangling from the area just about their mouths, or be actively used to manipulate or even pick up small items. In essence, their trunks acted as their hands.

They averaged about six feet in height, with the males slightly larger than the females, but their bodies lacked the ponderousness of traditional pachyderms, and often were slender and agile. They walked normally on all-fours, but could easily sit up on their hind legs for extended periods of time—and usually did so during meetings or performances. They sported bright, bold, light red eyes that sparkled with intelligence. None of them had tusks.

"You are the ha-humans of whom Mellie-dala spoke," one of them "said"—in reality, no sound emanated from their mouths, but the voice echoed clearly in my mind—as well as those of the others present. I could understand almost all of their communications from the very beginning. The "dala," I learned, was an honorific automatically assigned to all intelligent beings.

"We are the ones you call the 'ha-Pachyderms', although we term ourselves ha-Pollýxerri," it said. "What are your names, o gentle-ones?"

"Couldn't you get that information from our minds?" I asked.

"We could do so, kind human-from-another-place, but it would be contrary to our laws. We do not invade the minds of sentient creatures without their permission, or unless some crime has been committed against one of our own."

"I'm called Morpheús," I said. "What's your name, Sir?"

"I am Piramatikothetikopistemokyrio-dala, but you can call me Pirama-dala," he said, explaining that the "o" ending of his full name signified a male. "You, gentle Morpheús-dala, might well say that I am a kind of joint-sub-coordinator of this region, which is named the Kalliwill; but I do not, of course, claim any legal or other authority over you or your kind, or even over my own. Our females choose our coordinators, and when they become displeased with them, they replace them with another."

"That seems like a wise system, Pirama-dala," I said.

"It works for our kind," he said, "although perhaps not as well for others. We have not enough experience of such things to tell, really."

"You don't travel off-world yourselves, then?"

"Everything that we desire is present on this world, gentle-human, so why would we wish to be somewhere else?"

"But you must have done so at one point in your history, Pirama-dala, since your existence is known in this Circle and beyond," I said.

"Ah, yes, that could well be true, good Morpheús-dala," the pachyderm said, "but we have no knowledge personally of such things. There are stories, of course, there are many stories of eld, and some of them reflect experiences that now seem strange or *outré* to us; but that is part of the natural evolution and devolution of the universe itself, is it not? Within any closed system the entropical forces gradually denigrate into nothingness, only to begin again, and so on *ad infinitum*; but how can we—how can I—know such things as fact rather than fancy?

"This is why we sing our songs of *fête* and fable: to acknowledge those truths that can only be expressed in such ways. That truisms exist beyond our personal ken or observation is obvious to any thinking being, but how to measure such verities against reality is always a challenge. Some may call our tales flights of fantasy or myth; we prefer to think of them as hallmarks of past existences."

"Such as the great Eggs, Pirama-dala?" I asked.

"*The Song of the Eggs of the Elephant* is a part of our legendary repertoire of chants, o wiser-than-wise off-worlder, but we know the Overawing Ova to be real as well, and so they do not fall into quite the same category as *The Tale of The-Shaker-of-Stars Beyond the Sixth Circle* or *The Coming of Aradathamaiharu-dala the Mother of Music-in-Tongues* or *The Vengeance of Káthar-Jolárson the Slayer-of-Souls* or *The Story of the Maker and Weaver of Dreams.* We understand the difference between the real and the fabulous, and the not-quite-real and not-yet-fabulous, and all the permutations in and of between. This is not to say that we realize more than you do, o skater-through-the-æthersphere; but we have lived here a very long time, and perhaps this has salted our experience with the occasional tang of wisdom."

"What can you tell me about these marvelous artifacts?" I asked.

"Alas, not here and not now, blessèd Morpheús-dala," the leader said. "We must sing our songs as part of the Great Cycle of the Chants, which are performed in good time and at the appropriate ceremony, according to our ways, however miserly and miscalculated they may seem to others; but if you have the time to wait, o great one, a performance of that particular piece is scheduled for the month of Asynaritetu, on the sixth day, at the twelfth hour, and we should very much welcome your presence and those of your companions then."

I had no idea of the creatures' calendar, so I looked askance at Master Melanchthon. "About four months from now," he said.

"We hope to be gone by then," I said.

"You are, of course, free to depart at any time from our lovely world," Pirama said, "although we cannot assist you in doing so, per our common law. But just as you traveled here of your own free will, you presumably can also travel elsewhere in the same way, and we applaud your spirit of adventure.

"And now, I am very pained to say, it is the time of the Perripalanesisi, and so we must leave you until later in the day. You are welcome to enjoy the freedom of our abode here in Kalliwill for as long as you wish—and we so look forward to visiting with you again, dear Morpheús-dala, whenever that occasion should arise. Be seeing you."

And then they turned around as a group, and marched off across the field until they were lost from our sight, their trunks waving amidst the waving vegetation.

"What a curious people," Shah'rah said.

"Curiouser and curiouser," was Scooter's comment, and I didn't think that the wherret was being overly cynical at all.

CHAPTER FORTY-TWO
"SINGING THE EGG SONG"

"They're a bit full of themselves, aren't they?" Shah'rah said.

"Well, they are an extraordinarily ancient race," Master Melanchthon said.

"Not as ancient as our people," Mistress Zalmanna said.

"I'm not at all certain of that," the mage said. "Neither of you can accurately track the dates of your respective origins, so who can be sure?"

"We were the first!" the Tyro emphasized.

"But how do you know, really?"

"It's a matter of logical progression. Our world is clearly the paradigm of all the other worlds in the Circles that progress through ætherspace, each of them diverting more from our prime example than the last. This place is so far removed from Tyrotarichos that the creatures that dwell here are abominations, mere reflections of the non-sentient pachyderms that once inhabited our world."

"Although there's something in what you say, it's perhaps less than you might imagine," he said. "I've seen enough of the Sixth Circle to understand the utter chaos and randomness of the universe—and the subtle hint of purpose that underlies its structure.

"Somewhere beyond this sphere is a counterbalance to your planet—another prime, if you will. I have no idea who or what inhabits that place. Nor do I understand what role these peaceable philosophers on Pollýxerr play in the great game in which we're all mere pieces being moved by some invisible grand-master. But it seems impertinent to me to assume that we realize all things about our situation, or understand their role in the scheme of life.

"When I was a young man, I was taught that certain constants governed the rule of magick. And when I practiced the art, I found that this was so, within the variations of personal style and knowledge. But then I came to the Otherworlds, and discovered, much to my surprise, that the so-called 'rules' sometimes didn't apply, or that actions and words that had one effect on my homeworld or on Nova Europa would have a different result here. Why?

"You people explain such variations with great aplomb and sophistry and rationalization, but never with any certainties that might tell me—or others—exactly what's happening when my commands misfire, and/or how I could prevent that from happening, and/or gain the outcome that I desire. Words, meaningless words, that's all you have to offer. But you don't *know*, Tyro. That's what bothers me.

"I'm not certain that the Pollýxerri know either—in fact, I don't think that they do, not in any way that I would find comfortable. But they have a kind of wisdom that you don't share. When you listen to their songs, really *listen*, you find therein a comfort wholly lacking in the cold Tyro technology, however sophisticated and powerful it might be."

"But the pachyderms indicated that they wouldn't be singing the Eggs song for four months," I said.

"Ah," Melanchthon said, "well, that's true of the Kalliwilli band, but there are many such tribes on this world, and they all have their own legend cycles. I'm sure we can find one that will be conducting the appropriate fest within the near future. Besides, you can't leave this place anyway, so why does the time matter?"

"We'll find a way," I said.

"There's nothing here to find. I've spent years looking for an exit. It doesn't exist."

"Then tell me something, mage: how did the eggs travel from Pachydermia to the other Circles?"

For once I caught him speechless. "I...I don't know," he finally said. "I honestly don't know."

"Think about it."

Then we went up to the house of the Kalliwillis. I wanted to see how they lived, because one can tell much about a person by examining the ruins of his abode. Of course, as with all of the structures on the planet, this was a living construct created by sentient interaction with several species of plants.

"Astonishin'," Hawk said, which was an odd comment coming from a soldier whose appreciation of the finer arts had never been evident before. But he was right.

I'd thought, from seeing the outside of the "building," that the prevailing color would be green, but in fact the pachyderms employed a wide range of flowers and vines and leaves to create patterns of what could only be considered a slow but constantly developing painting or sculpture in vegetation. Some of the rooms were decorated in swatches of broad stripes and squares and circles of emerald and ivory and ruby hues, while others clearly had portraits of animals and beings from this world—and others! The variety was simply too great to be accounted for by the fauna of Pachydermia. So how did they know about the others, unless they'd actually seen them?

One room contained a pond formed by a small waterfall emanating from the ceiling, with brightly-hued newts and fish paddling therein, and a kind of ramp leading down to the "beach." Another was full of dangling vines that writhed even as we entered the space, evidently just as a piece of moving artwork. And still another was decorated with little sparkles of light—illuminati bugs, I later learned—that flashed on and off as we watched, forming almost a conspiratorial communication.

Each room seemed unique, but all were common to the group as a whole. I spied nothing in the alcoves that contained anything that I'd regard as personal. And, as Master Melanchthon had already indicated, there was nothing technological in evidence anywhere: no stone or metal or composite artifacts, only dead and living matter that had originally been vegetative.

We stayed the night, but without the pachyderms, the place seemed almost dead to me—and their ghosts constantly roamed the open spaces, moaning with the wind that gusted every so often through the apertures. I found the house very disquieting, and when I finally fell asleep, was disturbed with nightmares of wandering through great buildings looking for someone or something that was always just one more step ahead of me. They reminded me in some ways of my quest.

On the next day, we didn't wait for the inhabitants to return, but went back to Melanchthon's more "human" home, while he began making inquiries about the next performance of the song we wanted to hear.

CHAPTER FORTY-THREE
"LET'S SEE WHAT THE MAGIC SPIGOTS CAN OFFER US TODAY"

Melanchthon departed at noon, flying on a libbéll to question some of the nearer tribes of pachyderms regarding their schedule of song cycles. I called together the members of our group as soon as he was absent.

"We need to find a way off this world," I said. "I know what the old mage has said, but there has to be *something* we can do."

"If we had enough metal, we could forge a new transit-mirror," Zalmanna said.

"Have yet to see fire here," Hawk said. "They don't seem to cook or heat anythin'."

"A good point," I said. "Maybe they won't allow us to burn any of their wood."

"But even if we could," the Tyro said, "how hot would the flames actually be? Certainly not warm enough by themselves to fuse metals together with gold."

"We could increase the heat magically, Master," Scooter said. "After all, there are three mages and two wherrets present."

"But would Master Melanchthon and Grit agree to help?" I asked.

After a pause, the little creature said: "I don't see why not, Sir. They may wish to remain here themselves, but I don't believe that they'd try to block us from leaving."

"Then we need to take an inventory of the metals that we carry with us," I said.

So everyone emptied their packs, and when we'd accounted for everything, I said: "Well, we have enough gold to make a start, and just possibly enough silver, but the rest is mostly iron, and I've never heard of a transit-device fashioned from such base ore. It simply wouldn't work.

"We might be able to create a thinly-layered *argentaurum* mirror, but on Nova Europa that particular alloy can only be used for local jumps on the same planet—and we already know that we have to go off-world."

"We do not know precisely *how* far," Mistress Zalmanna said, "and we should not assume the worst. Just possibly, the next world with a transit-station or suitable receptacle might not be situated that far distant in the æther."

"We could descry through the sky-orb, and see what's out there, Sir," Scooter said. "We've done that once before on this journey."

"With very mixed results," I said. "But yes, we could try that. We also still have the power of *The Necropompeion* and its medallion. That might boost our chances of making a successful transit once we build a mirror. I think we have to try."

"You do realize that if we make such a device and attempt to use it," the Tyro said, "we could scatter our bodies and souls across the net if the energy level is too weak or the focus imprecise. We have no real way of calibrating the thing."

"Yes, we'd have to guess at some of the parameters," I said. "But which would you prefer, Mistress: trying to find an exit from this world, or spending the rest of our lives here, as Master Melanchthon has apparently chosen to do?"

She frowned and looked down at the green floor of the mage's living manse. "What about the other implements you carry, Master Morpheús?" she asked. "Do you have anything else that could assist us?"

I pulled out the pouch that I carried around my neck, and shook out the silver Hand of Morlock and the Firedog Pathfinder that I'd purchased from the itinerant street vendor.

"What are *those*?" the woman asked, her eyes growing large

with wonder. "Where did you find them?"

Everyone gathered 'round, oohing and ahing over the strange devices that I held in each hand.

I told them the circumstances behind their discovery. "The Firedog could undoubtedly tell us *where* we need to go," I said, "but I'm not as certain that it understands the concept of distance in the same way that we do. As far as the Hand of Morlock is concerned, the only application I've found for it thus far is locating *The Necropompeion*."

I didn't mention the fact that I could also call on the ancient mage Parakôdês, my ancestor, whose image I had back at my home, to provide me with advice—but just on two more occasions. I was reserving that option for real emergencies.

"So you see," I said, "we don't have very many choices. And that also assumes, of course, that we can find some information here about the physical location of the Eggs. There's no point in us running off to another world if they're actually hidden somewhere on Pachydermia."

"Maybe the Hand would be useful for that," Mistress Zalmanna said.

"Perhaps—if they're actually here. However, I'm getting hungry. Let's see what the magic spigots can offer us today."

I wanted to try an experiment. I went over to one of the walls, and thought very hard and very clearly about a lovely lamb shank that my mother had fixed for us when I was about ten. It was complemented with onions and olives and spices of all kinds, and I could still imagine quite clearly the luscious odor that it generated. I shut my eyes, and willed the dish to reappear.

"Master!" Scooter suddenly exclaimed, and I came out of my reverie to find a hard gourd full of what appeared to be a steaming mix of meat and vegetables resting in an alcove. Of course it wasn't *quite* meat—I realized that with the first bite—but it was warm and delicious nonetheless, and I showed the others what I'd done—and how it could be accomplished.

Some of our comrades had better luck than others in replicating my effort, but all of them applauded the idea of having some reasonable facsimile of their native cuisine available for the first time in weeks.

"Oh, this be *so* good!" Shah'rah said, the juices dripping down her chin. She was eating what appeared to be some kind of roasted fowl covered with herbs. "Sorry for mess." She laughed slightly at her gluttony—but the truth was, we were all partaking of that particular sin, and with great gusto, too!

I imaged in my mind a cup of fresh, ripe berries, and when the gourd appeared, shared them with my "wife" and others. We were still trying to stuff ourselves when Master Melanchthon finally appeared.

"Oh," he said, "you've discovered the trick of the dispensers. Amazing, isn't it? They seem to be able to recreate almost anything edible."

"Have you tried it with inorganic materials?" I asked.

"Of course. It doesn't work."

"I was wondering, Sir," I said, "If you might be able to assist us." Then I told him about our musings on the possibility of making a transit-device.

"You have enough *aurum*?" he asked.

"I believe so. But we have a little less silver, and no other metals except for iron and some small trace elements of a few miscellaneous things—nothing that would make any difference."

"How would you forge the vessel?"

I explained to him our theory.

"No, they won't let you burn anything. That I already know."

"How could they stop us?"

"Believe me when I tell you that you don't want to know. They have quite effective defenses when they wish to employ them," the mage said. "However, you could fashion a mold from inert clay, and then bake it in the suns. It might be hard enough to hold the pattern. Generating the heat is a bit of a problem, of course, but Grit and I will help you to concentrate our energies together—maybe that'd be enough to forge the alloy."

"Could we link the energy from the two books together

through the token?" Zalmanna asked.

"Maybe—yes, yes, that just might work. With the medallion on hand, we have possibilities that wouldn't otherwise be available. Let me think about it.

"Oh, by the way," Master Melanchthon said, "the Jellibell tribe is chanting the piece you want to hear in three days. I suggest that several of us travel there."

"You have heard it sung before?" Zalmanna asked.

"I have—but not for some time. I'd like to refresh my memory again."

"Sir, I believe you have one of the Eggs in your possession already," I said.

"Who told you *that*?" he said.

"You did, in the memoir that you left on Erésvepe."

"Oh, right," he sighed. "Very well—yes, I own what I believe to be one of the First Eggs."

"Can we see it?"

"After the singing," he said. "Then things will be clearer to you, I believe."

CHAPTER FORTY-FOUR
"CHASING VERY YOUNG LADIES THROUGH THE HOLY TUBBERY"

For some reason that I couldn't fathom, I suddenly had an urge to call "home." I used the sky-orb I'd been given by the Tyrosians to seek out the Magister of Mages Geraklíd, my former magical superior in Kórynthia, and reached him, much to my amazement, without difficulty, without even a hint of static in the connection.

"Morpheús!" he said when he recognized my image. "You're alive!"

He looked haggard and tired and just plain old. "What's happened?" I asked.

"The Queen is ill," he said. "Duke Zoltán has proclaimed himself her heir, and is being contested by Count Víka, Count Istiál, and Prince Zacharias of Mährenia. The contestants are cementing their positions in bedrock: Zoltán controls the area surrounding Paltyrrha, Víka has his base in the Southwest, Istiál in the North, and Zacharias in the far West. The latter probably has the strongest legal claim, since he's descended in the direct male line from the old House of Tighris, and has the backing of his brother, the Grand Duke Ferdinand xiv. The Kingdom is on the verge of civil war. I need you back right away. My position here is tenuous at best."

I didn't understand how this could happen. "But...but I descried the Queen's future," I said. "She had years left to live."

"Morpheús, it's been three years since you departed. She was struck down with an attack of paralysis a few months ago, and has been confined to bed ever since. She has enough sensibility left to provide some minimal direction to the state, but nothing close to the strong hand that we need. When she dies, everything will quickly fall apart."

I was stunned at this turn of events. Three years? For me it had just been a few months. I told him this, and gave him a brief outline of what had happened to me.

"Time for you runs slow," he said. "It must be the effect of chronoætheric displacement. Have you found the Eggs?"

"No, Sir, I have not," I said, "although I may be close to discovering at least some of the answers about their nature. But you need to understand that this world has no transit-mirrors—or any other means of reaching through the æther, except for this sky-orb I'm using. I can't get back there quickly, if at all, I'm sorry to say. I would if I could."

"If you wait too long, there may be no Kórynthia left to return to," Geraklíd said. "Already there are rumors of the Liets gathering their forces to seize the eastern provinces."

"What about the Emperor in Julianople?"

"The Autokratôr Julian has succeeded his father, but he still spends his days chasing very young ladies through the Holy Tubbery. There's no help there—and if his reign continues for many years, the Empire will have difficulties retaining many of *its* appendages as well. King Sinuballít of Asshyria is already drooling over the prospect of grabbing the Syrian coast. If it weren't for Julian's cousin, Prince Antiochos, they would have lost it already."

I suddenly heard a distant knocking coming through the link. "I have to go," Geraklíd said. "Urgent business—it's all urgent these days. Come back, Morpheús. I need you more than ever, my boy."

"I'll try," was all I could say. I knew that it wasn't enough. And then he shut down the link.

I attempted next to reach Niobë, and again was able to make the connection without difficulty. There was something about this world's aura that seemed, ironically enough, to facilitate ætherial communication, despite what Melanchthon had said.

"It's begun," she said, when her image finally appeared.

"What's begun?" I asked.

"I told you last time about Princess Tema's Garden, and how I've been allowed to exercise there with Sable. I had a notion, since the men here know so little about magical theory, to try a small experiment—and now I have. And it works!"

"What did you do?"

"We have a winged insect here called the bella-bella. It's a silly little thing, really, about as big as my outstretched hand, and has a call ('bella-bella') like a small bird. It helps pollinate our flowers.

"Well, the other day I spotted one flitting from plant to plant, and I waited until it alit on a bright yellow blossom, seeking to sip its sap; and then I grabbed its mind and brought it under my control. It's hard to manipulate even a small creature like this without losing oneself in its minute consciousness. But I did it, and I was able to fly with it beyond the walls of my confines, and visit other gardens around the great palace—and even saw Sadokéy walking with one of his advisors.

"Next, I need to figure out how to transfer from one insect to another, or from insect to rodent or bird—or to grab an avian mind directly."

"This is a very dangerous exercise," I said. "I've done it also, but only under close supervision, and I had to be retrieved several times as a student from losing my own perception of myself."

"Of course it's dangerous!" she said, "of *course* it is, Morphy, I know that! But I find that that's part of the attraction. I did the same thing several times when I was a young woman. Other than the contacts that I have with you, my existence is so bland as to be almost unviable. Even this garden has become 'old' now, it's so confined and limited. There's something within me that demands to get out, to live again. And it has to be soon."

I explained to her what had happened to us in recent days,

and the dilemma that we faced. "Once I have more information about what exactly the Eggs are, I may be able to make better decisions—but right now we have no way off this world, and are as much prisoners here as you are there."

"I don't think so," she said. "You have no concept of what long-term confinement is really like. There've been times when I've actively wished for death—just to end this interminable waiting. And waiting for what?—for you to rescue me? I'm not a sixteen-year-old girl, Morpheús. I lost my illusions a very long time ago. You don't even know where I am, much less how you're going to free me from my chains."

"All of that is true," I said, "But so what? I've made my commitment to you, and I'll find a way. I always seem to muddle through, no matter what the difficulties."

"But how long, Morphy? How long?"

"I don't know, Lady. I'll be there when I'm there." I was the one who cut the link this time.

So many responsibilities—they seemed to multiply with each passing day. Everyone wanted me to do something to help them. What about Morpheús? I thought. What does *he* want? That was the question, wasn't it?

But I had no more answers to that than the rest of the boobs, and no more wisdom either. "*Dum vivo, vero*"—"While I live, I hope." That was the only philosophy that made any sense to me in an ever-changing environment. The universe might revolve around me—although not literally, of course—but I still had to find the pathway that would bring the best result. And damned if I knew what that was!

I decided that I needed to talk to my ancestor Parakôdês again, but I didn't know whether I could reach him from this place—or how to make the contact. When I was back home in Barstölný, I'd focused on the marble bust of him that I'd had mounted there. But that was gone now, and it wouldn't have been available to me here in any case.

What I did instead was to call Scooter to me, and ask the wherret to link with and guard my consciousness, while I opened myself to the æther. Then I intoned the words of the formula given to me by my father:

"I invoke the name of he who gave me flesh, faith, and fore-sight. Parakôdês of the Red-Lands, awake thou from thy sleep!"

Nothing happened.

I tried again, this time augmenting my call with the power of the sky-orb.

Again—nothing but static.

Finally, I gave up and dismissed my familiar.

That night, the Great Mage came to me in my sleep.

"For the second time, I answer your call, my son," Parakôdês said to me. This time he appeared before me as a clean-shaven young man of perhaps five and twenty. We were walking together beside a canal lined with bushes on a pathway carved betwixt the shrubbery and the water. It might have been Nova Europa on a glorious, sun-splashed day in spring or summer. No one else was visible. He was dressed in gaudy robes that resembled in style the togas of ancient Byzantium.

"Sir," I said, "I've located the world of the Pachyderms, but every question I ask there is turned back on itself; and even if I do find the Eggs, there appears to be no way to take them off this world. These creatures have no metal and no technology, and certainly nothing resembling transit travel through the æther."

"Yet, most of the Eggs have been dispersed throughout the Five Circles," he said, "including your own world. How was that possible?"

"I don't know, Master," I said.

"Think, Morpheús! Use your brains, boy!"

I considered the problem for a moment, before finally saying: "Either someone brought them there, or the artifacts were able to transit the æther on their own."

"Yes," he said. "And if that's so, what conclusion would logi-cally follow next?"

I thought some more. "There has been travel from this world to other worlds in the past. What's been done once—or more likely, many times—can be accomplished again."

"Yes."

"But how, Sir?" I asked.

"I'm not allowed to answer questions of that sort directly, my son," the mage said. "All I can tell you is that the path is present somewhere. It's up to you to find and utilize it. You're an imaginative and inventive man, Morpheús. You can do this."

I turned to another pressing topic: "What exactly are the Eggs, Sir?"

We walked another hundred yards before he responded. In the far distance, I could see a longboat coming 'round a bend in the watercourse, slowly working its way towards us.

"Again," Parakôdês finally said, "I cannot respond to you in the way that you want. Some things you must discover for yourself. You have the means to solve this problem, if you consider the issues carefully."

"Are the Eggs present on this world, Master?" I asked.

"Everything that you need to move to the next stage, you already have, Morpheús," he said. "What you lack is the vision to understand."

The boat was getting closer now, but I could see no one visible on the deck.

"Our time is running short," the ancient mage said. "Speak now, boy, for I must leave when my transport arrives." He nodded at the approaching vessel.

"*How* do I understand, Sir?"

"The Pachyderms will tell you," he said. "You may call on me just one more time before you cross the River, Morpheús. Take care and be well. You'll do just fine, son of mine."

Then he stepped out over the water of the canal and vanished as the boat sailed by; and I was left, once again, with trying to make sense of what the old mage had told me. It bothered me so much that I finally woke up, and I couldn't get back to sleep again that night, no matter what.

CHAPTER FORTY-FIVE
"THE MAKER-OF-THINGS,
HE CAME TO POLLÝXERR"

I'd met too few of the pachyderms as yet to distinguish the individuals among them, so when we were introduced to the Jellibell tribe, they seemed the same to me as the Kalliwill. All were indefatigably polite, as they welcomed us to their "arena."

On other worlds, the site of a performance might have been a circle of stone seats, a fabricated stage, or a building constructed specifically for that purpose; but here, as always, places were "grown" to meet the demands of their makers. We gathered in a circular garden filled with low bushes and sparkles of flowering light, with the players wandering among and between us as we plopped down on the smooth grassy spots intended for that purpose.

The first thing that I heard—or rather, felt—was a low, rumbling sound emanating from the creatures' bifurcated trunks, very deep on the scale, to the point where the vibration of the music seemed to permeate the soil, the plants, and even our bodies. Scooter shook his head violently once on my shoulder, as if to rattle the racket from his ears.

And then came the voices in my mind—or were they real?— blending in and amongst each other in perfect polyphonic harmony, ranging above and below the underlying rumbling of the background music.

This is what they sang:

The Maker-of-Things, He came to Pollýxerr.
He sang to the sky, "I've given you stars."
He sang to the earth, "I've fashioned you well."
He sang to the sea, "I've sanded your shores."
He sang to Himself, *"I've made this too still."*

    The Fixer-of-Things, She sang to the Maker:
    "If things are too still, if song must be shared,
    "Then toot with Your trunks, then slap with Your ears,
    "Then trumpet Your soul, and banish your fears.
    "Let free all the sound, let music be heard!"

The Maker-of-Things, He sang to the Fixer:
"I'll let there be life, so music be heard,
"But never too much, and not to be feared,
"I'll just have a chirp, a peep, and a hoot,
"I'll open my ears, and savor the flute."

    And so He did make a world full of sound,
    And so He did fashion more and more life,
    But still there was stillness rather than strife,
    And too many times the quiet was found.

The Fixer-of-Things, She waved her two trunks,
She wanted to help, she wanted to try
And so She made us, but fashioned such spunk,
She made a mistake, She made a great lie.

    Pollýxerri found,
    Pollýxerri lost,
    When trumpets do sound,
    What shall be the cost?

The Maker-of-Things, He came to Pollýxerr,
He heard a great noise, He winced at the sound,
He blazed through the air, He blared his unrest.

The Fixer-of-Things, She fled from His ire,
But being his half, She had to rebound,
She twirled 'round and 'round, She couldn't find rest.

He couldn't reach Her, She couldn't be there,
He couldn't hold Her, She wouldn't be bound—
But They were one Word, one Being, one tier.

    Pollýxerri lost,
    Pollýxerri found,
    What can be the cost,
    If we're not around?

The Maker-of-Things, He sang to the Fixer,
He made a great noise, He hummed a sweet tune,
He sang to make music, He brought her along,
They came to this place, then found the right song,
They found the right notes to transform the moons:

They made the great Eggs of four parts of night,
Of four parts of day, of amorous plight,
Of faithfulness true, of balance in life,
Of love without end, of end without strife.

The first Egg They made in ninety-six shards
That kept safe the keys the universe guards,
And each piece thereof was fashioned of light,
That opened the door that led through the night.

The next Egg They made had sixteen great sides,
And all were the One, and One still abides.
The hope that They gave them shown with the sun,
That all should have life, that lost should be none.

The third Egg They made was fashioned and spun
From earth and the sky and sea-foam and dung.

In eight great readings, They fashioned their cars
To power the transit from earth to the stars.

The fourth Egg They made as One cut in twain,
The He and the She that must still remain,
So we can be healed, and we can be cured,
Of dissident sounds that They find absurd.

The Maker-of-Things is Mate to the Fixer,
One half of the whole, one whole of the half.
When Four Eggs are One, and One shall be Four,
Our world will be whole, forever and more.

    Pollýxerri found,
    Pollýxerri lost,
    Who else is bound
    To water and dust?

And that was *The Song of the Eggs of the Elephant*, but I cannot and have not conveyed the power of the piece as it permeated our very souls. When the music finally ceased, we collectively gave a great sigh—of sorrow that the song had ended, of relief that we could bear to hear no more, of joy that we had experienced the performance in the first place. Never have I been so moved by any singer or actor or juggler. Never have I felt the mix of emotions that I did on that one occasion.

I do not pretend to the title either of philosopher or theologian, or to ken the mysteries of faith and religion. Yet I felt instinctively that if only I could understand what was being sung in this piece, I would finally attain some small measure of wisdom in my life.

But perhaps I was only fooling myself. I still didn't have any notion of where to find the Eggs, or even what they were, except that Master Melanchthon had claimed in his memoir to have owned one—an artifact that he presumably still carried with him. Now, I knew, was the time to discover what he *really* knew—and how much he understood of the mysteries of the Eggs.

CHAPTER FORTY-SIX
"CURSED WAS THE DAY..."

Now more than ever, I wanted to know what it was that Master Melanchthon had found on Erésvepe, and so when we returned to his home-grown home-in-the-woods, I asked him straight out whether he'd found one of the Great Eggs.

"I do believe so," he finally admitted to our group of adventurers. "You must understand that the events commemorated in the song that you just heard may have happened—if they actually occurred in history (and I have no way of knowing this for certain)— millennia ago. However, the present-day Pollýxerri have very little real information to give us on these matters. They have no sense of the past or the future at all—they always live in the present.

"They also don't travel off-world, and have no notion of how to do so—nor do they care to, if truth be told. They believe in the absolute existence of the Eggs, but none of them has ever seen one themselves, or held it in their proboscides—and none have any idea of how to locate these artifacts. The implements were present at one time in their distant past, and now they're not. They're not curious in the same way that humans are.

"But their stories convey clues, if you examine them closely. For example, there's an ancient connection of some kind between this world and Erésvepe, although I still don't know what it is. Perhaps that's why one of the Elephant's Eggs wound up in the latter place, wandering from its point of origin on Pollýxerr.

"All I know is that I was browsing in an old shop one day in

Kashundkerri, and I spotted something sparkling on top of an open counter. This struck me as very odd, because everything else of value in that store was quite carefully sequestered and protected.

"'What's the story behind this one, eh?' I asked the proprietor, pointing down at the gem.

"'Ah, Master,' he said in Marsian, 'that's the "Star of the Pachyderm." Cursed was the day that I purchased the thing, because no one now will buy it from me.'

"'Why?'

"'It simply cannot be sold in the usual way, Master, unlike all the other merchandise here.'

"'What do you mean?' I asked.

"'Try to pick it up, Master,' he said

"And so I did, and was immediately drawn into a well of infinite depth. I finally jerked myself abruptly free from the compelling call of the jewel, and caught the vendor looking at me very strangely.

"'You're the first person, Master, who's been able to touch the "Star" since I bought it. All of the other potential buyers have been "stung" by it.'

"'Then I wish to make you an offer,' I said, and as is the custom on Erésvepe, gave the man an absurdly low figure for the artifact, figuring that I would now endure an hour or two of serious haggling before settling on a price that was considerably higher than my initial tender.

"Much to my surprise, however, he shouted the word 'Done!' and held out his flipper-hand to seal the agreement. I plopped the coin on his palm and pocketed the 'Star.' I've had it ever since."

"Can I see it now?" I asked.

The mage grimaced suddenly, as if I'd threatened to violate the secret love of his heart, but very slowly, and obviously with great reluctance, he retrieved the pouch hanging 'round his neck, and pulled from it the pulsing jewel known as the "Star of the Pachyderm"—or perhaps I should just label it now as what it clearly was, *The First Elephant's Egg*!

It called to me! I can't describe the feeling in any other way. It beckoned to my soul, to my very being, and I felt a rapid, rabid response from deep within. I knew somehow that I was mated for life to this thing of crystal and light.

But at that moment it seemed to me almost alive, beating regularly with systematic throbs of color that matched the blood-rushing pulse of my own internal pump, keeping time with my body's needs. And I needed the "Star," needed it right away and for always and ever.

I grabbed it out of his hand and held it in front of my eyes— and I lost myself in the center of the thing, lost myself as finally and as completely as an adolescent falling in love for the first time.

"No!" shouted Master Melanchthon, and he immediately tried to snatch the gem back; but when he touched it, a spark of flame leapt from the surface of the jewel to his finger, stinging him to the quick. "Nooo!" he moaned, now acutely aware of his loss. His dear one had finally renounced him for a better Master.

This is what I wanted, no question. *This* was the final settlement of the first leg of my long journey. And I knew that the First Egg could tell me the secret of where to find its sister, *The Second Elephant's Egg*. All I had to do was create a means of leaving this world—and it might be able to help me there, too.

Joy swept through my being, flushing out my soul.

But then Master Melanchthon pulled out a dagger of hard wood, and plunged it without warning into my chest.

"You may *not* take the 'Star' from me!" he yelled, while my friends pinioned his arms to his side and wrestled him to the ground. "You may *not*, Morpheús!"

But even as my consciousness faded into gray, I knew the triumph of victory. *The Egg would save me! I had another destiny yet to fulfill*, was my last thought before oblivion swept me away.

CHAPTER FORTY-SEVEN
"LET ME (*FALASHTI*) HIM"

I have little memory of the next few weeks. I seem mainly to recall faces and parts of faces—of Niobë (but how could that be?), of Shah'rah, of Mistress Zalmanna, of Scooter, of the Yowler, of several of the pachyderms, even of the lad Boupho who had hitched a ride with us from Erésvepe—all of them peering and poking and crying and talking (they were *mostly* talking, and *mostly* as if I wasn't there). And I remember the Egg—soothing, purring, telling me to live, healing, energizing, and, well, loving me. I think the wound must have putrefied, but…but in the end, well, it seems that I lived.

The first conscious thought I had was of someone—the dancer, perhaps—leaning over me with a wet towel, and squeezing it to drip some sweet nectar onto my tongue. Her shift opened as she bent, and I thought the sway of her bare breasts was the most erotic image that I'd experienced in a great many years. Then I dozed again.

The second time, I could hear someone humming off to one side of the room, where I couldn't see. There were no words, just the sound of the music, and I felt my consciousness drift as the waves of the tune washed over me, cleansing my pain.

The next day (perhaps), I awoke in earnest, and found myself hungry for the first time since my, uh, accident. I tried to speak, but all that emerged from my throat was a quiet croak.

"What was that?" someone said.

"Nothing. Just a thromalid," came the response.

I didn't know what a "thromalid" was, and attempted to say so, but found I couldn't. Then I slept again.

And again, I found myself awake and feverish, and cried out instinctively, and Shah'rah rushed over with some cool water to touch my lips and brow.

"He seems a bit hot to me," she said, and I heard the voice of Pirama-dala echo in my mind, "Let me (*falashti*) him," whatever that was; and then I felt myself being dragged back down over the cliff of consciousness once more, and I remained there, I know, for several more days at least.

Finally, I emerged yet again from the gray aura of healing, and found myself fully awake and alert and yearning for food and company, not necessarily in that order.

"Is anyone there?" I whispered, my mouth so parched that I had to force my lips open.

Shah'rah's quiet features appeared above me. "You're awake!" she said. "Scooter!" she yelled over her back. "Zalmanna! He's awake!"

The wherret scrambled up next to my head. "We feared for your life, Master," it said.

"It is good to have you back among the living men, Master Morpheús," the Tyro said.

"And what do *you* say?" I asked Shah'rah. But then I saw the tears rolling down her drawn cheeks, and I found that I couldn't face them—or her—directly.

"How long?" I finally was able to gasp.

"Three weeks," Zalmanna said. "Three weeks and a few days more."

"And Melanchthon?"

"No one knows," she said. "He disappeared after the attack. I asked about him, but the pachyderms would not tell me anything. I visited his house, but it was gone as if it never had existed—already the trees were growing up over the mound."

"Grit went with him, Master," Scooter said. "I don't know where either of them has gone. I can't 'feel' them any longer."

"The wound was very deep," the Tyro said. "It pierced your

left lung. I had nothing with me to cure that kind of injury. 'They' did something to fix it, or you would have died. And then you got the putrid sickness, and would have died again, save that the Pirama-creature came and somehow infused you with his will. You owe your life to him and to the others of his kind."

"I'm hungry," I said. "Can you find me something to eat?"

Shah'rah brought me a mixture of greens and pseudo-meat, which I wolfed down until I started getting drowsy again. Then I just drifted off into a quasi-nap.

While I was dreaming, I somehow saw Niobë again, looking at me with her wry concern—or perhaps I was just recalling something that I remembered from the deepest depths of my illness.

"I heard about your little adventure," she said. "I can't let you die, Morphy, or my hopes die with you. So I send you one of my bella-bellas."

And in my mind's eye, I saw her lift the veil from her face, and open wide her mouth, twice the size of a normal yawn; from within there issued forth one of the insect-like creatures that she'd found in the locked garden in Mirabö. It slipt the bonds of ætherial space, and transited straight to Pachydermia—although how, I have no idea. It landed on my mouth, and ever so daintily, pried open my lips and deposited its eggs on my tongue. I could feel them growing within me, helping to restore my energy once again.

"And that's how we make love on Naprimér," she said, before cutting the link. The bug flapped its wings over my face, buffeting me with its brief breeze, and flew away.

Then I saw the Egg again, pulsing in place of my heart, becoming one with me as it massaged my consciousness with its fire. Suddenly I knew what I had to do.

"I believe in you," I said. "I believe in the justice that you bring to the universe.

"Tell me, First One, tell me true: where is *The Second Elephant's Egg?*"

I found myself spinning through space and time, backing

away from the image of the Six Circles, outlined before me like great bands of light, each shadowing the next—and linked and tied to the outer limits of the Sixth Sphere was a series of other groups of Circles—and linked to them were ever more Circles, all spinning around each other in spherical harmony, an infinity of universes within an infinity of cosmoses.

But within the web of *my* Six Circles were enmeshed sixteen bright lights, each of them pulsing with a slightly different color.

"Which is the nearest?" I asked the Egg.

And then I knew where I had to go.

CHAPTER FORTY-EIGHT
"MY PROBOSCIDES
INTERTWINE WITH GLADNESS"

I was so debilitated by my ordeal that I found myself requiring assistance to move around during those first few weeks after my awakening. Even the slightest exertion tired me, and my skin color was decidedly paler than normal. I'd also lost considerable weight. My "wife" asked the pachyderms to grow me a cane, which they did, and I found that having a third "leg" to stand on helped considerably.

But I didn't actually encounter any of the natives for quite some time; indeed, I had the sense that they were avoiding me, perhaps because they thought that I had some uncomfortable questions that I wished to pose.

Gradually I regained my strength, and about a month after my consciousness had been restored, I sought out the spokesman for the local Kalliwill tribe.

"Greetings, o gracious ha-human mage Morpheús-dala," the pachyderm said psychically. "I am so overcome with joy, having seen your recovery from the basest putridity, that my proboscides intertwine with gladness. The Maker-of-Things and the Fixer-of-Things are indeed wondrous in their works."

"Indeed, o great Pirama-dala," I said, "I marvel at the mustiness of your apertures"—the creature's flat ears flapped several times at hearing my praise of him—"but I was wondering, as I lay upon my sickbed, what has become of my colleague, the Master Melanchthon."

"Ahhh," the native sighed, and then sighed again: "Ahhh. Gentle-being, we do not permit the exercise of violence upon our world, and when our sensibilities are polluted by the foul act of another's transgression, which is rarity indeed, we react instinctively, and banish that individual from our society forever. Thus do we keep the taint from spreading."

"I do understand, most eloquent spokesman of the Pollýxerri," I said, "but still, my innate curiosity and concern for members of my species make me want to inquire about *where* he was sent."

"Ahhh, ahhh, ahhh." Pirama obviously was caught in a dilemma between speaking a falsehood—forbidden in his culture—and revealing more than he—or society—wished. "He is gone!" he finally blurted out, significantly omitting the introductory, obligatory honorifics in his growing consternation.

"Yes, o great pachyderm of pachyderms," I said, "but *where* has he gone?"

"To Obashaw!" he screamed, actually using his trunks to speak this time, and not his mind.

"Where's that?"

"The farthest place we know: the other side of the Sixth Circle."

"So you *can* breach ætherspace!" I said. "But how?"

"*No, sirrah, no!*" He let out his breath in a great whistling "huff" of air. "No, no, no, most clever, most devious Morpheúsdala. I cannot travel through ætherspace. Neither can any of my brethren. But if we put our minds together, we can sometimes send another being far away, if we don't consider overmuch what we're doing."

"Then you can transit me and my party to another world!"

"*No*, mage of mages!"

"But you said…."

"It is an unconscious act on our part when it happens, o ha-human mage. We cannot control it. We do not understand how we do it. It does not happen but once in a generation or less.

It is abhorrent to us, as are the individuals who are transited."

"We need to leave your world. What do I have to do to gain your assistance?"

"I cannot respond to you at this time, Morpheús-dala," he said. "I must consult with the brethren. I will return in three days with my answer."

"Very well," I said.

When I returned to my room in the great Kalliwill complex, I had Shah'rah gather our people together, and related to them my recent conversation with Pirama.

"What do you want us to do, Sir?" Hawk asked me. He and his men still had their weapons, and had continued their daily exercises to maintain their form and physique during my lengthy illness. The young man named Boupho had been practicing with them as well.

"Just be ready," I said. "I don't really want to harm these gentle people, if I can avoid it, but at the same time, we must find a way to leave this place soon.

"How did Grit get transited?" Shah'rah asked.

"Was he perched on Melanchthon's shoulder when the mage attacked me?"

"Yes," Hawk said.

"Then the action of the pachyderms must indeed have been swift and instinctive—they acted so quickly that they couldn't distinguish between two such closely-connected beings. Although I did wonder why Grit didn't act to restrain his Master."

"Master Melanchthon also moved without thinking, Sir," Scooter said. "You can't stop something you don't foresee."

"My last memory of the attack is observing you folks pulling Melanchthon to the ground."

"He and Grit vanished from beneath our paws, Master. They were just gone—completely without warning."

"Well, I hope they're still alive. I don't blame Melanchthon," I said. "I probably would have done the same. The Egg is, well, it's different from any other artifact that I've ever held. It's almost as if it's alive."

"I think it is," Zalmanna said.

"What?"

"I think it is. I think it has a consciousness of its own. It chooses its masters. It wants to be united to its fellow Eggs, and so it picks the path that it thinks will best take it there."

"I remember what Master Efferitas told us, about how Melanchthon talked to the First Egg," I said. "I thought that story was odd, until I encountered the thing myself. Now I find it haunting my dreams. It showed me where the Second Eggs are."

"What!" Zalmanna said. "You know where the Seconds are?"

"Yes, I think so. All we have to do is figure out a way to get there."

CHAPTER FORTY-NINE
"OH, DON'T BE SUCH A SISSY!"

Pirama-dala returned to us as promised three days later.

"Greetings, o noble ha-human Mage-dala," he said to me. "I have shared your thoughts with my fellow Pollýxerri. We are appalled at the idea that we might become the occasion of random acts of coercion on your part simply to attain an objective that might otherwise be unrealized. Yet, we cannot actively help you create a technology which we currently do not have—and certainly do not wish to possess ourselves.

"However, we do understand your need to leave our world and pursue your quest, and even agree with you that the possibility exists that your journey might be a desirable or necessary end that would benefit the cosmos as a whole, and thus be approved by the Maker-and-Fixer-of-Things.

"We understand that you have the energy to transit off-world, and only lack the raw materials to create some kind of gateway to facilitate your travel. Is this correct?"

"That is correct, most honorable spokesman of the pachyderms," I said.

"Then we can assist you to this extent without violating our laws: we will give you access to our storeroom of metal-based objects, and you may use whatever you need of these materials to achieve your objective—provided that when you leave, you never return to this world again, and that if any of you decide to remain, which you are certainly welcome to do, you will stay here until your natural deaths. Is this acceptable?"

"It is, o great Pirama-dala."

"Very well, then: please follow me, gentlebeings."

He led us outdoors into the open fields that adjoined the great house, and whistled shrilly through his twin trunks. A few moments later a flock of the libbélli appeared and landed in front of us. We mounted the saddles, and then they launched themselves into the air, soaring over a nearby line of trees.

"This is wonderful," I said to Scooter, who was hanging onto my shirt with all four paws dug in as far as they would go. I watched the fields below us seem to turn as we suddenly banked to change course.

"I don't like heights, Master," the wherret yelled into my ear. "I don't like flying. I want to go home!"

"Oh, don't be such a sissy!" I yelled in return.

"I'll remind you of that the next time we're stuck in a pipe somewhere with the rats."

I didn't like rats, particularly the big ones, particularly in confined spaces.

So I didn't say anything more, but just enjoyed the trip. We were flying towards a distant mountain range that gradually loomed up before us, until finally we settled right in front of the first major rise, which was overgrown with vegetation.

I should have realized then that the "growth" was actually a kind of door—and the entrance to a large cave that penetrated deep into the rock. It showed signs of having been enlarged significantly to allow the passage of the pachyderms.

"I thought you folks didn't do this sort of thing," I said.

"Others did this for us," was Pirama's response, and then he was leading the way into the interior of the mountain.

We entered a huge open cavern that had obviously been sealed around the sides and top to prevent seepage. The central part of this dry storage area was filled with metal artifacts of all kinds, jumbled together in no particular arrangement.

I was astonished: "Where did you get these things?"

"They came to us from many places over the millennia, o grand and noble Morpheús-dala," the pachyderm said.

"How long have you people been here?" Zalmanna asked.

"We do not measure time in the way you do, Tyro-dalu," he said. "But by your accounting, perhaps a very long time indeed."

There were swords and shields and knives and pots and armor and utensils and things that I couldn't possibly identify. The variety of metal objects was simply amazing. One pile consisted of nothing but ragged scraps (large and small) of things that obviously had been torn or blown apart.

"What are those?" I asked, pointing to the jumble in question.

"Sometimes beings came to us in manufactured vehicles that crashed on our world. Those are the remains of their transportation devices."

I'd never seen such marvelous materials. We spent hours roaming through the heaps of junk (at least they were considered junk by the pachyderms), feeling the metal ores and testing them for composition; and found that we had plenty of possibilities to smelt into a transit-mirror.

"How do we transport these things back to Kalliwill?" I asked.

"We can make all the arrangements, wise and gracious Morpheús-dala," he said. "Just mark the pieces that you wish to use."

I consulted with Scooter and Zalmanna, and we chose a number of items that we thought might prove suitable.

When we returned to base, I told Pirama of our other requirement. We desired clay that could be molded into the forms we needed and was durable enough to endure baking in the sun— and still be serviceable as the receptacle for the molten metal that we would create and pour to generate the transit-mirror.

"Can you do this?" I asked.

"We can do this," he said.

CHAPTER FIFTY
"OHHH—IT FEELS LIKE DYING!"

Thus began what I came to regard as the "Great Smelting," although Shah'rah soon was calling it the "Great Smelling," due to the overripe odors that were generated by the process. But— first things first!

Before we could start the actual melding of the alloys, we had to select those pieces that might prove suitable for the process. I gave Hawk and his men (who had the physical strength to shift and sift the junk back and forth as needed) a detailed description of the kinds of things that we were hoping to find, and they made several more trips back and forth to the storage cave, looking for additional metal chunks and orts and anything else that might help the project. I, Zalmanna, and Scooter joined them when they'd made a rough sort of the materials, and we three made the final pick, marking the selections with colored vegetable juice.

Within three days, the pachyderms had transported the scraps to our worksite. How they got them there, I have no idea, because some of the pieces had considerable weight and bulk, far more (or so I thought) than any of the "bugs" could move. But—move they did!

I'd decided to return to the clearing along the riverbank where Master Melanchthon had lived, and I asked the Pollýxerri to restore his dwelling for our use, which they did within two weeks thereafter. We resettled there as our supplies began to arrive.

Then they brought me several samples of clay taken from different places around the globe. Zalmanna and I tried a number of combinations, and when we found one that seemed to retain its shape well under pressure, we asked them to ferry a large supply of this material to our site. Again, they responded almost immediately.

Pirama-dala was quite clear in telling me what we could *not* do: we could not create any fire that consumed the local vegetation, we could not destroy or harm any plant or animal life in the process of molding the mirror, and we could not use the larger native creatures as "mules" while building our transit-device. Although, come to think of it, what Pirama's people had been doing already almost amounted to the same thing—but the pachyderms seemed to be quite adept at tiptoeing over their philosophical tightropes.

I promised them that we would not do any of these horrible things, but just to be sure, suggested that they place an official observer on site to monitor our activities. This was an acceptable compromise, and Pirama introduced Tillusu-dalu, a female apprentice of his species, who would be his eyes, ears, and trunks while the work progressed.

"Your people are not very handsome, o great Morphy-dala," the young pachyderm said in her straightforward way.

"That is an enormous sorrow to us, o beauteous Tillusu-dalu," I said, "but somehow we live with the pain."

Scooter snorted on my right shoulder.

"What is that appendage that you have sitting up there next to your head?" she asked, focusing on the little creature's rude noises.

"You mean the wherret? Ah, well, they're the ones who actually control our species. We exist only to give them pleasure."

"But why do you tolerate such indignities?" she asked. "No being should be allowed to torment another in such a manner."

"Ah, but you see, we enjoy it," I said. Scooter could hardly restrain itself at this point—at any moment, I knew, the little creature could lose complete control. "Without this pain, we could not propagate our species. Mating between our kind is so excruciatingly pleasurable that we need the restraint in order to complete the act. Otherwise, we would soon die out, exhausted by our efforts to achieve total coital collapse."

"How terrible for you! I cannot even imagine such a situation. You poor, poor people!"

Scooter snorted again, a very long guffaw this time.

"Why does 'he' do that?" she asked.

"Those are its commands to us—it says that I should not be revealing our secrets to outsiders in this way."

Then I turned to the wherret: "O Scooter-dala, great and terrible, I accept my punishment. I bow down before your superiority."

Then I abruptly ducked my head, dumping it to the ground.

"Why did 'he' leave you?" she asked.

"I displease it. I offend it. Oh no, Scooter-dala, please, not that, not the pleasure principle! Ohhh—it feels like dying!"

Then everyone started laughing.

"Why...?"

"They are so happy for me, now that I've resolved this conflict, thanks, o wise and gentle one, thanks to your kind intervention. Without you, I could never have achieved such unsatisfaction.

"But now, alas, I must get back to work."

* * * * * * *

Over a period of days, we were able to create the clay mold without difficulty, placing it in a pit that we excavated for that purpose. We allowed it to bake in the suns' glare for several days, but I knew that it wouldn't be hard or firm enough to take the weight and heat of a smelting without adding something further.

"Back home," Hawk said, "such constructs are often strengthened with the fiber of certain plants, such as straw."

"Yes, but Pirama was quite explicit in his instructions to me: we can't employ stalks or stems in any part of the construct."

"What about some of the iron?" Zalmanna said.

"I don't know how we'd mingle the two elements together without using very high temperatures—and the mold itself might crack in the process."

So we decided to leave the clay structure as it was, and to experiment with smelting some of the iron, since we had an overabundance of that metal.

Among Melanchthon's surviving property was the second copy of *The Necropompeion*, so we linked all the humans and wherrets together psychically, leaving only the Yowler (who was incompatible) out of the chain; and then I forged a double pathway through both books into the medallion, and brought the enormous energy to bear directly on the ore. We had more than enough power, as it turned out, to heat the iron to the point where it began to run; but as soon as it started to settle in the mold, I heard a large snapping sound, and immediately halted the operation.

With great difficulty, since we couldn't employ any of the local beasts, we managed to pry the half-smelted iron out of the clay cup, using some of the scrap weapons as levers; and we immediately spotted a long fracture zigzagging up the side of the structure.

"Well, that's not going to work," Scooter said.

We all looked at each other with consternation smeared on our faces. If we couldn't create a mold that would hold, I knew, we wouldn't be able forge a transit-mirror. It was as simple and as complicated as that.

And I didn't have the faintest notion at this point of how we were going to solve the problem.

CHAPTER FIFTY-ONE
"THE RUNNING
OF THE ROACHES!"

I finally decided, after careful examination, that the mold had cracked because it had had too little support underneath. We needed something that would provide a foundation to hold the concentrated weight of a large piece of metal.

So I got Hawk and his men busy excavating the pit, before realizing that we were just too close to the adjoining streambed— the underlying water table was way too high. We would have to find an area where a rocky stratum emerged at or near the surface.

Ironically, the best place that we could quickly locate seemed to be the region near the base of the low range of mountains where the storage cave was found. We moved our camp there, and asked the pachyderms to shift our materials once again. On a rocky bluff we found a concave declivity that could be smoothed and polished into the rough form that we desired. This took weeks of painstaking effort, but when we were done, we lined it with the clay mold, and baked the construction in the light of the suns for a week, and then using some applied magic from myself, Mistress Zalmanna, and Scooter, fired the apparatus once more at high temperatures. I was convinced that this new shape would withstand both the heat and weight that would have to be applied to it in order to create the new transit-mirror.

We again experimented first with iron ore, and had no problem in fashioning a dummy device. Our primary structure survived completely intact. Then it was time to begin smelting the real metals.

I picked some pieces of the unusual remains of one of the alien craft that had crashed on this world at sometime in the dim past. The scraps were an alloy of something that I didn't recognize, but I sensed the potencies in the materials, and began trying to melt them down in earnest. This act required considerably more effort and energy on our part than previously, but when we began adding the *aurum*, I was pleased with the psychic signature I was receiving in return.

"Mistress Zalmanna, look at this!" I said, showing both her and Scooter the brownish-gold tinge that the new mixture was acquiring as it blended together. "I think it's a kind of *fulvaurum*." This was another very rare alloy of magical gold that had been thought by thaumaturgophilosophers to be theoretically possible—but had never actually been encountered by anyone I knew.

"Do such things exist?" she asked. "Our people were never able to create this one."

"I know nothing of this either, Master," the wherret said. "How do you control it?"

"I guess we'll find out," I said.

The key in fashioning a transit-mirror, something that I'd only done previously as a post-graduate student at the Conlegium or College of St. František in Polek, is making certain that the individual components of the alloy adhere to each other properly, and that the consistency of the mixture is the same throughout. Otherwise, while the finished product may indeed work in some fashion, the results can be catastrophic if any unevenness causes the destination-signature to lack focus, or if the power levels fluctuate or create anomalies while a transit is taking place.

And even when a mirror is supposedly finished to a high level of consistency and smoothness, it must still be calibrated, and this was going to present us with another major problem—because quite simply, we had nothing to measure it against. We would have to guess at a set of values as we fixed the internal "clock" of the device.

But a rat is as good stewed as it is fried, as my friend Barlévin was wont to say, so long as it's kosher; and so we concentrated all of our efforts initially on stirring the molten metals together until we were satisfied that they would now harden into a common and consistent composite.

This took us three days, by which time we were all ready for a break. I asked our young observer, Tillusu-dalu, for some recreational suggestions.

"Welladay," she said, "there's always the running of the roaches!"

Now, I must admit in all truthfulness that the image of the creature that she projected in my mind was not technically that of a "roach," as we know and love the ubiquitous little critters in Nova Europa (and most other worlds)—but it surely looked like one to me, save that *these* wee buggers were at least two feet in length.

I don't think that I've mentioned previously that Pachydermia has a superfluity of insect life, or at least some arthropod-like creatures with the general appearance of our "bugs." Many of these are small and unobtrusive, just as they are back home, except that they're *everywhere*, moving in and out of the open "houses" of the pachyderms at will, with strict rules forbidding their harm. I remember that Hawk accidentally tripped over and killed one of them—well, it was pitch dark and the "bug" was over a foot in length—and that was the first time that I'd seen Pirama or any of his fellows actually angry, at least until he was convinced that the incident was quite unintentional. And then Hawk was required to "recycle" the beast, which meant that he either had to eat it himself—or get us to join the feast. It was not a happy occasion.

Others of these creatures, such as the libbélli, are quite enormous in size, but none seem at all harmful to other life. We were shown some small scavenger insects that appeared to be a cross between our ants, termites, and bees, but were twice their physical size, and like them dwelled mostly in underground nests.

They would only "attack" and eat flesh that was already dead, however. I called them the "carrion crew."

I awoke in the middle of one night covered in a swarm of these things, and thought for a moment that I was somewhere else; but when I generated a finger-light, I saw immediately that the buggers were just conducting a "sweep" of the place, one of their periodic cleanings that helped maintain our environment and swept away all the decaying plant and animal life.

But I had no idea what the "running of the roaches" might be. For one thing, I'd never actually encountered this particular "bug" before, and I wondered why. When I asked Tillusu-dalu, however, she wasn't able to make me understand the reason.

"It wasn't (*rafalfi*) yet, unhandsome Morpheús-dala," was all I could understand. "You ha-humans don't (*malléto*) the (*darrýllo*)."

We certainly didn't!

However, the racing of the roachy rapscallions sounded at least unique and interesting, and so the next day, I gathered together our merry band of adventurers into the unknown, and we rode out with the pachyderms perched on one of several thirty-foot-long caterpillar-*cum*-centipede crosses (the wiji), heading from the main compound to a point about seven miles distant, I would guess, or maybe closer "as the crow flies." Several of Hawk's men experienced a kind of *mal de mer* similar to seasickness, caused by the constant undulation of the bugs' backs as they inched their way forward over the terrain.

We finally came to a flat bluff overlooking a deep gulley with steep sides, where we stopped and passed out baskets of a long-overdue lunch of flowers and fruits and odd-shaped vegetables. This was obviously a vantage point that had been employed on previous such occasions.

"How often do the roaches run?" I asked the young pachyderm.

"Just twice each year, o gentle mage, they make this journey from east to west and back again, whenever the (*billabongi*) emerge from their rest."

I had no idea what she was talking about.

We first heard some crackling and rustling sounds, as if dried plant stalks were being dragged over the ground. They emanated from our right, and so we all peered down the narrow rill to see what was happening. At first I couldn't make any sense of what I was observing. What appeared to be a band of large leaves was moving rapidly towards us in a wave of flagrant vegetation. I didn't feel any wind, and I didn't see how they could be traveling so quickly otherwise.

Then I realized that they too were "bugs," apparently disguised as plants (or maybe on this world they were one and the same thing), and being carried on a set of a dozen or more little legs each. In their smooth but swift movements they almost seemed to flow across the earth.

They were almost abreast of us before I saw the "roaches" racing swiftly after them, jumping slightly up and down as they tried to trap the squirming leaves beneath them. One roach succeeded, and then proceeded to put its mouth right down on the trembling emerald creature, obviously to begin feeding.

I turned to Tillusu-dalu: "I thought that no creatures here feasted on any others, save the scavengers that clean away the dead."

"How very wise and observant you are, o Morpheús-dala," she said.

"But…." I pointed to the mini-drama being enacted below us. "What's that?"

"It is their way of sustaining themselves, o traveler-from-afar."

I looked over the edge again, this time more closely. One of the "roaches" was licking the leaf with its twin proboscides (shades of the pachyderms!), sucking up some minute drops of yellow nectar that the plant was exuding, and several of the "legs" of the flat bugs were doing something nasty to the under-side of the larger creature.

Shah'rah started giggling, while Mistress Zalmanna looked greatly offended. "That's just how they 'do' it, husband," my "wife" said.

"But if...then...w-what about the Pollýxerri?" I stammered out, turning very red in the face at the thought.

The young pachyderm looked at us very strangely. "Why would you think this practice is so odd, ha-humans who have traveled from afar? Do you people not do something very similar?"

Then Shah'rah laughed out loud, and so did Hawk and his men, Boupho, the Yowler, and Scooter. I finally had to recognize the absurdity of it all, and joined in the general merriment myself. Only the Tyro frowned, but then, she was rarely amused by anything.

"Do you and that dog-creature conjoin to maintain your species—or perhaps with the smaller furry thing—or all three of you together?" the observer wanted to know. She was deadly serious, which of course made us howl all the more.

"Our, uh, 'conjoining' is between members of our own kind," I said, "and further deponent saith not!"

"Why is that?" she asked.

"Oh, I don't know," I said. "In the end, you just wouldn't understand why the mortar ultimately needs the pestle."

"You ha-humans are very strange," she said—and I suppose that from her point of view, that was undeniably true.

CHAPTER FIFTY-TWO
"A PLEASANT PLACE
TO PLOP AND POOP"

We resumed work on the mold the next day, inspecting how the molten materials that comprised the new mirror had hardened and gelled overnight. Overall, I was quite pleased with the result, and so was Mistress Zalmanna.

"Once it is polished and calibrated," she said, "we should be ready to try a transit."

I agreed, but we had none of the materials available that were traditionally used to sand down and smooth the surface of the metal. Again, we would have to improvise. Our inability to employ the local vegetation, some of which was sufficiently raspy to abrade the surface of the device, was a real handicap, but I decided that we could accomplish the same thing through an application of psychic force twisted sideways.

Once again we lined up the two copies of *The Necropompeion* together with its controlling medallion, and linked together the human and wherret members of our group—and then Scooter began carefully focusing the energy signature to plane away the rough parts of the surface. We had to scrape the bumps and ridges off the top of the mirror to enable it.

Then came the delicate process of transit calibration, which the Tyrosian Overseer supervised. She had the most knowledge of such esoteric matters, both theoretically and in terms of local signature addresses; and so she patiently tested one parameter after another until she was satisfied we'd done the best we could to focus the thing.

"We will not know, of course," she said, "until we activate the mirror, but I think this will work in some fashion. I just hope we can travel to someplace that can receive and reconstitute our signal."

"So do I," I said, "or it's going to be a very short trip indeed."

Before we reached that fatal day, however, I gathered the group together one evening, and asked if anyone wanted to remain on Pachydermia.

"I think I speak for everyone, Sir," Hawk said, "when I say that, while this is a pleasant place to plop and poop, none of us feel any ties here. We all want to go home when our journey's done."

I looked around the room, and saw the nods and heard the murmurs of approval, and said: "Very well, then. We all go to the next stop together, wherever that is. Mistress Zalmanna, do you have any idea of how to find the nearest transit station?"

"Nearest? I have no idea. But I am aware of a major site at Nolland in the Bardhöl Sector of the Sixth Circle, and if we can generate sufficient power, we might be able to reach there."

"We need to find a world called 'Mayharyn,'" I said. "That's where one of The Second Elephant's Eggs is supposed to be located."

"I am unaware of it," she said, "but surely someone will know where it is."

I decided to set the "launch" date for our enterprise some two days hence, and told everyone to gather together their few belongings then.

After our meeting broke up, Tillusu-dalu told me that Pirama-dala wished to speak with me before we left, so I asked her to arrange for a libbéll the next morning, and returned with her to Kalliwill.

Sitting tight behind a pachyderm on a high-flying arthropod is not something that I would recommend for a casual journey. I had to encircle her hind legs with my arms to keep from falling off the back of the "bug," which had the effect of pressing my face right up against her you-know-what. I discovered what should have been obvious to me: that pachyderms generate a considerable effluence of gaseous emissions from all the plants they eat. Gad, the torments that I'm forced to endure for the sake of science!

When we landed, the Pollýxerri spokesman was waiting for me.

"Greetings, o wise Morpheús-dala," he said.

I returned the compliment.

"Why do you seek The Fourth Elephant's Egg, o ha-human mage?" he asked.

"What do you mean, honorable Pirama-dala?"

"It is a simple question, seeker-after-truth."

"The Tyros desire it for their own purposes," I said. "We've signed a contract that requires them to send me to any place that I wish to go in return for acquiring that particular artifact for them."

"But have you never asked them *why* they want the Egg?"

"No. Should I?"

"Of course. If you become someone's slave, should you not understand the reasons for which you sold your birthright?"

"I'm no man's slave," I said. "This is a *quid pro quo*, pure and simple. I wish to save a great lady from her captivity, and this is what I have to do to locate her."

"Are you certain of that?" the pachyderm asked.

"No, of course not. How can I be certain of anything?"

"You cannot acquire the Eggs unless they permit you to take them. They were created for specific purposes, and they have powers that you cannot imagine, ha-human."

"What powers?"

"I cannot tell you."

"What purposes?"

"I cannot tell you."

"If you can't tell me anything," I said, "then why are we having this conversation?"

"Because, o gentle mage, the acquisition of anything worthwhile requires sacrifice, wisdom, and understanding, and that is as true of your quest to save the Lady Niobë as it is of your hunt for the Four Great Eggs. They are one and the same, and unless you achieve some modicum of balanced consideration during your trip into the æther, you will attain neither."

"How do you know this?"

"Suffice it to say that I do," the pachyderm said. "The journey exists so that you may learn enough of the universe and its creations to reach for something beyond yourself. The Tyros want the Eggs to control other sentient beings—and the Eggs will not permit this. You must want the Eggs in order to control yourself and your own desires, to bring peace both to your own being and to those who share our existence, and to restore order to the Circles. Without that balance, you will never find what you seek."

"I don't understand," I said.

"No, you do not, at least not yet. But you will be forced to make hard choices in the days to come. You see everything as some kind of elaborate game, with winners and losers, puzzles and solutions, and questions and answers, all of them easy to make and easy to decide—but life is not a game, great Morpheús-dala. When you make choices, as everyone must, sometimes the outcomes have real and lasting consequences.

"Mellie-dala and Grit-aslo are gone from this world—because of something you did. Your people now follow you—because of something you did. The Lady Niobë-dalu depends on your future intervention to save her life—because of something you did. Your former superior-dala waits vainly for your aid—because of something you did.

"But you have no real feelings for any of them, so when they vanish or die or are hurt on your behalf, you simply move on to the next task, without considering the cost that has been paid. What kind of person so divorces himself from the ebb and the flow of life that he can readily slough off all pain and joy and attachments? Are you so empty, ha-human, that you connect with no one? Have you never considered that your closest relationship is with an alien being?"

He was right, of course, but to have the facts of one's drab existence stated so baldly was a shock to my system and my sensibilities. I didn't want to hear what he had to say, because I knew, deep down inside, that he was right—that I was a cold son-of-a-bitch at heart, and that *that* fact underlaid all of the discontent that I now felt. The excitement of the chase hadn't changed anything, really. It had just blurred my perception of the inherent emptiness of my soul.

"What should I do?" I asked.

"That must be for you to decide, o semi-wise Morpheús-dala. It always has been so. But you must alter your being if you wish to find the rest of the Eggs, and if you want to attain the destiny that potentially awaits you. The Maker-of-Things and the Fixer-of-Things, or whatever creative principle you acknowledge, will show you the way."

"Tell me, great Pirama-dala," I said, "What exactly are the Maker-of-Things and the Fixer-of-Things?"

He didn't answer me as such, but instead stepped back, hissed a word through his twin trunks, and turned sideways to me. Suddenly his form changed right in front of my eyes, and I gasped when I understood what I was seeing.

It was a pachyderm, to be sure, but one with a head located at either end of its body.

"We are the Maker-and-Fixer-of-Things," it said.

CHAPTER FIFTY-THREE
"I'M TIRED OF THIS 'PARADISE'"

I knew that the image being shown me wasn't physically real, just a projection in my mind, but I was still shocked to the core at what I saw. The pachyderm was telling me, in essence, that his deity consisted of two beings in one body—and that half of this mixture was female! Of course, our own theologians talked about God having three different aspects—the Father, the Son, and the Holy Spirit—so I suppose this wasn't that far removed, although I always had had great difficulty in wrapping my mind around the three-in-one theory.

Then Pirama-dala was himself again, and he said: "I wish you and your companions well on your journey together, o great Morpheús-dala. May you find what you seek—and may you be satisfied with what you find."

I thanked him for his consideration and courtesy, and returned to our base—but I didn't brief my comrades on what had transpired between us. I didn't think it would help matters any.

It was now time to start testing our new transit-mirror, to see if we could find a signature in ætherspace to which we could establish a hard link, because without that focus at the other end, traveling anywhere would be impossible. The operation was dangerous enough that we could only attempt the scrying by putting together our little group of individuals who possessed some magical abilities—myself, Mistress Zalmanna, and Scooter—with each providing backup and protection for the others. It was also very tedious work; each session consisted of trial-and-error probes into the surrounding net of chaotic leys that made up the interlinked state of the Sixth Circle.

It was weeks of utter tedium interspersed with moments of absolute terror. Every so often we'd encounter some other entity "out there," doing precisely what or how or why we were never quite sure. Such individuals were better left alone, we knew, and we would immediately sever the link.

Except...there was one occasion when we tried to cut the connection, and the being at the other end (whatever it was) refused to allow it to lapse, but instead tried to force its consciousness through to our side, presumably to seize our minds and knowledge. We had to fight with every ounce of our strength to push it back again, and then psychically shut the door in its face.

Finally, though, after a month of probing and retreating and probing again, we discovered an address that seemed to provide a possible haven for us.

"What do you think?" I asked Scooter and Mistress Zalmanna, after we'd closed down the session.

"We'll definitely want to revisit this one again, Master," the wherret said. "I have one concern, however, in that I could not myself determine the nature of the receptacle at the other end."

"I had the same problem," the Tyro said, "and that bothers me. Of course, it could just be the variant nature of the devices available to us in the Sixth Circle."

"I think we need to keep looking," I said.

We discovered three more possibilities in subsequent weeks, and were able to determine that one was a pool of water, one a static (i.e., powerless) mirror, and the third a prism. But there were problems with each of these, not the least of which was the absence of any obvious focal point on the far side to generate a transmission image to resend us somewhere else. Pools of water can be used for transit, but only under certain conditions—and similar limitations applied to the other two media.

So we went back to the first site that we'd found, but couldn't activate it again. On the third try, it was "live" once more.

"This is very strange," I said. "I wonder if it's a machine

being turned on and off."

"If that is the case," Zalmanna said, "then we could have our transit there interrupted midstream, and find that half of our crew has been stranded on Pachydermia for the rest of their lives. We have to take the power source with us when we leave this place—but that means there can be only one possible jump from here to there."

Over the next week we tried connecting to the strange address again and again—and sometimes we were successful, and sometimes we weren't! There seemed to be no pattern to the periods when the signature was active. We managed to catch the device just after it was made functional again (we'd tried several quick links in a row), but were only able to determine that it remained "live" for just over an hour. On another occasion the session lasted the better part of three hours. And then again, we had one "blip" where the machine was active for just five minutes.

"Why don't we try sending a message there," I said—but when we did, we received no response. Either they didn't understand Tyrosian, or they weren't feeling sociable.

"So what's it going to be then, eh?" I asked our entire group, after laying the evidence before them. We'd been working more than three months now to construct the mirror and find some possible off-world connection. "This could still be a trap of some sort."

"I say we go, Sir," Hawk said, and his men murmured their echo of acquiescence.

"Yes, let's go," my "wife" Shah'rah said. "I'm exceedingly tired of this 'paradise'."

"Still want to find brrotherr," Arrgruffruff said. "He not herre."

"We need to continue our quest for the Eggs," Mistress Zalmanna said.

"I want to know what happened to Grit, Master," Scooter said.

"I'm still looking for adventure, Sir," Boupho said.

"Very well. We'll depart on the morrow, if the receiver has just been turned on—and if not tomorrow, then as soon as possible thereafter."

The next day, we started the process of loading the internal capacitor within the transit-mirror with energy, linking the two copies of *The Necropompeion* with its controlling metal token. Once I felt we'd gathered enough power to generate the leap, Mistress Zalmanna began probing the signature that we'd found.

"Not active," she reported—then "Not active" again—then finally, "Active!"

"Prepare to transit," I ordered, as she warped the leys to match the address at the other end of ætherspace.

And then we stepped one by one into the great mirror lying on its side in the rock and soil of Pollýxerr, the planet of the pachyderms, and left that place for good.

EPILOGUE
"THE ART AND SCIENCE OF ANGLING"

When I was about ten, my father, the great Julian warrior Kallíkratês, who was home on one of his rare leaves, took me on a fishing expedition into the countryside south of Zmyrna, not far from the ancient ruins of Ephesus. "For it is well past time," he said to me, "that you learn the art and science of angling."

Now, my Da' was one of those rare individuals who followed this piscatorial avocation whenever he had the chance—and by all accounts, he'd taught the skill to a sufficient number of the men under his command that his troops never starved in country where a free-flowing stream could be found.

He crafted his own poles and lines and hooks, for his magical talent, although not comparable to my own, ran to the fashioning of implements, as he later amply demonstrated when he retired from the Autokratôr's army. He could take a piece of scrap iron, and somehow twist it between his fingers, heating it with his own energies without ever burning himself, ultimately producing a perfectly-curved, sharp-pointed instrument of fishy terror. I was never able to replicate such work, much though I tried.

We rode southeast out from Zmyrna, Da' on an old mule, I perched on a brownish donkey, and after a half-day's journey, stopped by a creek called Strabo—or the twisted one. This was one of several small streams that ran all year, although many others of similar size in the region withered into dustways by early fall. We tethered our mounts under some trees, and then my father unwrapped the two poles he'd made, one long (for himself), and the shorter one for me.

He'd brought some dried strings of salted lamb in his pouch to provide bait—but also to give us sustenance if we failed to lure the small swimmers from their aqueous hidey-holes. When I tried to ask him a question, he shook his head, putting one finger to his lips in the universal signal for "silence."

We both wore old, droopy hats to protect us from the early summer sun. Da' strung both poles, attached the hooks, showed me how to bait the end without sticking myself (it took several tries for me to get the knack), and then we both settled down, side by side. My father pulled some line out with his strong left hand, and with a quick flick of his right wrist sent the baited hook out into the center of the Strabo, letting the mild current carry the tempting morsel downstream. Every so often he would jerk on the pole just slightly, to tell the hungry fishies that "something good was floating their way, if only they would bite."

And bite they did, after a time, and then Da' would jerk back on his stick and hook the swimmers in their lip or cheek, and gradually and carefully pull them back in. The small fry he pardoned from their fate, releasing them to grow for a few weeks or months more; but the rest he put into a sieve-pouch that he'd anchored to a branch that dangled into the cold water, the better to preserve them.

When he'd caught three or four medium-sized prey, he set his pole aside, and motioned for me to follow suit. But although I tried for several hours to garner even the barest nibble from the stupid, inconsiderate creatures that kept ignoring my treats, I snared nothing. Finally, I cast my pole down on the bank, ready to cry at my frustration and my anger.

"Hmm," my Da' finally said, "hmm. Sometimes, my son, the fish just swim their own way, and they favor one pole or one person more than another, for no reason that anyone can see. Life is often like that, and you can't let yourself feel angry because a cold, dumb creature zigs when it should have zagged.

It's never personal, Morpheús. The fishies don't care about you or me in the same way that we feel about each other.

"I've had days when I couldn't catch anything at all, and just a little ways down the creek someone else—some pikeman as dumb as an old ox—drops a stick in the water with a makeshift hook baited with a roly-poly bug—and boom!—out jumps the biggest critter I've ever seen taken from that stream. It happens, all too frequently. So, let's just forget about this afternoon and fix dinner, and then we'll try again."

He made us a fire from a flint and bark shavings, cleaned the fish he'd caught, cut and stripped a stick from a nearby bush, impaled one of the creatures on the prong, and roasted the thing over the fire, taking care not to burn the flesh. He brushed off a flat rock nearby, and deposited our meal one by one on the top, as he roasted each fish. When the meat had cooled enough, we picked it apart with our knives and fingers, and I consumed one of the best meals of my life. There's nothing to compare with a fish cooked right after it's been caught.

And in the few hours of daylight yet remaining, I caught my first fish—nothing special, mind, just a young adult—and we cooked that one too, not long before bedtime, just to celebrate my small victory over the animal realm.

* * * * * * *

For some strange reason, I kept recalling that boyhood trip in the hours before we transited from Pollýxerr into the unknown reaches of the æther. Just like the fishies that I'd tried so hard to snag, the pachyderms felt nothing towards us that was really personal. I doubt that they actually wished us ill, but they didn't much wish us well either. They were the most supreme examples of self-satisfaction that I'd ever encountered. I don't know whether that made them any happier than we, but I certainly had no desire, having met them, to share their lives for any longer than necessary. Neither did my fellow-travelers.

There was something very cold about the way that they

looked at the universe, something very unsettling to me. And yet, I'd spent much of my life to date running away from life— and I could see that more clearly now, having had their example placed before me.

I didn't know what the future would bring, or whether my quest to find the "Lady" would succeed or fail. I didn't know why I was doing what I was doing, save that it seemed to me a necessary act if I was ever to grow inside. It's not enough to be talented or successful, I was discovering—not nearly enough. Money, fame, the adulation of others—they all fade with time, and in the end you find yourself yearning for a simpler life with someone who actually and truly cares that you live or die. In reflecting on my past, I couldn't find very many instances where I'd made a positive difference in someone else's existence—and that seemed to me suddenly important.

But each new venture into ætherspace offered new possibilities. Maybe the universe or God or whoever governed the cosmos would give me another chance! I had to believe that—or grovel into a storm-shrouded corner in the ultimate despair.

I had to go forward—with my friends. I had to find what was out there. I had to believe that my life was worth living. I had to keep trying.

"Prepare to transit," I said—and then I smiled…smiled at everyone, both to give my friends heart and to give myself strength, as I shepherded them through our makeshift transit-mirror.

"To the stars—through difficulties!"

AFTERWORD
"STIRRING THE ELEPHANTINE OMELET"

According to my notes, I penned the first few pages of this novel on March 24, 2006. I was intrigued with the idea of a long-distance romance, of creating the story of an impossible liaison between two individuals separated by an enormous void that was nearly unbridgeable.

Now, there have been many such tales in the literature, stories of star-crossed love spanning the bounds of time and space, and I'd already read many of the classics, including such works as Richard Matheson's *Bid Time Return*. I knew all the conventions, and I wanted to do something different with them.

So I started with two words, "Help me!"—and went on from there. As I recall, I either wrote the entire first chapter or the first two pages thereof—and then set the story aside, until I had more time to develop it.

That time didn't arrive for more than two years.

I wrote the actual book in three stints spread over another two years—two weeks in July, 2008, just over four months beginning January 1, 2009, and from December 18, 2009 through May 7, 2010. By then the text had accumulated almost 600 pages and just under 200,000 words—and, strangely enough, I found myself continuing the thread of the tale in a kind of sequel set back in Nova Europa, right *after* Morpheús and crew have returned from the æther; and this went on for several more chapters before I realized (with some horror) exactly what I was doing. I was just having too much fun with the characters to want to abandon them. I'd never had this happen before.

So, I shut things down immediately, capped off the narrative with an appropriate ending, and sent off part of the first section of the manuscript. My then-agent said that she liked the beginning chapters, but that the book was too long to market as is.

A month later, I retired permanently from Cal State SB, and moved into full-time editing and writing, something that I'd wanted to do all my life. But *The Fourth Elephant's Egg*, as I was calling it, just sat there gathering literary motes. What to do with it was the problem—but that problem applied generally to all of my creative writing.

Of course, this wasn't my first fantasy of Nova Europa. I'd previously published three other long novels set in roughly the same *milieu* (but at different times and in different places) through a small California house, Ariadne Press. They'd made very little impression, although several had garnered excellent reviews from Tom Easton at *Analog*—and from a few others as well.

It was my dear wife, Mary, who suggested that all of my long fictions needed to be divided into trilogies to make them more palatable and salable to present-day readers. We started the process with *Invasion!* (this one had actually been penned as three separate books, although it had only been issued in omnibus form), and then turned to the unpublished fantasy, *Elephant's Egg*, which just a few individuals had then seen.

This novel, it turned out, also had potential breaking points at the one-third and two-third marks in the narrative, and was relatively easy to fracture. So I divided the manuscript into roughly equal sections, re-edited the text, and added the appropriate Prologues and Epilogues, as well as some small pieces of additional copy. I renamed the three parts as: *The Cracks in the Æther*, *The Pachyderms' Lament*, and *The Fourth Elephant's Egg*. And that's what I offer to you now.

* * * * * * *

The puzzle of what constituted the four elephant eggs actually plagued me throughout much of the writing of this novel. I didn't want to make the thing just another Hitchcockian MacGuffin—a plot device that starts the action off with a "bang," but winds up becoming relatively meaningless to the development of the rest of the story. The eggs had to *mean* something, both to Morpheús and to the others carried along with him. Therefore, they had to be instruments of power, albeit a focused kind of power that only a handful of individuals could access.

The question arises when our hero mage first manages to travel off-world at the beginning of *The Pachyderms' Lament*. The elephantine creatures, which Morpheús spends the entire novel trying to locate, are either the creators or guardians of the eggs—or perhaps just of the secret of the eggs. That the pachyderms possess great magical powers is obvious when one of the humans is abruptly sent packing into another sphere—without warning and without any judicial hearing. He's just... gone—and the creatures are unable to tell Morpheús how they accomplished this task.

I wanted to make the pachyderms truly alien—very strange and very *outré* to the humans they encounter. And yet Piramadala, the "speaker" for the elephant-like critters, tells Morpheús a truth that he's unable to hear from anyone else: that he has no connections with others, that he has essentially divorced himself from the human race, from all feeling or understanding. This shocks him—as it should. It changes him—as it must. It makes him look at life, the universe, and everything...differently. It prepares him for the next stage of his journey.

For the mage to make a difference—to himself, to others, to the universe at large—he has to find some connectivity with his fellow thinking beings—and ultimately with himself.

This is his challenge as he enters the third stage of his journey, and proceeds towards the peeling of *The Fourth Elephant's Egg*. I hope that you'll find the journey as rewarding in the reading as I did in the writing. I like Morpheús: beneath everything else,

he's an intelligent, decent man.
    Is that ever enough?
    Well, perhaps!

—Robert Reginald
San Bernardino, California
30 April 2011

ABOUT THE AUTHOR

ROBERT REGINALD was born in Japan, and lived in Turkey as a youth. He starting writing as a child, and penned his first book during his senior year in college. He settled in Southern California in 1969, where he served as an academic librarian for forty years. He currently edits the Borgo Press Imprint of Wildside Press, and has also penned more than 125 books and 13,000 short pieces. His recent works of fiction include twelve Nova Europa historical fantasies (2004-11); six science fiction novels: The War of Two Worlds Trilogy: *Invasion!*, *Operation: Crimson Storm*, and *The Martians Strike Back!* (2007/2011); two Human-Knacker War SF novels: *Knack' Attack* (2010) and *"A Glorious Death"* (2011); and *Academentia: A Future Dystopia* (2011); two Phantom Detective period mysteries: *The Phantom's Phantom* (2007) and *The Nasty Gnomes* (2008); a comic mystery, *The Paperback Show Murders* (2011); a horror novel, *Hell's Belles* (forthcoming); and four story collections: *Katydid & Other Critters: Tales of Fantasy and Mystery* (2001), *The Elder of Days: Tales of the Elders* (2010), *The Judgment of the Gods and Other Verdicts of History* (2011), *Dead Librarians and Other Shades from Academe* (2011). He has also edited the SF anthology, *Yondering* (2011) and the mystery anthology, *Whodunit?* (2011). You can find him at:

www.millefleurs.tv

And watch for the other
volumes in *The Hypatomancer's Tale Trilogy*:

THE CRACKS IN THE ÆTHER (Book One)

THE FOURTH ELEPHANT'S EGG (Book Three)

www.ingramcontent.com/pod-product-compliance
Lightning Source LLC
Chambersburg PA
CBHW020204270626
47157CB00028B/1097